To those without homes.

We see you.

NSCV

Please return/renew this item by the last date shown on this label, or on your self-service receipt.

To renew this item, visit **www.librarieswest.org.uk** or contact your library

Your borrower number and PIN are required.

Amanda Berriman, author of *Home*

How to Find Home

MAHSUDA SNAITH

BLACK SWAN

TRANSWORLD PUBLISHERS
61–63 Uxbridge Road, London W5 5SA
www.penguin.co.uk

Transworld is part of the Penguin Random House group of companies
whose addresses can be found at global.penguinrandomhouse.com

Penguin
Random House
UK

First published in Great Britain in 2019 by Doubleday
an imprint of Transworld Publishers
Black Swan edition published 2020

A CIP catalogue record for this book
is available from the British Library

ISBN 9781784162580

Typeset in 11.27/15.68pt ITC Berkeley Oldstyle Std
by Integra Software Services Pvt. Ltd, Pondicherry.

Printed and bound in Great Britain by Clays Ltd, Elcograf S.p.A.

Penguin Random House is committed to a sustainable
future for our business, our readers and our planet. This book
is made from Forest Stewardship Council® certified paper.

MIX
Paper from
responsible sources
FSC® C018179
www.fsc.org

1 3 5 7 9 10 8 6 4 2

No matter how dreary and grey our homes are, we people of flesh and blood would rather live there than in any other country . . . There is no place like home.

The Wonderful Wizard of Oz, L. Frank Baum

Home

This is a happy story. This is an adventure.

It began the night Rusby was released. Word got round that Jules was having a few bevvies at her squat and, by the time I got there, it was crammed with half the homeless of Nottingham.

It was kind of electric, the air that night. I could see it as soon as I stepped in: bundles of energy hanging from the ceiling, little sparks flickering from the living-room doorway and on to the stained carpet in the hall. I decided to hover near the entrance, hanging up coats that had been dropped on the floor; I'm not a large-groups type of person. But then Big Tony craned his neck into the hallway. His bald head was shining with sweat, eyes so wide you could see the whites circling his irises.

'*Molls*,' he hissed.

I smoothed down the back of a sheepskin coat and hooked it over a peg.

'Hi, Tony,' I said.

He reached for my arm, nodding back towards the party.

'*Quick.*'

He's a strong, beefy man is Big Tony, neck thick as an ox. But his grip was gentle as he led me through the dancing bodies and past those slumped against walls peppered with graffiti. Sweat and alcohol soured the air, lights low, music thumping through boxy speakers. I walked on tiptoes to avoid the debris and then spotted Jules by the boarded-up windows. She was jumping up and down with a can in one hand, her other hand slicing backwards and forwards to the beat. Her chestnut hair, usually pulled tight in a ponytail, had come loose on the sides. Ash fell down her camouflage jacket as she puffed away on a cigarette. She didn't seem bothered by it. That's the thing with Jules: when she's in the zone, she's not bothered by anything.

I wanted to get her attention so we could talk but Big Tony was taking me over to the corner of the room where a lava lamp, purple with fluorescent pink wax, sat crooked on a beer carton.

'Speak to this fella, Molls,' he said. 'I can't handle him.'

I looked down at the lad sitting cross-legged on the floor. He can't have been much older than me – early to mid twenties – and was wiry, like one of those dolls with legs and arms that stretch into spaghetti. His skin was a pale caramel brown, his Afro square like Lego. 'LOGIC' was stencilled in bold letters on his canary-yellow

T-shirt. I looked at Big Tony: mid-forties, six foot four, convicted of grievous bodily harm at least four times in his youth. He looked back at me, dabbing the sweat from his head.

'Bloody teetotallers,' he said, sticking a cider can in my hand before stumbling off to the bathroom.

I sat down next to the lad and crossed my legs, feeling my phone vibrate against my thigh. I knew it was a text because of the short single buzz but I didn't want to read it. Not then. Instead I asked the lad his name. He stuffed a lime jelly baby in his mouth and looked at me with narrowed eyes.

'Why?' he said.

His face was dead straight but I smiled anyway.

'Why what?'

'Why do you want to know my name?'

His voice was airy and light like a BBC news reporter's. I tried not to let it distract me.

'So I know what to call you,' I said.

I stretched my neck high and grinned, happy with my answer. He carried on staring at me, Afro glowing lavender in the lamplight, then stuffed a red jelly baby in his mouth. When I looked down I saw he was barefoot, a line of socks laid out across the floor in front of him. They'd been flattened into J-shapes, spaced out equally, each sock a different colour and pattern from the rest. One of them had little scurrying turtles; another pineapples.

It didn't seem as though the lad was going to say much else so I looked back at Jules, who was still dancing like she'd been possessed. The cuffs of her oversized jacket were flapping as she swung her arms, the too-full pockets of her cargo pants threatening to empty with each jump. I wanted to talk to her about the whole Rusby situation; I'd heard nothing from him for three years and now he was messaging me non-stop. His words had an intensity that made it hard to breathe. I sipped my cider as the music pounded. It was a throbbing track that made me want to get up and dance with Jules, to dance so hard that I'd forget Rusby, to dance so hard that I'd forget everything.

'Luca,' the lad said.

His back was still straight but his shoulders had slackened, eyes looking square into mine. It was like he could see right inside to the wires feeding round my body, the lump of my heart pounding in my chest, the ball of my mind rippling with activity.

I licked my lips.

'Luca's a nice name,' I said.

'Thanks,' he said. 'Do you like jazz?'

I frowned.

'I don't think I've heard much jazz.'

His lips curled as if I were twisting his fingers back.

'But yeah,' I said. 'I guess so.'

His face relaxed.

'Do you have any special skills?' he said.

'Like qualifications?'

His expression flickered with irritation.

'No, *not* like qualifications.'

I fiddled with the ring-pull on my can.

'I don't think so,' I said.

He sighed and looked away; whatever test he'd put me through I'd failed. I stretched my legs, ready to push myself up.

'Do you believe in fate?' he asked.

The lavender light illuminated the side of his face as he waited for my answer.

'No,' I said.

His face relaxed, lips pursing into an 'oh'.

'Do you?' I ventured.

His expression became serious again.

'Belief is an illusion created by humans to legitimize a totally meaningless existence,' he said.

Bundles of energy crackled around us. I could see why Big Tony couldn't handle this but I was finding it funny. Not funny ha-ha or funny strange, but funny interesting, funny surprising.

The skin between Luca's brows shrivelled up like a popped balloon.

'Sorry,' he said.

He fiddled with a rainbow-striped sock.

'Why are you sorry?' I asked.

'For being weird.'

I looked down at the socks; there were eight in total, all of them the same size but none of them matching.

'It's not weird,' I said. 'It's interesting.'

5

He laughed. Not a nice laugh, sort of mocking.

'No,' he said. 'It isn't.'

He stared straight ahead as though I wasn't there any more, as though he was in an empty forest on a winter's day and not a room full of sweaty bodies.

I felt another buzz in my pocket. When I pulled my phone out I had twelve messages from Rusby. The last one rolled across the top bar of the screen.

Remember what we've been thru darlin x

I put the phone away, hoping that, if I ignored the messages, Rusby would figure I'd lost my phone or had it nicked or that it was just plain broken. That he'd give up. But I also knew that, when he really wanted something, Rusby never gave up.

The room grew darker. Nobody noticed but me.

Things you should know about me:

My name is Molly Jenson.

I've been homeless since I was fifteen.

My favourite book is *The Wonderful Wizard of Oz*.

My favourite place to sleep is in hospital chapels.

Sometimes, I see things that other people don't.

I try not to think about the last thing too much.

'Can I tell you a secret?' asked Luca.

Jules was across the room, collapsed on a children's bean-bag, fuzzy strands of hair in a mane around her blotched red face. Private Pete was sat beside her delivering an intense monologue and sloshing Special Brew all over the already-stained carpet. He swayed from side to side, the hood of his coat draped over his forehead, his three-legged Border terrier dozing on the floor in front of them. As he spoke, his hood crept backwards, revealing the psoriasis that covered his scalp.

'Can't get a break, Jules,' he yelled.

Slosh!

'Can't get a fucking break.'

Slosh, slosh!

Luca's expression was wide and expectant.

'Sure,' I said. 'You can tell me.'

Luca leant in so close that the curls of his hair tickled my cheek. I could feel the energy again, hovering above us.

'I'm going on a mission,' he said.

'I mean really, Jules!' Private Pete was shouting now, Special Brew shooting out of his can. 'You wouldn't believe what I've got now.'

Slosh!

'Have a gander.'

Sllloosh!

He pulled on the elastic waist of his jogging bottoms. We call him Private Pete because he can't keep anything private. It's what you call an ironic name (unlike Dodgy Mike's, which is based on fact). One of the things Private

Pete shares is his skin infections. Not literally, of course, though I'm sure there've been cases. He's had it all: scabies, street feet, gangrene and – what seemed to be the case this time – crotch rot.

Jules was so far gone she didn't even realize Pete was showing her the contents of his underpants until it was there right in front of her. The look on her face suggested it wasn't a pretty sight. Her body jolted so hard that her right foot jerked out, kicking Pete's three-legged Border terrier in the back. Pete had found the dog a few weeks earlier, abandoned in a shoebox by the canal. He'd named the dog 'Boy', even though she was a girl, in order to make himself seem harder on the streets. His theory was people treated females like delicate little things while males were to be steered clear of. Of course there was no logic in this; Pete was a man and soft as a pile of feathers. And you couldn't really be afraid of Boy, so small and scraggly with wide floppy ears and one leg missing. Even when she leapt up and barked at Jules, everyone just looked over and smiled soppily. Everyone except Jules.

The thing with Jules is she's the competitive type, so as soon as she clocked Boy she was down on all fours yapping like a Pekinese. She would've been more convincing without the camo jacket. She looked like a soldier in one of those war films who's shot one too many villagers, running off into the jungle to go mental.

Luca was oblivious to the barking and yapping. He was gazing at me like we'd known each other fifteen years instead of five minutes. I have to be careful sometimes; I'm too good a listener. I'm not beautiful but I have these big pale eyes that draw men in. Child's eyes, Jules says, which is why I pull in the perverts. But there was something different about this lad. It wasn't how he looked (the worst perverts look the straightest) but how he *was*. Like he knew about things – both painful and beautiful – that made him kind of sensitive. Don't ask me how I knew this; I just did.

'A mission?' I said.

He nodded.

There was a whimpering from the other side of the room. Boy was walking towards the kitchen, snout down, tail hanging between her leg and stump. Jules was on her beanbag, head rolled back, panting.

'Do you want to come?'

Luca was staring at me through the squares of his glasses. The energy was crackling again, brightening up the room.

'Where are you going?' I asked.

He grinned.

'Skegness.'

The energy exploded above us, sparks showering us like confetti. Nobody could see it but me.

'Are you fucking with me?' I said.

I must have said it harsh because his lips trembled. He shook his head.

'I'm deadly serious.'

I took a deep breath.

'Why Skegness?' I asked.

Luca smiled.

'I've got a map and a key.'

I nodded even though I didn't know what he meant. My thoughts were scattered. Skegness – Izzy. Nottingham – Rusby. Skegness – Izzy. Skegness. Skegness.

I must have missed something because suddenly Luca was pulling at a chain around his neck.

'My grandfather gave me this,' he said.

There was a key – small laced head; thin bronze body – attached to the chain.

'I've got a rucksack with all the necessary equipment,' he said. 'I know where it is. I just need to get there.'

'Wait,' I said, shaking my head. 'Where *what* is?'

Luca paused, then chuckled as though realizing he'd forgotten the most important part.

'The fortune!'

The music was so loud now that it rattled through my ribcage. If there's one thing I've learnt from life it's this: you can't do much about the past but you can make sure the present is filled with so many good things that they drown out all the bad. It makes sense, proportionally wise. Like how a drop of ink can turn a puddle black, but in the sea it just spreads out and becomes more sea. It was as if I had waves in me. The ink was being washed away.

'OK,' I said.

Luca frowned.

'What?'

Sizzle. Pop. Hiss.

'I'll come!' I said.

The pressure built up, the energy released.

Wheee. Zip. BOOM!

'You're messing with me?' he said.

My cheeks ached with how much I was smiling.

'I'm serious,' I said.

Luca's expression was caught between joy and disbelief, like he'd been hitchhiking for five hours and I was the first car to pull up. He lowered his head as he took the chain from around his neck.

'Here,' he said, draping it over my head.

He put the key in my palm and wrapped my fingers over it like a present.

'Welcome to the mission.'

I felt it there, cold and solid. Luca's face glowed and, when I looked down at our hands, I saw light glimmering through our fingers.

'Wanna dance?' I asked.

Luca watched me stand up. You could tell he wasn't the dancing type. Every inch of his gangly body wanted to hide in the corner of the room and disappear. He looked down at his socks, then pulled on one with balloons and another with bumblebees.

'You only live once!' he said.

The music continued to throb. We danced like crazy people until midnight.

11

The Council with Jules

If you sit by Nottingham Castle where the tourists stand
with maps and baseball caps and eyes that look without
seeing, you'll hear a busker who, when he sings, bleeds
his soul. You have to look real hard but, when you do, you
can see tendrils of liquid light running out from the cloth
of his parka and the wire of his beard. They seep into the
ether like magic.

When he batters the strings of his guitar, the earth
trembles, the sky cracks into pieces and the tourists look
away. They pose for pictures at the Robin Hood statue, with
V-signs and forced grins. They pretend they can't see the
man with a flat cap, bleeding all over the cobbled streets
below. But behind the grins you can see panic because,
even though they can close their eyes, they can't shut their
ears. It scares them, this voice, because they've never heard
singing where the heart is being drained, never heard notes
bellowed from the pit of something dark and wonderful.

Jules says the busker's psychotic. That he glassed a man once for telling him his shoelaces were undone. She says I should quit watching him every time I pass, that my sobbing will be the undoing of us both. I tell her it's not sobbing, just a quiet emotion. She says that's enough.

'Emotional people can't cope with the emotions of others. Best keep your distance, doll.'

But I can't keep my distance. I keep going to the castle to watch the busker, to let him know someone can hear him, to let him know someone can *see* him. You become invisible when you live on the street. People avert their gaze when they walk past, look straight through you when you speak. I used to think this was a good thing, that this meant you could truly disappear. But now I know that when you stop being seen, you stop existing and when you stop existing, that's when you give up.

Luca had seen me. He had looked deep inside and found something worth taking with him on his journey.

I guess that's why I said yes.

The next morning, Jules was on a berserker. She goes on a berserker most days but, depending on her mood, the length and height of the rage can vary. Sometimes it can last for a few minutes, other times for a few days. One time she stole an Alfa Romeo, drove down to Bridgend and set the car on fire by the side of the road. That berserker lasted a good week.

This particular morning Jules was at about seven on the Richter scale. She stomped around the squat in her Doc Martens, creating little earthquakes wherever she went. Cigarette butts fell from ashtrays; beer cans tipped over, spilling golden pools across the floor that trembled with each stamp. At first she didn't say anything, slicing through the crowd in her oversized camo jacket like a viper through grass, tongue nipping in and out as if tasting the air for prey. Then, when she saw the lava lamp had been left on overnight, she swung her arms up to the ceiling.

'Would've served you FucKeRS right if you'd been BuRnt to FAg AsH!'

She kicked some beer cans out of the way and went into the kitchen where she found a dog turd sitting square in the middle of the steel sink.

'PEEEETE!' she screeched as she stormed through the squat.

She kicked open every door, checked down the side of every piece of makeshift furniture, until she found Boy curled up on the bath mat by the shower. Pete was nowhere to be seen.

For the next ten minutes Jules marched around the squat berserking. Spit shot from her mouth like embers from a volcano. She was trying to make a rollie but kept getting distracted by new branches of rage so that she had to continually restart it.

'BlooDY CHeek oF iT! YoU PEople taKe thE PiSS!'

The squat got emptier as people escaped. Whenever Jules turned to rant at one side of the room, the group behind her stumbled out until she was spinning around shouting at nothing but empty beer boxes and a couple of people too far gone to move.

I was clearing cans throughout the ruckus. It seemed the most helpful thing to do. If there's one thing Jules can't stand, it's mess. When we shared a shop doorway she couldn't have any old cardboard box beneath her sleeping bag; she had to have a fresh one with no rips and no battered edges.

'No excuse not to be neat,' she'd say. 'Sign of being civilized, that is.'

There were syringes splayed across the hallway floor. I wrapped them up, knowing if Jules saw them her Richter scale would go through the roof. But she saw me taking them to the bin, the way I'd wrapped them up in miles of loo roll and was carrying them all delicate.

'For FucK'S sake! JusT CoS You'RE a SMaCKHEaD dOn't MEAn YoU cAn't BE a LiTTle FuCKing TidY, DOeS IT?'

She looked straight at me, even though they were nothing to do with me. But there's no reasoning with Jules when she's on a berserker. She marched off and I dropped the needles in the bin.

I thought about checking my phone and then decided against it. Instead, I sat down on a wooden step-stool and played with the rubber bands around my wrist. I closed my eyes and tried to remember the story from when I was a kid, the one about a girl made of stationery. Her mouth was a paperclip, her eyes drawing pins, and her arms, body and legs were made of thick, wide loops of rubber band. She had two crisscrossing rubber-band plaits hanging from her rubber-band head and could stretch herself as tall as mountains and twist her way through the tightest cracks. She travelled to new places, befriended the locals and defeated moustachioed villains along the way. Each night she would staple herself to a tree and rock herself to sleep.

The Rubberband Girl belonged to no one. The Rubberband Girl was free.

Jules shouted from the living room.

'FoR LorD's sake! SOMeOne DO SOMeTHIng with This BiTCH!'

Boy ran into the kitchen and jumped straight on to my lap, nuzzling into me as she whimpered. Jules walked in and nodded her head, glad the situation had been dealt with. She was still trying to roll her cigarette, eyes flickering up and down, shoulders rolled forward. I stroked Boy's leathery ears and felt the stump from her missing leg digging into my thigh. Her whimpering quietened. Jules stared at me as though straining to remember some bastard awful thing I'd done. Then, Rizla stuck to her lip, she clicked her fingers.

'What's All this BOLLocKS aboUt you PissiNg off with PoSh BOy?'

She pulled off the Rizla and began rolling, sprinkling a bit of green bud in with the tobacco. She stared at me with her broken eye.

Most of the time you don't notice Jules's broken eye. It's only when she stares that you can see the right one looks off to one side. It's nearly all black from an accident with a pellet gun. She still has the vision of a bloody hawk though. Sometimes I think she can see my thoughts.

She made a clicking noise with her mouth.

'You know he's PSycHOtic, don't yA?'

I smiled in a cheery way. Jules says it's a nervous tic, my smiling. She says when I'm real worried I go on smiling-benders, like I've got a whole banana stuck in my mouth. Her skin blossomed with red blotches.

'BEing PSycHOtic is NO LauGHinG MattER, MoLLy!'

My smile dropped.

Jules is sensitive about psychotics on account of her being diagnosed as one at fifteen. She's been in and out of mental health wards ever since. Now she sees it in everyone.

I put Boy on the floor and went back to the living room to collect more cans. It didn't seem to matter how many I picked up, there were always more. Boy followed me and Jules followed behind, burning lasers into the back of my skull.

'He's all right,' I said.

I didn't look at her as I said it but I could still feel her bubbling up.

'You'Ve OnLy kNown Him FiVe BLeeDING Min-uTes, MoLLs. I mEAn . . .'

When I looked up Jules was standing in the middle of the room with her spliff hanging limp from her lips. She looked around, noticing for the first time that every other bugger had left.

'They took their time to **FuCk!** off, didn't they?'

She kicked as she blurted out the **FuCk!** as though kicking out the last of her rage. Boy sensed the change in atmosphere and began scavenging for pieces of food.

Jules lit her rollie and eased her body into a blow-up armchair. She gestured for me to sit on the children's beanbag. Her phone trilled with a little tune from the nineties. She pulled it out of her pocket, a boxy Nokia so old it was probably considered antique. She glanced at the screen and threw it on the floor.

I sank deep into the bumpy folds of the beanbag. Luca had said he needed to get a few things sorted and that he'd meet me outside the vintage shop near Broadmarsh Shopping Centre at twelve thirty. It was already ten thirty and I wanted to visit the castle first, so I didn't have much time for Jules's opinion, which would, no doubt, take some time.

'You're so soft, Molls,' she said. 'You haven't thought it through, have you?'

She listed all the reasons I couldn't leave with Luca:

The Social would get on my back when I didn't report in.

The Job Centre would get on my back when I didn't report in.

The Drugs Unit would get on my back when I didn't report in.

Rusby would be on my back quicker than the lot of them when he realized I'd gone.

Just hearing his name made me sink deeper into the beanbag. I was trying my best to forget Rusby; I'd decided not to mention him to Jules at all. But word gets around quick with the homeless and Jules knew more about it than I did. When he'd been released. Who he'd been crashing with. How he was on the search for me and letting every person he came across know it.

I picked at the dirt beneath my nails as I thought about the list Jules had given me. She'd forgotten I wasn't in touch with the Social, the Job Centre or the Drugs Unit any more. It was her and everyone else we knew that was. Truth is, I don't do well with the authorities. Just the flash of their badges makes the blood rush to my cheeks and my legs fill with an itch that makes me want to run to the edge of the world.

Jules's phone trilled again. She craned her head forward to look at the screen, then leant back.

'Who's that?' I said.

She pointed at me, hard and forceful.

'Don't change the subject.'

The tune carried on playing as Jules tried to think of other reasons I shouldn't leave. As the phone stopped, her expression crumpled, her bottom lip fluttering.

'What about me?' she mumbled.

I frowned.

'You?'

She straightened out her bottom lip and smacked her hand against her chest.

'Yeah, *me*. I'm only your bessie mate, aren't I? We take care of each other.'

I nodded quickly.

'Always.'

Jules's shoulders slackened. Her skin was back to a blue-white colour so I knew she was simmering down. Jules likes to pretend she's tough as granite but really she's soft as sponge. She'd rather die than show anyone. Which is half the reason she gets in all the trouble she does.

'I mean, you would tell me,' she said, 'if you were going to leave.'

She was looking at me as though this was an obvious thing, like telling her if she had spinach between her teeth. I nodded even though I hadn't planned on telling her anything.

Jules passed the spliff to me and I took a toke, staring straight up as I blew out a fountain of smoke. I placed my finger over the key hanging around my neck and closed my eyes. I saw the Rubberband Girl bouncing from one land to the next. Twanging across deserts, catapulting across oceans, using her rubber-band plaits to swing from tree to tree.

'It'd be nice though, wouldn't it?' I said. 'To get a change of scenery.'

I meant only to think it but the words slipped out. When I looked over at Jules she was staring at me with her broken eye. If you get real close to her you can see the universe in there, a string of gas and stars whirling around in the dark of her pupil. She waggled her finger at me.

'This is not like you, Molls,' she said. 'This is not like you at all.'

I know she meant it as a bad thing but I liked it when she said that. I looked at her broken eye and, maybe because of the spliff, maybe because I was still imagining the Rubberband Girl, I smiled.

Jules sat bolt upright. I tried to straighten out the smile but it was too late. Her skin turned volcanic red.

'I'm not allowing this!' she said. **'I ForBiD iT!'**

She hit her fist against the arm of the blow-up chair and it bounced up, nearly hitting her in the face. She blew her cheeks out, the rage ready to erupt. I shrugged my shoulders as though I hadn't seen any of this.

'I'm only having a laugh, Jules,' I told her. 'I don't even know the lad, do I?'

I sniggered to show how absurd this all was. She glared at me with the universe there in her eye. It made me shiver.

Boy came sniffing at Jules's feet, her little wet nose skimming the edge of Jules's trainer. I waited for Jules to bat her away but she was too intent on staring at me. I looked down at Boy's stump.

'You won't throw her out, will you?' I said.

Jules glanced down.

'She ain't my dog.'

'But you'll take care of her?' I went on. 'Like you took care of me?'

As soon as I said that, Jules's whole body relaxed and Boy, sensing her chance, jumped on to Jules's lap. You had to give it to Boy; that dog had guts.

'Honestly, Jules,' I said. 'I'm not going anywhere.'

She looked at me a little longer. Then she gave Boy a little rub on the head.

'**Too rigHt**,' she said.

The Cyclone

Knights surrounded the castle. Their helmets and polished armour gleamed in the sun. Some held shields bearing lion emblems; others wore digital wristwatches that showed beneath the cuffs of their costumes. Damsels stood beside them, wearing tall pointed hats with flimsy fabric soaring from the tops. They handed out flyers to tourists and beamed serenely, telling everyone to make haste to the medieval festival before gesturing to the ticket booth shaped like a dragon's head.

I stood on the mound by the castle, looking down at the cobbled street. I was hoping to see the busker with his flat cap and wild beard, to hear him bellow out one of his soul-cracking songs. His voice always smacked me hard in the stomach, so hard I could fold with the force of it. I suppose I shouldn't want that feeling but it can make you numb, the homeless life. From the cold, yes, but also the way no one sees you. To feel that hit brings everything into focus. It makes sense of things, and what I needed right then was to make sense of the whole Luca situation. Of what Jules had said, and what she hadn't. Of where I wanted my life to go, and how I planned on getting there.

I waited another ten minutes but a burger stand was moving into the busker's spot. I don't know why I thought he'd be there; he's not what you'd call the predictable type. Sometimes he gets into fights that land him in the nick and sometimes he's just too pissed: conked out in some gutter, a dented can clutched in his hand. One time I saw him climbing up the side of the castle walls with his guitar case strapped to his back like he was trying to invade the grounds with nothing but music as his weapon. I was pissing myself about it for hours.

I swung my camping rucksack on my back and made my way down the mound. As I was squeezing through the crowd I heard someone call for me.

'Aaaay, Molls!'

His voice cut sharp through the buzz. It bore right into my ear, splitting my skull in half and ricocheting through my spine. I knew it was him. I knew that he'd found me. But I also knew that if I stuck my head down low I could get away. I wrapped my jacket around my body, making myself smaller, weaving into the crowd and hoping its thickness would swallow me. The bodies enveloped me like a hug, but he was too quick, bouncing straight through them and landing in front of me. Rusby's like a weasel in that way. Fast and springy.

'Ay, Molls!' he said again, bouncing on the spot. 'Didn't you hear me calling?'

There was no hassle in his voice, which was some kind of blessing. I gave a twitchy smile and tried to act surprised. He was skinnier than when I last saw him which, given his nickname was 'Scarecrow', was saying something. I could tell just by looking at him that he was still on the hard stuff. His skin was zombie-white, his tracksuit hanging from his body like a flag from a mast. He was wearing the same red baseball cap he always wore to cover his receding hairline and, when he grinned, I could see that his teeth were yellowed and uneven like broken paving slabs.

That's what crack does to you. One minute your body's fat with life and then you're a mummified corpse.

'What happened to my beautiful little boy?' his grandma used to say when we visited, showing me pictures of a chubby toddler in a vest and shorts. Then she'd offer us a cup of tea with a plate of Jammie Dodgers. The biscuits tasted like sand after you saw her crying like that.

The smile on Rusby's face weakened. He had that pitiful look he gets when he needs a hit.

'You gotta help me out, Molls.'

Same old Rusby. I hadn't seen him in three years, not since he'd pissed off to Aberdeen with that Slovakian girl, yet it had taken him all of half a minute to ask me to help him score.

'I'm in a bit of a rush to be honest, Rusby,' I said.

He began bouncing quicker on his feet. A boxer once told Rusby he could be a world-champion featherweight if he ever got his life in order.

He held his hands up.

'Now I know things didn't work out between us but that doesn't mean we've got to have this wall of ice between us, does it, darling? Doesn't mean that we can't still be *mates*.'

I squeezed my shoulders tight and pushed out a smile to show there were no hard feelings.

'See you around, Rusby.'

He shot his hand out, fingers clamping on to my wrist. His sinking grip felt like pulling on old boots – snug but pinching in at the same old places. His pupils were dilated, eyelids twitching, and the stench of alcohol was heavy on his breath. He looked like he was ready to tear my head off. That's the thing with Rusby; he can be happy as Larry one minute and bashing your teeth out the next. He cocked his head to the side.

'Now don't be rude, darling. You know I hate it when people are rude.'

A man in jousting gear locked eyes with me. He'd been chomping on a burger, jaw frozen mid-chew, deciding whether or not to intervene.

I sailed into the jouster's body, seeing the image of me and Rusby before him. A tall skinny man in a polyester tracksuit with a hollowed-out face and me, a pathetic mouse of a girl with greasy hair and holes in her jeans.

We were barely people; just waste products on the side-lines of humanity.

I wondered how me and Luca would look to the jouster, standing at the station with our rucksacks. Suddenly the holes in my jeans were a fashion choice. We were students on a gap year and not two fuck-ups, which is all me and Rusby ever were.

Rusby loosened his grip. His eyes turned puppy-dog.

'Get us a bevvy at least, will you? For old times' sake.'

I looked back at the jouster. He was talking to a man in a fluorescent-yellow vest with a walkie-talkie. Legends tell us about knights in shining armour who come to a lady's rescue. But they don't tell you how the knight ends up glassed and blaming the damsel in distress for it. In a fight, when it comes to Nutter versus Honour, the Nutter wins every time.

I looked at Rusby.

'Just a quick one. Yeah?' I said.

His broken smile spread wide across his cheeks.

The medieval music played as Rusby draped his arm over my shoulder and guided me to Ye Olde Trip to Jerusalem. We all called it 'the Trip' but the full name is painted in old-fashioned script on the side of the pub with the words 'the oldest inn in England' under-neath. Rusby always loved this place. The winding stairs and warren-like cubbyholes where he could sit tucked away without the bar staff walking by, recognizing him and throwing him out because he'd already been barred.

We shot straight past the bar and up to a little room on the third floor. It was an arched cave made of the same sandstone as the castle mound it was attached to, with gauntlets hanging from metal loops on the wall and cases holding ornate swords inside. Rusby got all excited, planning to use the gauntlets to prise the swords from their cases. As I went back down to the bar, I could hear the clinking of metal against stone and hoped someone would catch him: the History Preservation Police perhaps, dressed in their own coat of arms.

There was a grandfather clock standing snug in an alcove by the bar. Twelve twenty-five. Luca said to meet him at half past for the train at ten to. I imagined him standing by the vintage shop, searching the crowds through the square frames of his glasses. I considered slipping out but then the barman asked what I wanted and I just went ahead and ordered. It was a good job because when I turned around Rusby was standing at the top of the stairs, peering down, as though waiting for me to leg it. Just leant up against the doorway, not caring whose way he was in or how dodgy he looked chewing away at his nails. He said it was better than using clippers but would always bite past the point any blade could reach. Then he'd start gnawing on the flesh.

As soon as he clocked me, Rusby turned around and went back into the sword room. If I ran now he'd only chase me. I'd seen him run from the coppers enough times to know how fast he could be so I followed him up.

He seemed to have forgotten all about the swords as I sat down opposite him. He was swaying in his seat, pissed already. I put the pint down in front of him, white foam spilling down the sides of the glass. He took a gulp and then started on about his mother and her depression, about how all he really wanted to do was settle down with a nice lass and a couple of kids.

'Maybe get a dog. A Chihuahua.'

I leant forward on the table trying to find an entry point into this monologue. I thought I could say I had a doctor's appointment, or a social worker meeting, anything so I could leave. But Rusby banged on like a hammer hitting a nail, driving his point in over and over again, tears in his eyes, hand clinging on to mine.

'You wasss the best thing that ever happened to mees, Moll.'

He held my hand for a few seconds then slammed his pint down on the table top. Brown liquid sloshed over the rim, fizzing on the dark wood. I wondered what had caused this revelation – probably the Slovakian girl dumping him when he got chucked in the clink for the umpteenth time. Or maybe it was genuine – you could never tell with Rusby. When we first met he was the sweetest lad, particularly considering all the troubles he'd been through – children's homes, then foster care, then more children's homes, youth detention centres and finally prison. But he had this thing about him when we first met, like, if someone gave him a break, he could be something wonderful. I wanted to be that person. I wanted to make him wonderful.

I watched Rusby rocking side to side and remembered what we'd once had. He caught me staring and squatted his shoulders low to the table. His eyes hooded over. It was a look I'd seen before. A look I'd seen too often.

'I will always find you, Molly,' he said. 'Anywhere you go, I will Sniff. You. Out.'

I tried my best not to move. I felt the horrors of our relationship rushing over me. The nights locked in our squat. The days walking up and down looking for the next hit. The anger when we didn't get it.

Rusby looked back at his pint.

'I've found a place for us,' he said. 'Nice little squat. You'll love it, Molls. It's *perfeck*. I've got a plan, see.'

Rusby always had a plan. A new get-rich-quick scheme, a new way to get clean, a new start. But I was already clean and I knew that I wouldn't stay that way with Rusby. It would start nice, of course. He'd move us into a bedsit, set it up neat and cosy. I could see it forming around him as he sat there in front of me: the Ikea shelves clinking into place on the sandstone walls, filling up with cereal boxes, cans and bowls of fruit. A dresser with a built-in mirror, fairy lights trailing over the top, a picture in a silver frame of us smiling to the camera. For the first few days he wouldn't even use in front of me; Rusby can do just about anything when he wants. Problem is he never wants to do anything for long. I could see the nice things disappearing from the dresser. The picture frame first, then the ornaments and lights. The fruit shrivelled black in its bowl as the shelves emptied. Rusby's *We can do anything, Molly!* expression replaced with a dark *Don't fuck me off* scowl. And then he was leaning towards me, body shaking all over, telling me to go to the charity with the food parcels, the one for girls who work on the streets.

And that's how it would begin.

The lights on the wall flickered and I was back in the Trip with Rusby. When I looked at his face I felt nothing but rotten disgust.

'It's going to be beautiful, Molls,' he said. 'A fresh new start.'

Pipes and lutes played from the streets. I looked up at the swords hanging from the wall. If I'd lived in medieval times I would have dressed as a boy and joined Robin Hood's outlaws. There'd be no pretty pointed hats and cross-stitch for me; no way, fella. I'd be the best archer and poacher in Sherwood and, when the unwitting rich came stumbling through, I'd be the first one to attack, screaming so loud the whole forest could hear.

I decided to be an outlaw. I reached for Rusby's pint and, gripping it hard in my hand, threw the contents in his face. The liquid hit him in the eyes, spraying out in a foaming shower. He yelped like a schoolchild, clutching his face. I held the glass up and released my battle cry.

'Yaaah!'

I smashed the glass against the wall behind him. The shattering noise silenced the whole pub. I picked up my rucksack and ran down the stairs, hoping the barman would run up to the cave room, recognize Rusby and delay him.

I ran across the cobbles, away from the castle mound, dodging the traffic on the main road as everyone hit their horns. I ran past the Navigation pub, across another road and down the slope towards the canal path. I thought I'd made it, that I was free, but then I heard his voice over the noise of the traffic.

'Mollleee!'

I imagined Rusby running up to the railings, looking down and spotting me as I dashed towards the station. So I ran for the bridge instead, disappearing underneath and leaning against the inside wall. I took a deep breath, trying to think of what to do next. Then I pulled my phone out of my pocket and began to text.

Jules says don't come to hers. She's fuming at you.

I pressed send and threw the phone in the canal. It made a funny *plo-unk!* noise. Circular ripples swam across the green water. It felt good to do that; throwing away that phone was like throwing away Rusby.

Above me, I heard squawking. Rusby had picked a noise like a parrot being murdered for all his notifications.

I could tell he was close, from the volume. I closed my eyes. If Rusby believed the lie, he'd head to Jules's after he'd read the message. If he didn't, he might stay up there, waiting for me. Pigeons sat in the rafters near my head, cooing and ruffling their feathers. I'd bunked under that bridge so many times that the noise sounded like a lullaby, calming me down. I placed my hand over the pocket of my denim jacket where my pillbox sat, with its flower motif painted on the front.

I knew what I needed to do.

I took off my denim jacket and rammed it into my rucksack. Then I put up the hoodie of my jumper and walked out from under the bridge. If Rusby was still watching, he wouldn't know it was me unless I ran, so I tried to walk normally, just like another person in the crowd. The wind picked up, pulling me backwards. But then pigeons flew out from under the bridge, as if they were leading the way. As if saying, *You can do this, Molly. Fly.*

I came to the slope before the magistrates' court. I tried not to think about the last time I walked through the big glass doors, eyes turning to look at me. The way they'd looked.

I shook my head. The past was tugging at me, or perhaps it was Rusby. He had this magnetic power; he could always pull me into his grip. And then the wind changed.

Instead of dragging me back, a huge gust lifted me up. I hovered off the ground and my body sailed over the canal path to the main road. I passed buses, bikes and the train station tower as its clock hands pointed to twelve forty-three. I flew with the pigeons towards the vintage shop with gold print glittering on the window. There in the doorway, by a rusty giraffe sculpture, stood Luca with a navy-blue trench coat, a leather rucksack on his back and a trumpet case by his feet. He'd waited for me.

The wind lowered me down beside Luca. I flung my arms around his neck and he yelped as I squeezed tightly.

'Thank you, thank you, thank you,' I whispered in his ear.

When I let go, he looked confused, happy and annoyed. I pulled down my hoodie to show him it was me. His expression didn't change.

'You're late,' he said. 'We'll have to wait for the next one now.'

My chest heaved as I tried to catch my breath. My cheeks were stinging, a stitch aching down my side as if someone had punched me.

'I thought you weren't coming,' he said.

I still couldn't speak so I gave him a wide, apologetic grin. He tried to be serious, but it wasn't convincing because he didn't have a serious face.

'I'm not mental,' he said.

It was an odd thing to say but, at the same time, it wasn't.

'I don't care if you are,' I said.

There was something broken in him. You couldn't see it at first but if you looked real hard there was a hairline fracture running through his soul. Perhaps I could see it because I had one too.

Luca shook his head.

'We'd better go,' he said.

The Road to the Station

I was born in the customer lounge of Nottingham train station. My mother was waiting on the platform for the 6.52 to take her to an important meeting in London when the contractions she'd been trying to ignore throughout the previous night became so strong that she keeled over, amniotic fluid trickling down the inside of her thighs. The other passengers reared back as a puddle formed at her feet. As the train pulled up she was ready to straighten herself up and walk calmly on board to continue her journey. But when the rail guard arrived, face ashen, she felt the rush of the next contraction clamping down and knew there was no getting out of it. He escorted her into the customer lounge, eyes bulging, before radioing for help and sitting down on one of the benches.

'It's the last week before I retire,' he said. 'I was hoping for a quiet one.'

My mother loved telling me this story because it was proof, she said, that I was trouble from the start. Whenever she got to the part with the guard she'd look at me, shaking her head, as if I'd done it all on purpose. She said I liked to ruin things: her important meeting, the guard's retirement; it was my way of drawing attention to myself. I even ruined Nottingham for her. After she gave birth to me in the customer lounge and the local newspaper put her story on the front page, we moved away from the city. She didn't like attention, my mother, which explained why she didn't like having a child; people can't help but see children.

So my mother gave me Stillness Lessons, teaching me how to disappear.

I usually like going to the train station. I feel connected to the tracks and cables, the café with its high ceilings and stained-glass windows, the noise of the trains whizzing past. When I ran away, I ran to Nottingham station, not Nottingham itself. I knew my parents would never look for me there. It was my safe place, the place no one could touch me. I hung around the platforms, slept in the toilets, looked up at the departure boards as though I was a passenger at the beginning of a journey when, really, I'd just finished one. Nottingham station wasn't home, but it was the closest thing I had to one.

But this time, as I walked towards the station, I didn't feel that I was going home. I was on edge; every baseball cap, every glance my way, every wiry body that brushed my shoulder was Rusby's. Even people who didn't look like Rusby were Rusby. Their eyes turned gaunt and wide, their teeth turned to broken slabs ready to rip right into me. It's as if I give off a scent that only he can smell and no matter how hard I try to scrub it off, Rusby will do just as he promised: Sniff. Me. Out.

'Do you know what makes us human?' asked Luca.

He'd stopped walking and was stood by the wall under the tram bridge. He looked quite smart with his leather rucksack and buttoned-up trench coat.

I watched as a crowd of Rusbys walked past.

'Say again?' I said.

Luca dropped his rucksack on the ground, looking as though he'd just asked the Most Serious of All Serious Questions.

'Do you know what makes us human?' he repeated.

'Is this a riddle?' I asked.

He shook his head. I thought about it for a bit.

'I don't know,' I replied. 'What makes us human?'

He opened his mouth as if he was going to give me the answer, then shook his head again.

'Think about it.'

Luca picked up his bag and began walking. He was an odd fish, that was for sure, but some of the best people I knew were the oddest.

We didn't walk to the main station entrance, but to the platform footbridge at the side. The smell of just-brewed coffee wafted past in takeaway cups. It was another hour until the next train but Luca had wanted to be early because time was relative.

'When you have lots to do you have less time, and when you have nothing to do you have lots.'

My mind sprang into gear.

'Like when you're in a waiting room for twenty minutes and it seems like hours?'

Luca nodded.

'But when you're having fun,' I continued, 'hours go by in seconds.'

Luca frowned as though 'fun' was a foreign word.

'Like when we were dancing at the party,' I said. 'We danced for ages but time just zoomed by.'

He thought about this for a second, then licked his lips, nodding as though he'd tasted something amazing and that thing had been my words. That's how I got caught off guard.

There was a figure standing by the exit, talking to a man with long dreads, holding some *Big Issues*. I didn't recognize him, but I knew the woman straight away. If a cat was sitting by itself, Jules would start talking to it.

She caught sight of me and leant her shoulder against the wall.

'All right, Molls?' she yelled. 'Fancy seeing *you* here.'

She had slicked her hair into a neat ponytail and rolled up the cuffs of her oversized jacket. Her army rucksack was by her feet and stuffed as if she was ready to hike Mount Kilimanjaro. I wrapped my arms around my waist and smiled.

'All right, Jules,' I said.

I could feel Luca twitching beside me. Jules saw it too, though she didn't let on. Instead, she looked him right in the eye.

'All right, Posh Boy?' she said.

This didn't seem to help matters. He looked down at me, trying to keep his voice low.

'We've got to go, Molly,' he said.

Jules rocked back on her heels.

'Oh yeah?' she said. 'Where are you two lovebirds off to?'

The man with the dreads shuffled to the middle of our group. He looked sort of sorry and cross at the same time.

'No offence, guys, but you're ruining my trade.'

He rolled his eyes towards all the people walking in and out of the station. We nodded and moved to the other side of the road. The *Big Issue* folk take their jobs seriously and one thing they don't like is other homeless ruining their trade. Pedestrians can't stand groups of homeless together, especially when they're trying to flog something. They like to think of us as lonely types with no community. If you're by yourself, people can identify and sympathize, but if you're in a group then they feel alienated and resentful. Simple psychology really.

'Having a dirty weekend, then?' Jules said real loud for the whole world to hear. She was swinging side to side. It can look hostile the way she rocks about, but it's a technique she uses to keep herself alert. If she stands still for too long her defences drop.

I kept my voice light.

'Just going away for the day,' I said.

She raised her brows, showing off the black iris in her broken eye.

'Anywhere special?'

Luca stuffed his hands in his coat pockets and mumbled through the side of his mouth.

'Skegness,' he said.

Jules did one of her broad grins.

'*Brill-i-ant*. Love a bit of Skeggie, I do. Got an aunt up there, ain't I, Molls?'

She slapped me on the side of my arm as she carried on grinning.

'You remember? The one with the figurines.'

I nodded, watching the electronic board that publicizes the departure times.

'Don't mind if I come along, do you?' she said.

She scanned both our faces, waiting for us to grin back. Luca clenched his jaw.

'No way,' he said.

Jules stood tall. Her broken eye bulged.

'ParDON mE?'

The edge in her voice was sharp as a butcher's knife but Luca didn't hear it.

'This is a two-man mission,' he said.

Jules screwed her jaw tight.

'As far as I can see there ain't no **mEN** around here.'

There was once a woman called Medusa who was beautiful in that way women in myths and fairy tales always are (flaxen hair, fair skin, virginal as a nun). This woman was cursed and transformed into a hideous monster with snakes for hair. She became ugly in that way women in myths and fairy tales always are (old and withered). If you looked Medusa in the eyes she'd turn you to stone, mouth spitting hatred, face filled with venom. That was like Jules when she started a berserker in public. I knew it wasn't going to be pretty.

'Give us a minute, Jules,' I said.

I pulled at Luca's sleeve and made him follow me to the other side of the pavement. He was huffing and tutting, like a kid who wasn't getting his own way.

'You don't want to get Jules mad,' I said.

He shook his head.

'I am *not* letting her come.'

I looked over my shoulder. Jules was back with the *Big Issue* seller, jabbering away as he tried to ignore her.

'She won't be any trouble,' I said.

'Ha!' said Luca.

I glanced back and saw Jules swinging her army rucksack on to her back. It was about three times bigger than her body. She looked over at us.

'When we setting off, then?' she yelled. **'I ain'T GoT aLL dAY!'**

Luca shook his head again. I wanted to tell him to listen, not to me, but to the edge in Jules's voice.

This is the thing they don't tell you about Medusa: she was cursed after being raped by Poseidon in the goddess Athena's temple. This enraged Athena and it was Medusa who bore the brunt of that rage. It's always the women who get blamed, you see, and always the women who become hideous and revolting. Like Medusa, Jules had reasons for her venom. But Luca didn't know any of this and I didn't have time to explain.

'Time!' I said loudly. 'You're right; it's relative. The more time we stand here arguing, the less time we have to get on the train.'

Luca looked at Jules and back at me, then at his watch and then back at Jules. Before I could say anything else he marched towards the footbridge.

'Moody sod, ain't he?' Jules said as we tagged along behind.

The first few nights I was homeless I slept in the train-station toilets. They smelt of piss and disinfectant but the worst part was the cold tiles. I'd brought a sleeping bag but I'd forgotten silly things such as a hat and a decent pair of gloves. My fingers were tinged blue by morning so on the third night I decided to chance the waiting room and sleep on the wooden slatted seats. When I woke up, two policemen were standing over me in black uniforms. It near gave me a heart attack.

They started saying things about the law and rough sleeping. I nodded my head and pretended to listen but

I couldn't look at them; I can never look a policeman in the eye. Then they said they'd give me an Anti-Social Behaviour Order if I was found there again. I'd never been threatened with an ASBO before. I didn't realize you could get one without speaking to anyone, but it turned out being anti-social didn't only mean being abusive but making people feel uncomfortable, which seeing someone sleeping on a bench could do, apparently. I suppose it makes sense; being homeless is the most anti-social act you can commit.

I was shaking as they watched me get up. When I felt like this as a child I'd make Rubberband Girls, dozens and dozens of them, to calm my nerves. I'd hide them under my bedsheets or in the bathroom, stick them in flowerpots and desk tidies, hoping my mother wouldn't find them and throw them away.

I found one of those Rubberband Girls as the police watched me pack. I hid her down the crack of the bench before they escorted me out, a knotted arm sticking up in a half-wave as I left her behind. I imagined her joining the other Rubberband Girls I'd left behind. I imagined her forming an army.

And then I stopped shaking.

Our train was at Platform 2, past the shelter of the station and out alone at the bottom of the tracks. It was a tiny, two-carriage number, blue and boxy like a couple of sardine cans, and, seeing as it was sitting there waiting, we decided to get on.

Luca was still in a foul mood because Jules had blown a raspberry at him when he'd told her to get a ticket from the machines. He'd had to wipe the spit from his face with a tissue. As we walked through the carriage he didn't turn to me once. He thought the whole trip was ruined but I knew that with Jules on our team we'd be stronger than ever. She's small is Jules, but as resourceful as a Swiss army knife, flicking out her arm to reveal a bottle opener or kicking out her leg to reveal a tiny pair of scissors. Luca just needed a bit of time to see that.

The carriage was empty so Jules said we should take one of the tables. The seats were covered in a synthetic crimson material and had a grey plastic table between them, which left little space to squeeze yourself in. Jules pushed her rucksack on to the window seat and parked herself opposite. I sat next to her and Luca sat next to the bag, both wedging our rucksacks between our legs. He still wouldn't look at me, staring down the aisle like I was just another passenger. Like we were strangers, which I guess we were.

Jules began telling us about her aunt in Skegness.

'She's barmy as a parrot. Now me, I may be on the *eccentric* side, I admit it, but my aunt Janice is a proper *fruit loop*. All those bloody china figurines dancing and twirling about in that locked cabinet of hers. Bloody weird.'

Luca put up his hand, palm towards Jules as if he was a lollipop man and she was traffic. She stopped talking and looked at me like I somehow knew what was going on.

Luca looked at the rucksack beside him and then back at Jules.

'Your bag is panting,' he said.

Jules scrabbled over the table, flipping the top of her rucksack open to reveal a little wet nose.

'Jesus Christ!' Luca said, jumping to the back of his seat.

'Don't panic, Posh Boy,' Jules said, pulling Boy from inside. 'She's barely bigger than your head.'

Boy went crazy, front feet tapping against the plastic table, tongue lapping at Jules's face. I wondered how comfortable the poor thing had been, stuck in that rucksack for who knew how long, but I was dead chuffed that Jules hadn't left her behind. I made a big fuss over Boy, ruffling behind her ears and nuzzling her with my nose. This seemed to make her more excited, her body twisting from side to side as she tried to lick both mine and Jules's face. Her tail banged against the table as it wagged furiously.

'You've got to be joking,' said Luca.

'She's adorable, isn't she?' I said.

'A dog,' he said, gesturing at Boy. 'A *disabled* dog.'

I sat up tall.

'So what if she's disabled?' I said.

'She's going to get us kicked off.'

'Because of her leg?' Jules said.

'No, because she's a bloody dog.'

Boy lurched over the table, tongue heading straight for Luca's face.

'Keep your dog away from me!' Luca yelped as she licked him.

Jules reached over to retrieve Boy.

'She ain't my dog,' she said. 'Her owner pissed off so I'm just—'

Jules stopped mid-sentence and elbowed me in the side. She was staring ahead at the conductor making his way through the carriage. He was one of those petty official types; you could see it in the neatness of his uniform and the flaring of his nostrils. My throat twisted a little. We hadn't even set off and we were going to be chucked off the train. As he reached the glass doors, Jules slipped under the table. She's dead nippy, so by the time he got through to us she was balled up, Boy tucked against her body, her head covered by her camo jacket. They looked like another piece of luggage.

'Tickets from Nottingham, please,' the man said all loud even though we were the only people in the carriage.

My heart throbbed with a *de-dum-dum*. Luca searched his pockets. I didn't know what he was going to pull out but I had a feeling it wouldn't be good. I wrapped my fingers around the handles of my rucksack, ready to run.

A pair of orange and green tickets emerged between Luca's fingers. He handed them to the conductor, who scanned them slowly. I waited for him to tell us they were invalid, to either pay up or get off. Instead he stamped them with a curt 'Thank you' and then walked on down the carriage.

Luca must have got the tickets that morning. I thought that maybe I should thank him but he was sitting with a finger propped on his chin like he was having some deep thought so I decided not to disturb him. Instead I looked out of the window as the train pulled away from the station, the platform narrowing, the tracks crisscrossing. As we got further away from Nottingham, we got further away from Rusby. Concrete buildings turned to fields of green crops, his magnetic power waning.

A tiny yap came from beneath the table. I looked down at Jules's eyes peering up at me.

'He gone or what?' she asked.

'Oh, yeah,' I said. 'Ages ago.'

She slipped back out, disgruntled.

'Cheers for telling me.'

'You were so convincing we forgot you were there,' Luca said.

Jules sat up tall, taking this as a compliment.

'Bet you're glad I'm on your mission now, aren't you, Posh Boy?' she said.

Luca didn't respond, pulling a packet of jelly babies from his leather rucksack instead. He opened it and offered me one but Jules had her hand straight in the bag, rummaging around, pulling out a fistful and feeding a couple to Boy. Luca looked down at the bag as though it had been contaminated. He held it out to me again. I peered inside, taking a dark one the colour of a bruise, with a love heart moulded on its belly. It tasted of Berries and Pain. Luca made his way through what was left. As soon as he finished one sweet, he popped another in his mouth.

Jules nestled into the corner of her seat as Boy laid his head against her chest.

'So what's in Skeggie, then?' she asked Luca.

He raised a brow.

'You'll find out.'

She rolled her eyes.

'Don't be a tight arse. Just tell us.'

Luca paused, holding the head of a jelly baby between his teeth. He bit it off.

'It's got to be spontaneous,' he said, chewing. '*Unplanned.*'

Jules cocked her head.

'All right, Posh Boy, I know what *spontaneous* means. I'm not a fucking idiot.'

She carried on sitting all offended for a bit. Luca pulled a book from his bag.

'I'm going to read now,' he said.

He opened the book, eyes zipping from side to side behind his glasses.

Jules raised her brows as if to say *Look at Mister Lah-di-dah*. Then she skimmed the train carriage. She was getting twitchy.

'Right, I'm going for a *spontaneous* slash,' she said.

Luca pretended he hadn't heard but watched over the top of his glasses as she passed Boy to me and made her way down the aisle. When he caught me looking at him his eyes dropped back to his book.

'She's all right when you get to know her,' I said as Boy sat panting on my lap.

He squinted.

'So are serial killers.'

I giggled. He raised the book in front of his face. I don't know how I knew, but I could tell he was grinning.

After a while, Luca peered over his book as a woman with a snacks trolley came down the aisle. He started shuffling awkwardly in his seat. I leant forward so she wouldn't see Boy snoozing on my lap, smiling up at her but only briefly so she wouldn't get suspicious. She walked past and Luca sighed.

'Who is she talking to?' he said.

I craned sideways. Jules was chatting with two old women. They were prim-looking, with perfect grey bobs and tailored coats with fancy brooches. I looked back at Luca.

'Just two ladies,' I said.

I could hear Jules telling them about the pellet incident that had left her with the broken eye. It was one of her favourite stories. The women were listening politely, but at the same time giving her strong *go away* signals. Jules is rubbish at reading body language, but it was nice they were too polite to tell her to piss off.

'I think they're all right,' I said.

Luca looked at me all strict.

'You think because they're old they aren't dangerous? What do you think happens to criminals? They disintegrate at the age of sixty-five?'

I looked out of the window. He was getting intense again. I could feel him studying me, the same way he'd looked at me at the party, examining my organs. But this time, I didn't like it.

After a while, he leant forward on the table, fingers interlaced.

'The thing is, Molly, I've had a lot of things happen to me and I know you probably want to hear all the gruesome details but I don't really feel like going into it right now. And even if I did—'

He stopped, suddenly distracted.

'Why are you smiling?'

I didn't realize I was smiling until he pointed it out. I'd been looking at the scene outside: clouds skimming through the sky like froth on the top of a milkshake, sun streaming down through the gaps and dancing across the grassy hillsides. It was like something from a gallery.

'You don't even know what we're looking for,' he continued.

I tried to work out what he wanted me to say, but then remembered I'd stopped playing that game. The more you try to guess what other people want, the more you mess up. It's better to be honest.

'I don't mind not knowing,' I said.

He flinched a little when I said that, then his face relaxed.

'You're different from other people, aren't you?' he said.

I grinned.

'Look who's talking.'

Luca laughed. It was the first time I'd seen him laugh since the party. We eased back in our chairs, smiling at each other as the hills zoomed past. It was one of those rare moments when everything slows down and you both stop thinking and worrying and wondering about life or what's going to happen next and just *experience* it. In that moment, a tiny hand reaches out of your chest and touches the tiny hand reaching out of the other person's chest and you're both right there, the fingers of your souls interlinked.

But then the moment passed.

Luca's eyes went over my shoulder and widened. I began to follow his gaze but he shook his head.

'Who is it?'

'Just keep your head down.'

He lifted his book to cover his face. I tried to look back but he grabbed my hand. I could feel the pulse of his thumb as it pushed into my flesh.

'Don't!' he said.

His eyes froze on something behind me. I kept my neck stiff, staring ahead.

'*Run*,' he hissed.

I grabbed Jule's bag and the rucksack from between my legs as Luca jumped up. Boy leapt off my lap, yapping as she ran after him. Jules was still talking to the two old ladies but stopped when she heard Boy.

'What the fuck?' she said as we ran by.

The train was pulling up at a platform. I turned but couldn't see the conductor coming up behind us. I couldn't see who had spooked Luca either, only the ladies.

I chucked Jules her bag.

'We've only been on fifteen minutes!' she said.

The doors of the carriage slid open. Luca grabbed me by the waist and lifted me down on to the platform. It was unnecessary; I could have jumped, but I liked being held by him.

Jules sneered and hopped off, swinging her rucksack on to her back. Boy hovered at the train doors, looking at the platform but edging back into the carriage.

'Who you running from, Posh Boy?' Jules said.

There was a trill little beep. I leant forward and grabbed Boy just before the doors shut. She squirmed in my arms, licking my face. When I looked up, the train was already moving away. Whoever Luca had seen was gone.

'Jesus,' Jules said, looking down at Boy. 'Can't get rid of the bugger.'

But I could tell she didn't mean it, because she took Boy straight out of my arms.

It was a short platform, a lone metal bridge connecting one side to the other. There was only one exit so Luca marched towards it.

Jules groaned so I tugged at her arm. It was only when we got to the white picket fence at the exit that Luca stopped, staring up at the platform sign. He dropped his rucksack and threw his trumpet case on the ground. It clattered against the concrete, echoing around the platform.

'You're frickin' kidding me!' he cried.

I looked at the sign. In large blue capitals it said 'BINGHAM'.

The Dainty Land of Bingham

When I was eight, my parents took me to see my grand-mother. She lived in a small town in the middle of nowhere. By the car park near to her house was a mini-ature village with model shops, a model primary school, a model fire station and a cellophane lake. My parents stood by the lake arguing; my grandmother was dying and neither of them had wanted to make the trip. As they argued I could see their faces getting knotted up in that ugly way. Not fairy-tale ugly (my parents were well-groomed, good-looking people) but ugly in the way that makes you sick because of the nastiness behind it.

So instead of looking at them, I focused on the village. I studied the little bricks on the buildings and the cobbles on the roads. I examined the expressions painted on the figures as they waved to each other. I watched the little steam train chug around on the miniature railway, the train driver hold-ing out his hat as he rode past. Then I took a nearly finished

Rubberband Girl from my pocket, knitted her hair into two plaits and placed her by the Town Hall. This was her home.

Stepping into Bingham was like stepping into that model village. There was a cobbled square and black metal bollards with gold detail, spindly trees lining the streets and rows of dainty shops with hand-painted signs. There was bunting strung across the Post Office window and what looked like a fancy cookware shop. All it needed was a train chugging by, the driver waving his hat through the window.

Luca stood by a monument in the middle of the square. It was octagonal with stone pillars that rose into arches and then into a spire. It was a pretty thing but entirely useless. There were no benches inside for people to sit on and the arches were too low and narrow to work as a bandstand. Still, there was something nice about it. Like maybe it had been special to someone once.

Boy sniffed the ground, tail wagging as pedestrians shuffled past. There was the smell of just-baked food – sweet breads, meat pies and pasties – which made my stomach rumble.

Jules pulled a packet of Quavers from her cargo pants. The pockets were great for storing things as well as for shoplifting. Jules can be carrying half the contents of a corner shop before anyone notices the items are missing.

'Is this a village?' she asked, pushing a potato curl in her mouth. You could hear the crunch echo; the place was that quiet.

'Market town,' said Luca.

Jules nodded. I must have looked confused because she leant in close to me.

'Like a normal town, but posh.'

When I looked down at my feet I could see two rubber bands looped over each other in front of me. They looked up at me like eyes staring from the ground.

'What now, Posh Boy?' Jules said.

Luca blinked as though a fly was buzzing around his head. He scanned the square and then the road behind us. There was a part of him ready to run from this place and a part of him ready to hide in its darkest corner.

He straightened his arm in front of him, finger pointing ahead.

'Pub,' he said.

Luca began walking to a red-bricked building with yellow window frames. It had 'The Butter Cross' written across it in large golden letters. Jules shoved the packet of crisps inside her jacket and grinned. She nudged me in the arm.

'That's the best idea he's had all day,' she said.

These are the things my parents argued about.

How they needed to live in that detached house, in the nicer area.

How they couldn't afford to do that and whose fault that was.

How he always held her back.

How she never stopped complaining.

How he was sleeping with other women.

How she was crazy, like her mother, which meant she said crazy things like he was sleeping with other women.

How they should never have got married or had me.

How she was a terrible mother.

How he loved me more than he loved her.

How she was sick and manipulative.

How he was the same, but worse.

How, if he was so bloody awful, why didn't she just take this knife, right here and now, and slash his throat?

How she was tempted.

They would usually save these arguments for home. As soon as the front door shut they threw down their coats and tore into each other. They didn't need to tell me to go upstairs; I just went. After the argument at the model village I thought things might change; they'd revealed themselves to the world and there was no going back. Except, of course, there was. Back to smiling at other parents by the school gates, back to wrapping their arms around each other at parties. Back to pretending.

I guess it's hard to give something up when you've become so good at it.

It was a classy pub, the Butter Cross, even though it was a Wetherspoon's. Me and Jules had toured all the great

Wetherspoons of Nottingham and, even though we loved them, there were none we'd have called classy.

The booth we sat in was clad in strips of leather and tweed, the chairs around the other tables painted in muted whites and greens, and above us, hanging from the ceiling, were upside-down silver buckets that acted like lampshades and plant pots with long grass hanging from within. I don't think the plants were real but they still looked classy. Metal seats that seemed like they were once part of some piece of farming equipment were nailed to the painted brick walls. They had the words 'BLACKSTONE', 'MARTIN' and 'NICHOLSON' moulded on to them. I wondered if there was a tractor seat out there that said 'JENSON', which is my family name, but I couldn't ask because I don't tell people my real name. Not any more.

When Jules saw the menu she was happy as Larry because it was Steak Club Tuesday, which was one of her favourite days in the Wetherspoon's week.

'Eight-ounce rump steak with a pint of Stella.'

She slammed her hand down on the table as though that was the end of the matter and there was no persuading her otherwise.

Luca asked me what I wanted. I felt the coin purse I kept in my jeans pocket. It was as flat as a deflated balloon so I told him I wasn't hungry. Luca looked at me and grinned.

'What?' I said.

He pulled out a white card from his wallet and placed it on the table. It had silver numbers and 'PLATINUM' written across it. He tapped it gently with his finger.

'It's on me.'

He looked proud of himself, chest puffed up as though he'd been crowned King of the Pub. Jules grabbed the card off the table. She turned it over in her hand.

'Who d'ya nick that off?' she said.

Luca's chest deflated. He bent over the table and whipped the card away from Jules. His cheeks were flushed.

'I have my sources,' he said, before pushing it back into his wallet.

Jules's phone rang. It was that same irritating tune but it seemed louder here in the pub. She pulled it from her pocket, holding it close to her chest so that I couldn't see the screen before pressing decline. She seemed put out, suddenly agitated and twitchy. She scowled at Luca.

'You paying for **mE thEn**?' she said.

I looked at Luca, hoping he could hear the edge in her voice, but he was too busy staring at Jules as though she was absurd to notice me.

'Of course,' he said. 'You're part of the mission.'

Jules's brows rose slowly up her forehead.

'You know, lad,' she said, sitting tall. 'I thought you were a dodgy fucker when I first met you, but you're growing on me.'

Luca frowned, his mouth crooked. Then he relaxed. It was like watching your divorced parents getting along at Christmas.

Jules slammed her hand on the table again.

'Make that two pints, then!' she said. 'And a steak for the dog.'

Luca opened his mouth but stopped himself from speaking. When the waitress came over she looked down at Boy and said only assistance dogs were allowed in the food area. Then she saw she had a missing leg and went all soppy, bending down and ruffling behind her ears.

'You can have her for fifty,' Jules said.

The waitress laughed, though I don't think Jules was joking, and said Boy could stay if we didn't tell the manager. Jules winked, then leant over the back of the seat to watch the waitress's hips sway as she walked to the bar.

Jules turned back.

'See that?' she said. 'Pure chemistry.'

Luca shook his head.

'With who?'

Jules gestured behind her.

'Me and that lass,' she said.

When the waitress came back with our drinks and then our food, Jules grinned wide at her. I'd ordered the Chicken & Rib combo and a pint of cider. The plate was massive: half a rack of ribs, a diamond chicken breast, six beer-battered onion rings and a heap of chips, with coleslaw and sauces in little glazed pots. I tore straight into the ribs. The meat filled my cheeks as the sticky barbecue sauce coated my lips.

'Hungry much?' Luca said.

I looked up mid-bite. I wasn't sure if he was disgusted or impressed. Perhaps I was supposed to use a knife and fork instead of my fingers but then I'd never be able to get the meat clean off the bone. I licked the sauce from my lips.

'You bet!' I said, even though my mouth was still full of meat.

Jules pulled out a knife and fork from the inside pocket of her camo jacket. They were the pure silver ones she'd won in a bet with Dodgy Mike. She sat up straight, cutting her steak into cubes.

'Our Molls is a bit of a gannet,' she said. 'Can't tell to look at her, can you? Skinny little mite. Now me, I like to savour my food.'

She spiked a chip and a steak cube on to her fork and pushed it into her mouth. She closed her eyes all dreamy as she chewed, jaw chomping up and down like a television chef.

'This is proper *banger*!' she said.

'Spoken like a true lady,' Luca said.

Jules sat up tall, holding her fork daintily in the air. When she spoke, it was in her posh, royal voice, the one that always cracks me up.

'Why, thank you, sir,' she said. *'I do try my best.'*

Jules was on to her second pint by the time the food was cleared away. As the waitress collected the plates, Jules released an almighty belch. It vibrated right through the seat. The waitress giggled as she walked away.

'What did I tell you?' Jules said to Luca.

He rolled his eyes.

'You're right,' he said. 'Pure chemistry.'

Jules basked in the glory of a full stomach and all the chemistry before rummaging around in her cargo pants until she found a box of toothpicks. She passed them around and we sat there, picking the food out of our teeth. Then Jules sat up and slapped her hands together.

'I say we jump on the next train to Skeggy and rent ourselves a nice seaside B&B courtesy of Mr S. Bargate.'

I frowned.

'Who's he?' I asked.

Jules nodded her head at Luca.

'The man who just bought us dinner. Or at least his card did.'

When I looked at Luca his cheeks were rosy with embarrassment.

'*Good day to you, Mr Bargate,*' I said, mimicking Jules's posh voice.

We both snorted.

'*Why, how very gen-herous of you, Mr Bargate,*' Jules said.

This set us off in a bout of giggles. We get these sometimes, especially when we're a little tipsy. Every time a wave of laughter peters out we look at each other and start giggling again, except stronger and harder until we're cackling like fishwives.

Luca didn't see the funny side.

'We can't go by rail,' he said.

Jules was still hee-heeing.

'Why not, Posh Boy?'

Luca lowered his voice.

'We're being followed.'

There was a pause. Then me and Jules laughed again, our hooting ringing around the pub like a bell. This seemed to confuse Luca. He shook his head.

'I'm not joking,' he said.

Jules patted me on the arm and we both calmed down, wiping the tears from our cheeks. I focused on the mums with pushchairs and retired couples as I tried to control my breathing. They were glancing over at us, unsure whether they should get us removed or join in.

Jules crossed her arms.

'Go on then, Posh Boy. Tell us who's following us.'

Luca shook his head. He put his elbow on the table and pressed his fingers against his temples.

'I need time to think,' he said.

He looked down at the wooden table. Jules glanced at me and I glanced at Jules. I sucked my lips in so that I wouldn't get the giggles again. We sat in silence for a minute, stroking the rims of our pint glasses. I knew this was hard for Jules because she can't stand silence. It lets the voices in.

After a while she downed the rest of her pint.

'Right! While Posh Boy *thinks*, I'm going for a gander.'

Luca looked up.

'A gander?'

Jules stood up.

'A mosey. Shufti. *Looksee*.'

Luca shook his head.

'There's nothing to see round here. Trust me.'

She slid out of the booth, picking up Boy, who had gravy all over her nose.

'I'm great at finding the hidden treasures. Coming, Molls?'

Jules has led me on some great adventures. It's always kind of exciting, tagging along just to see where you might end up. But Luca still had his fingers pressed to his temples, his eyes swimming as though he was seasick.

'Best stay here,' I said.

Jules looked at me with her broken eye. I nodded to the glass in front of me.

'Still got half a pint, ain't I?' I said.

She paused and then nodded. Jules couldn't argue with half a pint. She clicked her fingers, pointing at me with a wink.

'Find you later then, doll,' she said.

I didn't ask where she'd find us. She didn't know that I'd thrown my phone in the canal and that there was no way of reaching me. But Jules has this great ability – she can find you in the unlikeliest of places. It's her superpower: sensing you're in danger, leaping in to rescue you right at the last minute.

I sipped at my cider. When I finished, Luca was still thinking so I ordered a pot of tea. I thought it might help him focus and I was right because when the waitress brought it over Luca sat up straight and poured it into the cups like a butler. I wondered if he'd learnt this in some posh school: Horse Riding in the morning, Latin after break, Tea Pouring in the afternoon. He took a sip, swirled the reddish-brown liquid round in his cup as if trying to find his future. Yasmin from Glasgow had taught me all about tea reading so I knew he was doing it all wrong.

'If I ask a question you are fully entitled to tell me to piss off.'

Luca had his hands laid out flat on the table with his fingers spread out like starfish. It had been so long since he'd last spoken that it took a while for me to respond. Jules would have told him to piss off before I'd opened my mouth. I was kind of glad she wasn't with us, because I knew what he was going to ask. And I wanted him to know the truth about me. I wanted to lay the broken pieces of my past before him like relics.

Luca paused. I took a gulp of tea.

'Who was that man you were with earlier?' he said.

I nearly spat out the tea. I didn't know how he'd seen me and Rusby without me seeing him. I felt grimy with the thought of it, as though it wasn't relics he was looking at but junk. I coughed into my hand.

'Rusby,' I said. 'My ex.'

Luca screwed up his lips. He picked up a napkin and ripped the corners between his fingers.

'Looked like an idiot.'

I smiled one of those nervous smiles when your face doesn't know what to do with itself.

'He's not that bad.'

I didn't want to look at Luca so I examined my nails, remembering how Rusby used to gnaw at his own until he got to the flesh.

'Do you still love him?' he asked.

Luca's lips were still screwed up tight.

'I never loved him,' I said.

His expression dropped.

'Oh.'

'It's OK,' I said. 'I don't think he loved me either. Not really.'

He thought about this for a moment before giving a half-smile.

'Then I was right. He's an idiot.'

I half smiled back.

Luca folded his arms. I knew he was having another think so I left him to it and drank my tea. I felt hollow, like someone had taken a shovel and scooped out my insides. Eventually he looked up at me.

'Let's go.'

What Yasmin from Glasgow had taught me about reading tea leaves was this: you had to drink slowly, meditating on the problem that was bothering you. Then, when you were nearly finished, you swirled the cup before turning it on to a saucer so that the leaves formed a pattern on the plate. I knew what to look for: the anchor, the axe, the star and the cup. And I knew how, when a certain symbol faced a certain way, it meant good luck and a safe journey, but if it faced the other way it meant you had to stop everything as there was something terrible on the horizon.

I listened and nodded as Yasmin explained, knowing that none of it was true. Life is as random as the pattern in a saucer; there's no way to make sense of it. But people like to feel that they're in control. Which I suppose was why Yasmin was mad into the fortune-telling stuff: the tea leaves; tarot cards; mediums with dodgy moustaches and flashy cars, who conned you out of your money and left you stuck on the street with the likes of me and Jules. The way I figure, there are only two things you'll see when you look into your future: what you want to see and what you're scared of seeing. I didn't say this to Yasmin, of course. Fortune telling was like a religion to her and there's as much point arguing with someone about religion as there is arguing with the wind. Neither of them can hear you.

When we got outside Luca led me down a side street off the main square. It was full of old buildings and led to a path running straight through a graveyard. The church beside it had stained-glass windows that reached high and tall. I love stained glass. If I had my own house I'd have stained glass in every window, door, glass cabinet, table top, even the oven doors. Not with the saints but with all the things I loved. An ice-cream sundae with sprinkles and cherries. A huge oak tree with branches that stretch far and wide. A newborn baby with ginger wisps of hair.

'It's peaceful here, don't you think?' Luca said.

I looked around at the gravestone slabs, feeling the silence of the place.

'Nobody bothers you in a graveyard,' I said.

He nodded.

We walked around slowly. The air still smelt of baked food, now accompanied by a musty smell coming from the gravestones. Each slab was large and foreboding; they all dated back to the 1800s and had moss growing up their sides and cracks lightning-bolting through them. I like walking around graveyards. I like imagining the lives of the people who ended up here, what they did, who they loved, *how* they loved, their talents, their hopes, their dreams.

'Have you thought about my question?' Luca said. He kicked some pebbles across the ground. 'The one about what makes us human?'

It was strange that he kept bringing this up but I figured it must be important. I thought of the bodies lying beneath us. I thought about them being eaten by worms and beetles and how they weren't really people any more and that they never would be again. But we cared about them anyway. Places like this were proof of that.

'I'm still thinking about it,' I said.

Luca nodded. Then he pulled a piece of bread from his pocket. It was a crusty white roll from his meal at the pub. He broke it up and threw some pieces on the ground. The birds came instantly. Little sparrows, finches and pigeons. The pigeons were fat grey clouds with deformed feet. They seemed to be following us everywhere.

People say pigeons are the rats of the skies. They say they're common and dirty but if you look real close you'll see that they're spectacular creatures. Their feathers are awash with iridescent colour and their bodies are shaped like hearts. If you think about it, they're really grey doves and no one calls doves the rats of anything. That's why pigeons are one of my favourite animals.

'Maybe we should stay here for a bit,' Luca said.

I looked around and nodded. We could kip beneath the big oak tree; I reckoned we could all bunk under it for the night. I suggested it to Luca.

'No, not in this graveyard,' Luca said. 'In Bingham. I think we were meant to get off the train here. I think we should stay.'

He paused and then added, 'Just for a bit.'

He stuffed the bread back into his pocket, happy that he'd come to this decision.

I looked back at the oak tree. Its branches were looped together with rubber bands. Not all of them but some of them, twisted and tied tightly with different colours and thicknesses. I felt an uneasiness in my stomach; it was knotted as tight as those branches. We weren't going to Skegness anytime soon.

I told myself that it didn't matter, that it's the journey which matters and not the destination. But it really felt like the destination mattered most. It felt like the destination was the only thing that mattered.

I curled my fingers around my wrist and snapped the rubber band against my skin.

'Sure,' I said to Luca.

When we got back to the square we stood by the monument so that Jules would be able to find us. There was writing around the top of the arches, fancy capital letters in a language I couldn't understand.

'I wonder what this monument's called,' I said.

'Buttercross,' Luca said. 'The pub's named after it.'

I looked at the pub and then back at Luca. I wanted to ask how he knew this but he was too distracted by all the people glancing at us. He curled his shoulders, turning up the collar of his navy-blue trench coat.

'Nosey bastards,' Luca said, lowering his head. 'I wish I could disappear.'

I thought for a second.

'No problem,' I said.

I sat down on the cold slabs, legs crossed, and pulled a paper cup from my camping rucksack. Luca watched me, and then sat down in the space I patted beside me. I put the cup in front of us and would have pulled out my little

71

sign asking for money, but I didn't need to; everyone had already stopped looking.

'Ta-dah! My first trick in becoming invisible,' I said.

Luca rolled his shoulders back.

'And you told me you didn't have any special skills,' he said.

I remembered all the shop doorways I'd sat in, how I used to watch passers-by. They tried so hard to pretend I didn't exist that they would walk into things. Once, when I was sitting under the bridge by the Navigation, a young lad knocked over my cup, sending coppers scattering across the pavement. It was a Monday morning and everyone was on their way to work and one man, dressed in a nice suit, briefcase in hand, started laughing like he'd just seen the world's greatest comedy show.

'Good on you, mate!' he shouted.

The young lad bent down to help me collect the coins but he still didn't look at me or speak. He was more embarrassed about me being there than he was about knocking over the cup.

'Have a good day,' I said as he stood.

He shoved his hands in his pockets and walked away. I suppose I can't really complain. I ended up on the streets because I wanted to disappear.

'Can you make *her* invisible?' said Luca.

When I looked up, Jules was striding towards us. I pushed him on the arm.

'Be nice,' I said.

She had a carton of beer tucked under one arm and Boy under the other. Jules is a Bevvy Wizard: she conjures up drink wherever she goes.

'Found any hidden treasures?' Luca said dryly as we both stood.

'I've done better than that, Posh Boy,' she said. 'I've found us somewhere to sleep.'

The Discovery of Manor Cottage

My favourite story of all time is *The Wonderful Wizard of Oz*. When I was little I'd read a chapter every night, clutching the book to my chest before I fell asleep. It was a hardback so the pointy corners stuck right into my chest but I loved the story so much that I didn't mind the pain. In the morning, I'd make the bed and stick the book beneath my pillow so it would be ready for me to pull out and read again later that night. Whenever I got to the end of the book I'd start reading from the beginning and kept going like this on a loop for a good year before, one day, Mother caught me reading it. She must have seen how happy it was making me because the next time I did something wrong – speaking too quickly, grinning at a stranger – she made me rip out twenty pages and put them in the fire. I recited the words in my head as I watched the pages ignite, trying to remember each and every detail.

I guess that's why parts of the story come back to me wherever I go. For example, when Jules led us down a lane off the market square and the cobbles had the sun shining all over them, it felt like we were walking down the Yellow Brick Road. Jules had passed Boy to me and, as I carried her, I realized she was like my own little Toto, but with three legs. It felt like a sign, not only that we were on the right path, but that we were on *the* path. The one that would take us to the Emerald City where the Wizard would wave a wand and fix all our problems – he would fix us. The more I thought about it, the more the bricks glowed yellow beneath my feet and soon my red canvas shoes began to glitter like Judy Garland's ruby slippers (in the book they were silver slippers, but I don't mind that they changed them; red looks better in Technicolor). I carried on staring at my shoes sparkling wildly like they were on fire, until I bumped into Jules who'd stopped walking. She made an *ummph!* noise, stumbling ahead before turning back to me.

'Back in dreamland, Molls?' she said.

She rolled her eyes. When I looked down at my shoes, they were still sparkling.

'What is this place?' Luca said.

Jules stood in front of a derelict building, her carton of beer still cradled in her arms.

'*Our new abode,*' she said in her posh voice, before bowing down real low and waving her hand out to the side.

75

It was a red-brick building, tall and wide, with crumbling posts at the entrance that ran up to a small peaked roof with broken tiles. Nailed beneath the peak was a sign that read 'MANOR COTTAGE'. It was probably a grand old house back in the day but now it looked bleak, like a doll with its eyes gouged out. There were metal sheets over the windows but Jules had prised the corner of a wooden board from the front door. It left a gap, like the mouse holes you see in cartoons. Boy sprung out of my hands, lowered her head and went straight through.

'I don't know about this,' said Luca.

He looked up and down the road. It was quiet with no pedestrians.

'What's wrong with it?' asked Jules.

'Anything could be in there,' said Luca.

'I've already given it a gander,' she said. 'Completely empty.'

Luca looked at Jules suspiciously.

'Don't trust me or summat?' she said.

Luca took off his glasses, cleaning them with the corner of his coat.

'Trust only leads to disappointment,' he said.

Jules wrinkled her nose, wiggling her head side to side.

'*Trust only leads to disappointment*,' she said, high and shaky like an old woman.

She shoved the carton through the gap.

'Get your arse in, Posh Boy,' she said before shimmying through.

I didn't look at Luca because I didn't want to give him time to object. It was easy for me to slip in and, as we stood waiting in the dark of the hallway, I wondered if he'd carry on standing out there just to prove his point. I heard a click and Jules's face glowed orange as she lit a cigarette. She looked at me with blazing eyes.

'Proper nervy little bloke, ain't he?' she said.

The flame clicked off. For a moment I could still see the glow of her face but then my eyes adjusted and I could only see the amber disc at the end of her cigarette, flaring every time she took a puff.

'Just a bit careful, I think,' I said.

We stood in the silence a little longer. I could hear Boy panting and sniffing.

'So,' Jules said. 'What exactly did you do to Rusby?'

It gave me a start, hearing his name.

'What do you mean?' I said.

The room lit up as Jules pulled out her phone. She was concentrating real hard as she scrolled through her messages.

'"Tell Molls I forgive her,"' she read. '"All she has to do is come say sorry."'

She looked up at me questioningly. The screen went blank.

'I threw a beer in his face,' I said. 'Then I smashed the glass and ran away.'

She went quiet for a second. I imagined her shaking her head, thinking about how I'd wasted that beer. Then a sudden panic swelled in my chest.

'You haven't told him we're here, have you?' I said.

There was a rustling noise at the door as Luca's trumpet case was shoved through the gap.

I felt a hand on my shoulder.

'Don't worry, Molls,' she said softly. 'That bastard ain't ever going to touch you again. That's a promise.'

The panic eased.

Another rustling noise, a rucksack being pushed through the gap, then Luca himself. His long body bent and twisted like a contortionist, the light glowing around him. I imagined someone walking past, seeing his legs wiggling on the other side like two worms trying to get through the same hole. Jules leant in close to me.

'He's making a proper meal out of that,' she said.

'He'll be fine,' I replied.

I opened the door to the main living room, hoping she'd follow, which she did. A lovely blue light was coming through the tops of the windows where the metal boards didn't quite reach high enough. We could make out the outlines of each other but not below hip level, only our faces and torsos.

'Right!' Luca said as he followed us through.

He knelt down on the floor and rifled through his rucksack, pulling out a camping light. It was a collapsible thing, which he straightened out and began winding with the handle attached to the top. It glowed kind of weak at first and then stronger until we could see the dust across the floorboards. We had a little look around but the only piece of furniture was a broken bureau with some washing machine instructions in the top drawer.

We spread our things into a circle on the floorboards and sat down on our rolled-out sleeping bags. Luca's bag looked new, no cuts or stains or patches to stop the draught, no blanket or liner to put beneath it. Rookie mistake.

Jules hummed as she ripped open the carton of beers and stretched one out for Luca. He shook his head.

'I don't do well with drink,' he said.

Jules snorted.

'Who does?'

She carried on holding out the can until eventually he took it. She was dead chuffed, as though she'd converted him to her religion.

People wonder why homeless people always have a bevvy in their hands but it's kind of medicinal. Drink doesn't only keep you merry but it also keeps you numb. If you're pissed, you don't really notice the pain and the cold. Crack does the same, but a hundred times better. There are worse side effects to that though, so alcohol's a good substitute. Or at least it's a *legal* substitute, which means you can get your hands on it easier.

When we all had a can, Jules yanked her ring-pull back and lifted hers up. I watched the universe twinkling inside her broken eye as she waited for us to do the same. Even in the dim light I could see it all: the spiralling stars, the gases spinning against the purple-black.

'To Bingham!' she cried.

'No,' Luca said, just as we were about to take a sip.

He looked down at his can.

'I can't cheers to that.'

Jules sat with her neck pushed forward, beer can inches from her lips. She slammed it down, amber liquid sloshing out of the top.

'Then what *can* you cheers to, you miserable sod?'

Luca got ruffled by that, neck suddenly straight like a chicken ready to peck. I lifted my can.

'To adventure!' I said.

They both looked at me, paused, then nodded. We all took a swig, the sour taste sitting on our tongues. As I tilted my head back for the second mouthful I saw something scurry along the back wall. It was big, black and furry. I decided not to mention it to the others.

The light was already fading on the lamp so Luca began winding it up again. It made a whirring noise like a broken-down fridge. It got me thinking about machines and how they work, and then people and how they work.

'Jules,' I said, 'what do you think makes us human?'

Luca stopped winding the handle. His body was stiff, as though telling Jules his Serious Question was the same as telling her he had herpes. Jules didn't notice though; she was too busy mulling it over.

'Like, what makes us different from animals?' she said.

Luca shook his head.

'Other animals,' he said.

'Say what?' Jules said.

'What makes us different from *other* animals. Humans are animals too.'

Jules snorted as if he'd told a joke; then she clicked her fingers.

'I got it!' she said. 'We *think*, don't we? Animals are stupid as fuck.'

She looked over at Boy, who had her head buried behind the bureau.

'Sorry, doll,' she said to her. 'But it's true.'

Luca's forehead crinkled.

'No, it's not,' he said.

Jules shrugged.

'Erm, yes, Posh Boy, it really bloody is.'

'What about dolphins?' he said.

Jules snorted again.

'Dolphins? They can't even walk. How clever is that?'

Luca looked over at me with wide eyes.

'What about chimpanzees?' I said.

Jules sneered.

'Smaller versions of humans. Haven't a thought in their head.'

Luca shook his head. You could tell he was trying to be patient.

'Gorillas?' he said.

Jules looked at him as though he was an idiot.

'They eat their own shit!'

81

Me and Luca were trying not to laugh, but there's something about the way Jules says things that's just freaking hilarious. We tried to think of more examples but Jules was getting to her feet.

'Right, I'm off,' she said, picking up her can.

Luca looked around.

'Off?'

She pointed a thumb behind her.

'Got to talk to a man about a dog.'

Boy was still sniffing the floor and, when Jules picked her up, began thrashing around so that she nearly fell from Jules's hands.

'See,' she said as she left. 'Proper stupid.'

Luca sat bemused. I shrugged, pushing myself to my feet.

'We should look for some cardboard,' I said.

Luca wrinkled his nose.

'Cardboard?' he said. 'What for?'

I frowned, wondering how many times Luca had slept rough. There were some homeless who managed to avoid it: sofa surfing, night buses, hostels and crisis accommodation. He must have been lucky so far; nothing can prepare you for that first night on a cold floor.

'Just follow me,' I said.

When the police booted me out of Nottingham train station I followed the crowd. I didn't know the city but, as I followed the masses, its layout became clear; how you had to walk through the shopping centre to reach the city centre, and cross the roads carefully because they weren't just for cars, buses and people, like normal roads, but for trams too. When I got to Market Square, the crowd dispersed so I walked in and out of the shops to keep myself warm. I moved on every half an hour so that the security didn't get tetchy and threaten me with an ASBO again. I tried to avoid the restaurants – the smell of food made my stomach ache – but every other shop was a fast-food joint so there was no escaping it. Then the shops started closing and, tired from all the walking around, I sat on a bench by the Town Hall and read a paperback copy of *The Wonderful Wizard of Oz*. I'd bought it at a pound shop before leaving home, an essential tool in my street-survival kit alongside duct tape and foldable cutlery.

When I was part way through the fourth chapter I saw him. A tall willowy man with a wispy grey beard and a knee-length jacket with rainbow stripes down its length. He had a purple beanie rammed low on his head and was walking up and down the street as though he had springs in his legs, two hessian bags clutched in his hands. I watched as he popped in and out of sandwich shops, his bags getting fuller with each visit, until eventually I lost sight of him. The Town Hall clock struck six o'clock and all the shop doors closed. I got back to my book but I couldn't shake the image of the man. The rainbow jacket, the bouncing motion, the bags of sandwiches clutched in his hands.

'Cheese and pickle?'

When I looked up he was standing in front of me, a soft grin across his face as he held a triangular package out to me. I felt my cheeks get hot; I don't know how he'd figured it out. My clothes were still clean, my hair brushed neatly behind my ears, I'd even made sure to spray myself with a tester bottle from the perfume counter in the shop, and yet he'd known I was homeless. I didn't say anything, just shook my head, grabbed my rucksack and rushed off as though I was late for an appointment.

As I walked the streets that evening I looked at all the homeless people sitting and lying in doorways. It felt strange that I was one of them now. Whenever I walked by homeless people as a child my mother would say, 'That's where you'll end up if you don't do as you're told.'

I did as I was told and I still ended up here, which shows how much she knew.

I didn't want to take anyone's turf or sleep in the open in case the police found me again so I went to one of the NCP car parks and made my way up to the top level. Most of the cars were gone by then so I found a corner away from the cameras and exits and bunked up for the night. I'd barely got in my sleeping bag when I saw him. The same man, thin and willowy, bouncing his way towards me across the black concrete. He didn't have the hessian bags any more but a large piece of cardboard in his hands. I thought about getting my things together and running away again but then there he was, standing in front of me just like he had been before, a big grin across his face. It stretched up into his cheeks and made his eyes glow so brightly he could have had a candle burning inside him. I wondered if he was homeless too. He didn't look homeless, just a bit of a hippy. I didn't know then that homeless people came in every form imaginable. There are people who sleep in cars, iron their suits in petrol station toilets and still go to work the next day without anyone knowing they have no place to call home.

'Don't worry,' the man said, seeing the panic in my eyes. 'I'm not staying.'

His voice was gentle, the exact opposite of the policemen who'd spoken to me earlier. It was soothing, as if it could guide you into meditation. He passed me the cardboard sheet from his hand. It was big, with a picture of a television printed on the front.

'That's your bed,' he said. 'Put it under your sleeping bag and it'll stop the cold getting through from the ground.'

Then he rummaged in his pockets and pulled out a woolly hat with a pink pom-pom on the top.

'Heat comes out of your head and feet,' he said, passing it to me. 'Wear it while you sleep.'

I'd already taken the cardboard so it felt rude not to take the hat.

'And I'd take those earrings out if I were you,' he said.

I felt my earlobes. I had a pair of teardrop silver earrings that my grandmother had given me for my thirteenth birthday.

'You don't want someone ripping them out in the middle of the night,' he said.

I took them out.

'Thank you,' I said.

He smiled again. It was an honest smile, a smile you could trust. But I wasn't ready to trust anyone, not then.

I watched as the man rummaged in his pockets again.

'Barbecue chicken wrap,' he said, pulling out a cellophane package and passing it to me. 'More your type of thing?'

I gave him a weak smile. I know it was weak, because I felt weak. But it was the best I could manage at the time.

'I like cheese and pickle too,' I said. 'I'm not picky really.'

He placed a finger on his forehead and tapped it.

'Noted,' he said.

He began to turn away.

'What's your name?' I said.

The man looked at me, then crouched down, pulling off a moss-green glove as he held out his hand to me. When I felt it wrap around my palm it was like a hot-water bottle. I looked into the man's pale eyes. He was the first person to touch me in days.

'My name is Martin Wallis,' he said. 'But they call me Robin Hood.'

We found some cardboard at a dumpster behind the pub, then went back to Manor Cottage and set up our beds for the night. I showed Luca how to layer a bin liner on top of the cardboard and checked his sleeping bag to make sure it didn't have any stitching coming loose. It still had the shop label on. I read the description: water-resistant down, a four-season rating and a pillow pocket in the hood. It was probably the best sleeping bag on the market but, all the same, I knew Luca was going to have a terrible night of it.

I told him it was best to layer up his clothing before he got into the bag but he still pushed his shoes off and started his ritual with the socks. He peeled each one off real slow then placed them across the floor in little rows like he had the night before. As soon as he'd taken off the last sock he began unpacking his leather rucksack. It was mainly full of opaque tubs. He laid them out in rows next to his socks. Behind him I saw something scurry along the wall.

I nodded to Luca's trumpet case.

'Do you play?'

'No.'

He carried on unpacking.

'Oh,' I said.

I was kind of hoping he'd pull out the trumpet and play a mini-concert for me right there in Manor Cottage. I love orchestra music. The way the strings flow and the piano music sails along, making you sit back in your seat and melt right into the fabric. My mother used to take me to see the Symphony Orchestra. She was a big fan of classical music, hated anything with lyrics. Now me, I love music that's got truth in it. Not the stuff about sexy women with big asses but the stuff about life. The kind of music that stirs a person up inside. I don't think the orchestra stirred Mother up though; I think it placated her. She was never interested in truth.

'My granddad used to play,' Luca said.

He'd stopped messing around with his tubs.

'Was he any good?' I asked.

Luca nodded.

'He was a genius,' he said.

He picked up his can of beer and crossed his legs, turning his body to face me.

'He was taught by Louis Armstrong. You've heard of Louis Armstrong?'

'Yeah,' I said. 'That's awesome.'

He grinned.

'He was a pretty awesome guy. He was the only person who really listened to me. I mean really *listened*. When he died he gave me this . . .'

He stroked the trumpet case beside him. I felt the key around my neck.

'That too,' he said.

I kind of knew the key was precious the first time I saw it, but now it felt heavy, like a weight attached to my soul. I let go of it, letting it drop over my top.

Luca was slurping at his beer. I could tell it was already getting to him because he kept missing his lips when he tried to drink. I knocked back the rest of my own. Luca looked at me with a mischievous grin.

'I'm going to show you something,' he said, 'but you can't look.'

I rolled my eyes.

'How can you show me something if I can't look?'

He sniggered.

'Just turn around for a second,' he said.

I rolled my eyes again, before swivelling away. A rat was staring right at me from the other side of the room. Its eyes were glinting red in the light, its front teeth long yellow buggers capable of puncturing tyres. I usually like animals but this looked like a right vicious bastard.

I kept real still, like I wasn't anything but a piece of furniture. That's what I used to do when Mother gave me Stillness Lessons. I'd sit in the corner of the room with my feet square on the floor and my arms crossed as she worked on her business proposals at the dining-room table. She'd put a twenty-minute timer on the edge and say she'd only let me go once it rang. I suppose twenty minutes doesn't sound long but it is when you're six years old and every time you shuffle or lick your lips or even just blink too quickly the timer restarted. So I learnt to pretend to be a piece of furniture. A cabinet or a book-shelf (being a fridge worked the best), all stiff and straight with no feeling in my limbs. You become less threatening when you become a piece of furniture. No living thing is threatened by a lump of wood.

Behind me I could hear Luca clicking his trumpet case shut and then the whirr as he wound up his lamp.

I couldn't help looking down at the key. It glowed around my neck, oozing light, perfectly in time with the lamp that got brighter with each turn. I watched it glowing against the walls and into the rat's eyes. But even with the glowing the bastard didn't move. It was creepy how it just sat there, staring at me instead of scurrying away. It was like it was waiting for something but I didn't know what. I heard Luca clicking the handle back into place.

'You can look now,' he said.

When I turned around Luca was sitting on his knees with an envelope in his hand. It was a big square thing, browned on the edges.

'What is it?' I asked.

He looked all excited.

'A map.'

'A map?' I said, smiling. 'For what?'

He leant in close as though we weren't the only people in the room.

'*The fortune,*' he said.

He ran his finger all around the edge of the envelope.

'Granddad put it in the case along with the trumpet and key,' he said. 'He sealed it up and put it in the attic with my name across it. It was his last gift to me.'

His eyes were bright as though he was full of a thousand stories. How they played games together, how his granddad taught him all his wisdom and left him little gifts that only the two of them understood. I took a deep breath and reached towards the envelope. Luca snatched it back.

'Is it OK if I'm the only one who looks at it for now?' he asked.

It seemed an odd request but I suppose it was all part of the granddad–grandson connection. I sat back and shrugged.

'Sure.'

'And you won't tell Jules?' he said.

I pulled my fingers across my mouth like a zip.

'My lips are sealed.'

He sighed and nodded as though he was pleased with how the exchange had passed. He shuffled on to his bottom.

'I'm glad you're here, Molly,' he said.

Then he looked at me all serious again.

'Can you turn back around?'

I wanted to tell him I knew he was going to put the map in his trumpet case but a part of me didn't want to ruin this little game. When I turned to the wall the rat had gone.

'None of them believe me,' Luca said. 'They never believe me.'

'Who?' I asked.

He didn't say anything but I could hear him winding up the lamp again. I turned around. He stopped winding. He took his glasses off, blowing on them before wiping them with the fabric of his T-shirt.

'I know it's there,' he said. 'I just know it.'

Luca climbed into his sleeping bag. I took off my shoes, put on all my layers and got into mine too. We both lay down on our cardboard beds, staring up at the ceiling.

I thought of the rat; there was probably more than one. On the streets they left you alone unless they smelt food. Private Pete got nipped on the thumb once, after falling asleep with a burger clutched in his hand.

'You haven't got any sweets left, have you?' I said.

Luca rolled over and rifled through his rucksack. I heard him yawn.

'No, I ate them all,' he said. 'I'll get some more in the morning.'

I looked up at the ceiling again. There was a circle of light coming from the lamp. It hovered golden, like a faraway sun. I found the metal pillbox in my pocket and pulled it out. On the front were hand-painted wildflowers against a pastel-blue background. I unclicked the latch. I couldn't see much so I used my fingers to stroke the hairs inside. They were still soft, like down. I put the box away and tried to get comfortable.

You get all sorts of problems sleeping on the streets; mine is my hip. As soon as I lie down I feel pain in the right side, aching and stabbing. It trickles all the way down my thigh. When it's cold I feel it twice as bad, like icicles pricking my nerves. The old Molly would have found something to ease the pain – something quick, something direct. Instead, I curled up into a ball and tucked my chin to my chest. I focused on the warmth of my body, lulled by the rhythm of my lungs breathing long and slow, waiting for the outside world to slip away. It's a strange kind of magic, my own disappearing act. It doesn't ease the pain as easily as the old way of course, but the hard tricks are the ones that stay with you the longest. If I've learnt anything in life, I've learnt that.

The lamplight faded, moonlight creeping through the edges of the boarded-up windows. As I curled up tighter I saw something glinting by Luca's side. I squinted until I could see the edge of it, sharp and smooth. It was only when I saw the black handle with a polished screw in the middle that I realized what it was.

We all need things to make us feel safe. For me, it was Rubberband Girls. For Luca, it was a knife.

The Deadly Row of Cars

Rusby had a knife. It was a handmade hunting knife with a ten-inch blade that his grandmother had given to him on his eighteenth birthday. He'd told her it was for whittling; then he sent her the link on eBay.

The knife was a thing of beauty, the curve of the bone handle designed to sit snug in the palm, a rippling marble effect on the Damascus-steel blade. He'd show it to people like it was a new watch, holding it flat out in his hands, angling the metal to the light.

Then one day it was stolen.

We were living in a squat at an old community centre and we'd had a few people over. It was a small building with an open-plan kitchen and a snooker table that stood by two toilets, one for boys and one for girls, though the girls' toilet was always out of use. Rusby had found us a bed frame and a mattress, and even a couple of falling-apart sofas with cushions that dipped down in the middle like crooked smiles. Across the window were bedsheets instead of curtains, which tinted the room with an orange, otherworldly light. You could almost call it cosy.

Everyone was drinking and shooting up, too far out of it to notice that Rusby had taken off the leather case strapped under his tracksuit and placed it on the snooker table before going into the boys' toilet. He always took the knife off before going in there because the blade dug into his thigh when he sat down. Usually he'd still take it in with him, leaving it on top of the cistern. He didn't realize his mistake until he came back out.

He was all obscenities when he saw it was gone, 'fucking' this and 'knobhead' that. Repeating the same thing over and over, getting louder and redder and flinging stupid things like pens and lighters across the room. Eventually he calmed down enough to do a head count. The only person missing was a small, scrappy lad called Stevie. He was new to the streets and had one of those fancy haircuts, two bolts of lightning shaved into the side of his scalp. He said he was seventeen but he couldn't have been much more than fifteen. He had one of those baby faces; you could just tell.

Rusby stormed around the hall, a broken snooker cue clutched in his hand, listing all the nasty things he was going to do to Stevie once he found his sorry arse. Things he would do with his knife; things he would do with his hands. Medieval-style torture with iron maidens and racks. How he would hang, draw and quarter the lad and how he knew exactly what that meant. The only bit of history Rusby knew was the gory stuff.

Yasmin from Glasgow was smoking a cigarette on the bed with me.

'Don't be so harsh, Rusby,' she said, waving her hand in the air. 'He's only a wee lad.'

Usually, Rusby wouldn't have said a word to her. Yasmin was a beautiful girl, flawless cinnamon-brown skin, cupid's bow lips and feline eyes accentuated by a dark flick of eyeliner. She's a high-class lass, way out of Rusby's league and he knew it. He could barely string a sentence together when he spoke to her, but he didn't mind her being around the squat. In fact, she was the only friend I was allowed to see.

A wave of calm seemed to wash over Rusby as smoke rippled out of Yasmin's pursed lips. Every muscle in his body lengthened; he seemed broader and taller than his usual weedy self, as though he'd been inflated. He pointed his snooker cue at Yasmin.

'Nobody takes what belongs to me,' he said. 'That boy is dead.'

He took his phone from his pocket and made a few calls. Two hours later there were ten men in our squat who I'd never met before. All of them were hunched as they swaggered in, eyes scanning the room, scars across their tattooed faces and necks. I'd seen men like this before, become friends with them, but there was something that radiated from this group – the detachment in their hooded eyes, an animal aggression brimming beneath – that made me shrink down. Yasmin felt it too. She made her excuses, picking up her Dior handbag and slipping out of the fire exit.

These gorilla-type beasts fist-bumped and shook hands, slapping Rusby on the back, talking in mumbles, grunts and head nods. Rusby stood, shoulders rolled back, clarity in his eyes; it seemed plausible that this scarecrow of a man might really be in charge. But then, Rusby can do just about anything when he wants to.

I sat there on the bed, hugging my knees to my chest, eyes skipping back and forth as I watched them plan it all. The locations, the connections, people in security, people in surveillance. They had networks all over the country so if Stevie decided to leg it they'd be right behind him, sniffing at his tracks. They'd hacked into his social media, knew exactly what part of Nottingham he was in and who he was meeting. They planned their attack, what weapons to use, the best alleys to hide in and how to escape without being identified. Rusby hardly said a word, letting his pack unveil the master plan. The poor lad didn't have a chance.

Rusby got his knife back a week later. He didn't tell me about it but I saw it by the kitchen sink, pushed into its case with a dark crimson stain soaked into the leather. He saw me staring and picked up the case, winding the leather strap around it, slow and deliberate. Then he looked back at me with that same hooded detachment.

'The boy's learnt his lesson,' he said.

I later found out this lesson had left the boy in intensive care. His parents had been called in because of his age: twelve years old. Tall for a twelve-year-old, but twelve years old all the same. I still think about him sometimes, that little lad, Stevie; I wonder if he went back home to his parents, if he was checking behind him, hoping lightning wouldn't strike twice like the bolts in his hair.

I didn't see the hunting knife after that. Rusby started carrying more basic weapons: crowbars, metal poles, nail files sharpened to a point at the tip. All of them were classified as offensive weapons and could put him in prison for up to four years if he got caught, but he didn't care. He thought he was invincible by then.

One day, after we'd gone to see his grandmother for the usual Jammie Dodgers and tears, I asked Rusby what had happened to the knife she'd bought him. He was biting his nails in that way he did, digging into the flesh.

'Dodgy Mike gave me fifty for it,' he said.

He said it so casual, like he'd sold an old bike he'd grown out of and not a hunting knife that some poor lad had nearly died for. But then I realized, it was never about the knife. It was like he said to Yasmin: *Nobody takes what belongs to me.*

In Rusby's mind, I belonged to him. Even when he didn't want me I belonged to him. And in running away, I had as good as stolen that knife myself.

*

I was woken by a nudging in my ribs. When you sleep on the streets you learn when to play dead. Nine times out of ten you get left alone. The one time you don't, your ribs get fractured.

Just before the nudging, I'd been having a dream about Bingham. I was walking down a cobbled street with rats scurrying along walls and gutters when I realized two police officers were following me. Whenever I turned around to look at them they spun on their heels and walked the other way, but a few moments later they'd be shadowing me again. I went around a corner and there were more uniformed police walking away from me, except this time they had doubled in number. The ground was littered with rubber bands. They were pouring from the police officers' shoes. The rats continued to scurry along the gutters but the officers didn't notice them. I tried to escape but everywhere I went there were more of them – police, police, police – none of them looking my way. The rubber bands rose around my ankles like a flood until soon I couldn't walk. The rats were squeaking, loud with panic. The police were coming at me, faces towards me but with no features. I was grateful to be woken because then I knew they weren't real. That they were nowhere near me. That I was safe.

The nudging got harder and I started to wonder what would be waiting for me when I opened my eyes. I got to planning how I'd grab my rucksack and bolt to the gap in the door. I had my hands primed when suddenly I felt a wet tongue licking my cheek. When I opened my eyes, I saw two dark dog eyes staring back at me.

'Get up, you lazy cow!' I heard Jules shout.

She was standing over me with a bevvy in her hand. Her voice didn't have the edge in it but her hair was sticking out at all angles and she was skipping from one foot to the other so I knew she was buzzing off something. Nothing as harsh as heroin, she despised needles, but some sort of pill that made her more hyped than usual. Even in a small town like Bingham, Jules could score.

As I pushed myself to sitting, the floorboards creaked beneath me and Boy, spooked by the noise, began barking. This woke Luca, who began rolling about, a squeaky moan leaking out of him. He searched the floor for his glasses. When he sat up his Afro was squashed down by the hood of his sleeping bag and, when he pulled the hood off, flat on one side like a tree with half its leaves blown off. His skin had gone deadly pale, his mouth dry and flaky; he looked like he was going to be sick.

'Can you tell your dog to keep it down?' he said.

'She ain't my dog,' Jules said.

She looked down at Boy, who stopped barking instantly. Luca unzipped his sleeping bag and pulled his feet out.

'Jesus, I think I've got frostbite!' he said.

Me and Jules examined Luca's feet; they were white on the toes, but the colour came back as he wiggled them. He screwed up his face with each wiggle. If he'd kept his socks on like I'd suggested, he wouldn't have this problem.

'Sensitive type, ain't you?' Jules said real loud so that her voice echoed off the bare walls.

This didn't help Luca's mood. He pulled on his socks, still laid out in rows from the night before.

I took the small plastic pencil case from the bottom of my rucksack and went to the kitchen. The light was brighter in there so I could see the sink, with its big square ceramic basin and brass taps inscribed with 'HOT' and 'COLD' in looping writing. My toothbrush was so old and used that the bristles looked like they'd been stepped on. I rubbed a bit of soap on it and ran it around my teeth. It tasted foul but it cleared the morning fuzz. I wet the soap and rubbed the suds underneath my armpits, breasts and around my groin. I wasn't going to get crotch rot like Private Pete if I could help it.

'Is there a toilet in here?' I heard Luca say.

Jules laughed.

'Where do you think you are? The Plaza?'

When I returned, Jules was still hopping around and Luca was sitting with his lips screwed tight. I gave him an encouraging nod.

'There might be one upstairs,' I said. 'It's worth having a look.'

'Yeah,' Jules said, softening. 'Won't hurt to have a look, Posh Boy. Though mind the rats. I saw a couple on the way in.'

Luca's mouth fell open, but Jules didn't notice.

'Talking about rats . . .' she said.

Jules's stories always start somewhere solid but get muddled along the way. She began this one with a man who looked like Flash Gordon outside the Costa Coffee. Then the story swerved to her twisting her ankle by falling over some lady's shopping trolley, and Boy having a fight with a tomcat in an alley. The cat nearly swiped a piece out of Boy but when Jules got down and began barking, the cat soon scarpered. It got her thinking about the brutality of nature.

'Cos I'd only just been telling you about how stupid animals were, right? I still full-heartedly stand by that. But there was something about the way this cat was going at Boy. Just like two lasses out on the lash on a Saturday night. Proper vicious it was. Proper *human* . . . So anyway, this Flash Gordon fella starts groping me and I nutted him smack on the forehead. I already owed him a tenner so it kind of killed two birds with one stone.'

She took a swig from her can as she took a breather. The thing with Jules is you don't know if what she says is true or whether half of what she says is memories of past incidents and, even then, not necessarily *her* memories. I swear sometimes she recites storylines from old soaps.

Luca began wriggling, squeezing down on his crotch.

'If you need to go for a piss, just do it in the sink,' Jules said. 'Don't mind us.'

But Luca did mind, checking over his shoulder as he went into the kitchen, then checking the floor for rats before checking over his shoulder again and angling away from us as he stood in front of the big enamel sink. There were no doors and he kept glancing over to see if we were watching – which we were. It was like seeing the fuse on a bomb burning except the explosive in this case was the contents of Luca's bladder.

Eventually he turned his head away and hitched his hips up. We heard the trickle as it hit the enamel, his body sighing as he got into a flow.

Then *Clatter! Crash!* A pigeon came flapping out of the rafters. Luca leapt so high that a streak of yellow arched through the air. Jules creased over, laughing hysterically, and I couldn't help joining in. It was like being at the circus and watching a clown falling over his big floppy shoes.

'Priceless, this lad,' Jules said, wiping the tears from her eyes. 'Price-*less*.'

I was glad Jules was in a good mood; it meant she'd taken her medication that morning. If she goes without it she can be a bloody nightmare. Even I find it hard to be round her when she's not on her meds.

I heard Luca zipping up his trousers. When he came back in he had a right cob on. His lips were screwed up again and his brows knotted in the middle.

'I'm not staying here again,' he said.

I expected Jules to get offended at his ingratitude. Instead she rummaged around her cargo pants and pulled out a few croissants covered with cellophane. Boy zoomed right over to her so she gave him one first, then chucked the rest to us. Luca examined the pastry.

'Ham and cheese,' Jules said.

I peeled off the cellophane and stuffed my mouth full. It was still warm, the cheese melted on to the cured ham and flaky, sweet pastry.

'Ta, Jules,' I said, spitting out crumbs as I spoke.

Luca looked down at the croissant.

'Yeah, *ta*,' he said before unwrapping it and taking a bite.

Jules sat down on the floor.

'What's the plan, Posh Boy?' she said.

Luca pushed one hand into his jacket pocket. He froze. His face, which I didn't think could get any paler, got paler. He pulled out coins and sweet wrappers and then rummaged through his rucksack and then through his tubs filled with screws and spoons, calculators and paper-clips. Me and Jules watched as we finished our croissants.

Eventually he stopped.

'Right, very funny,' he said with a half-chuckle. 'Can I have it now?'

He looked at both of us but he lingered on Jules. She shrugged.

'Don't know what you're talking about,' she said.

'The credit card,' Luca said slowly. 'Can I have my credit card back?'

Jules frowned.

'Why would I have it?'

He looked at us both again, examining our faces.

'You're serious?' he said.

He didn't wait for an answer but rummaged through his rucksack again.

'Shit, shit, shit!'

I felt for the lad. Jules must have too because she wasn't even slightly amused.

'Sorry, Posh Boy,' she said. 'That's pretty harsh.'

Luca sat down, head in his hands. I hoped to God he wasn't going to start hurling accusations at us. I could handle it, but Jules was right touchy about things like that. You couldn't say Jules wasn't a thief, she most definitely was, but she'd never take something from someone she knew. It was part of her code and she took on that code the way nuns took on vows. I crawled over to Luca, placing my hand gently on his shoulder.

'It doesn't matter,' I said. 'Whoever owned that card would have blocked it soon anyway.'

Luca lifted his head.

'We have to keep moving,' he said. 'I'm telling you: someone's following us. They've taken my card just to fuck with me. We have to leave.'

Jules was looking all sceptical.

'We'll just go on to Skegness,' I said.

'But that card was our *way* to Skegness,' Luca said. 'How are we supposed to get there now?'

Jules stood up.

'Easy,' she said. 'We move on to Plan B.'

She picked up her things. I could see she was serious so I gathered my things too.

'What's Plan B?' Luca asked.

But there was no time for explanations.

I first met Jules when I was waiting for Robin Hood's handouts by the Tourist Information in Nottingham.

Everyone calls him Robin Hood on account of how he takes from the rich (the posh sandwich shops) and gives to the poor (the homeless). Except Robin Hood was an outlaw and Martin Wallis used to be the CEO of a big company that sold computer parts before he became homeless and started visiting sandwich shops at the end of trading and asking politely for out-of-date food. You'd be surprised at the stuff they throw out: perfectly good wraps, salads and sandwiches that can't be sold because of the 'Freshly Made Today' stamps. You'd think they'd just take the stamps off and sell them for a couple of more days but customers can be picky buggers about things like that.

Robin Hood was the only person I knew on the streets back then. Every so often we'd have little chats about politics and the power structures of the super-rich but I was a bit of a loner so kept to myself. He was a gentle soul but strict with his rules for handouts. There were only two but he went over them at least three times an evening:

1) You take one item and wait until everybody has something before taking another.
2) You don't throw your rubbish on the ground or you will incur the wrath of all wraths.

He really hates rubbish does Robin Hood. He's a bit of an environmentalist. I've seen him threaten to push discarded sandwich boxes 'up your rectum' if he finds them on the ground. He says it softly but you can tell he means it.

The day I met Jules, I was standing at the back of the crowd, waiting for my turn. I felt someone staring; it's funny how you can feel this sometimes, a presence in your peripheral vision, the shape of a body, an unmoving gaze. When I turned around I saw Jules's broken eye focused on me. She was in full army gear, camouflage print from head to toe with a pair of black Doc Martens on her feet. She caught my eye and pointed at me.

'I know you, don't I?' she said.

She had a can of Stella in one hand and a cigarette in the other. Around her wrist was a threaded bracelet that I later learnt she'd got from a Hare Krishna. Jules is poly-religious in the sense that she'll try any religion once, especially if they give free food.

I was new to the streets and trying to keep a low profile. I wasn't in a good place in my head. When you're not in a good place in your head you're not in a good place to be around anyone. Besides, I wasn't very chatty back then. Truth be told, I was kind of scared of new people. You don't know what you're getting with new people until they give it to you and then it's too late. I'd already learnt that; already had jewellery stolen from my rucksack, already been kicked in twice for no reason. But as Jules would later tell me (and keep telling me) there are a lot of psychotics out there. Not just the homeless, of course, but in general. To be fair, you probably get a few more in the homeless category. It's partly how people end up on the streets and partly the result of living on the streets – hard to know whether it's chicken or egg in some circumstances. The trick is to differentiate between friendly psychotics and the dangerous psychotics. At that point, I couldn't tell with Jules.

She carried on looking at me, waggling her finger up and down.

'Honest to God,' she said. 'I know you from somewhere.'

I smiled and then shrugged, looking back at the crowd to see if I was any nearer to Robin Hood. I hadn't eaten for a while and was feeling weak. The hunger in your stomach goes after a few days but the weakness is constant.

That's when she came and stood beside me.

'You know Sheila Dugan?' she said.

I shook my head. She took a puff from her cigarette. Big fat clouds billowed from her mouth.

'Freddie from down south?' she said.

I shook my head.

'Dodgy Mike Gibson?'

When I shook my head, she jolted back as though I'd walloped her.

'*Everyone* knows Dodgy Mike!'

I didn't realize the crowd were listening until they all mumbled their agreement. I didn't like the way they were looking at us. I wanted to be invisible. I wanted to disappear. I was about to mumble that I had some place to be when Robin Hood called out 'Tuna steak salad with wasabi' and Jules stuck her arm up like a rod.

'That'll be for me, ta!'

She dived to the front as quick as a ferret. Her army clothes merged into the bodies as though they were trees in a forest. When Jules came strutting back she had two boxes. I didn't know how she'd done it but she'd managed to break Robin Hood's Number 1 Rule.

She stuck one out to me.

'For you, my dear.'

Robin was watching us as he continued to hand out sandwiches and, when he saw me looking, he gave a reassuring nod. I thanked her and took the box. It was from the posh deli place, sesame seeds over strips of purple tuna steak.

'Nobody ever takes these on account of them not being cooked,' Jules said as she opened her box. 'Sushi, it's called.'

She pulled out a lime-green plastic fish filled with soy sauce, ripped off its head and drizzled it over the chopped vegetables.

'But they are *right* nice,' she said. 'Especially with the wasabi. Got a proper *kick*!'

She jerked her leg as she said this, like a little ninja kick. She gestured for me to follow as she walked to a bench. I looked up and down the street for an escape. Jules turned.

'Get over here, you dozy cow!'

It was friendly, how she said it. As though she'd known me for years and I was her best mate. She'd already started on the sushi when I sat down, a pair of chopsticks held tight between her fingers.

'Private Pete?' she said, sugar snap held up to her lips. 'The one with all the infections?'

I shook my head. She popped the pea pod in her mouth and chewed thoughtfully.

'Jason Rusby?' she said. 'Skinny fella who nicks watches?'

I shook my head again.

She scrunched her face up, still confused.

'Jesus Christ, d'ya know *anyone*?'

I tried some of the tuna. She was right; it was delicious. I shrugged.

'I'm kinda new.'

Her face relaxed.

'That explains it. What's your name, then?'

Nobody had asked me my name at that point, not even Robin Hood. I didn't know whether I should tell the truth or lie like I'd planned. I looked over at Jules as she wiped her mouth with the back of her hand.

'Molly,' I said.

She squeezed her eyes shut.

'Molly Molly Molly,' she said before opening them again. 'Have to do that or I won't remember it.'

She tapped the side of her head.

'Got a lot of voices in here.'

110

I thought I'd heard her wrong, that she'd said 'names' not 'voices'. Of course, I'd heard right the first time.

When Jules finished, she stood up to throw her rubbish in the bin. Then she sat back down and slapped her hands together.

'Right!' she said. 'I'd better introduce you to the gang then, hadn't I?'

She began walking before I could say anything. She had a swagger that told me she wasn't afraid.

I wanted to be like Jules; I didn't want to be afraid any more. So I followed.

It was 6 a.m. Jules is always up at crazy times when she's buzzing and she likes to have everyone up with her. The sky was navy blue, with a few streetlamps shining orange light across the pavement. It was quiet so you could hear the birdsong real clear, as clear as the strings of the violins at the Symphony Orchestra.

We walked along the street that led back to the train station, me and Luca following Jules, Boy trailing behind us as she sniffed the pavement. Then Jules paused, turning to face the road.

'Which d'ya fancy?' she asked.

She fanned her hand out to the cars. I looked at Jules, then at the cars, then back at Jules. Luca's face was wide and excited. I shook my head. Luca paced up and down the street, eyeing the cars. Boy followed him as though this was a game.

'Yes,' he was saying. 'Yes, *yes*!'

He pointed at a four-by-four. It was a huge thing, shiny and black, with wheels as tall as a three-year-old. Jules laughed as though they were in on some joke together. Luca got to his knees and rummaged through his leather rucksack. I stepped towards him, arms wrapped round my waist.

'You can't, Luca,' I said.

He looked up at me.

'No, I can,' he said. 'I saw this guy do it once.'

But that's not what I meant.

I could feel something bad inside me. The feeling comes every so often – not butterflies fluttering but snakes slithering around my gut. It makes me queasy, like I'm about to be sick, a sour taste spreading across the sides of my tongue.

Luca stood up with a wire coat hanger in his hand. Jules stopped laughing.

'My God,' she said. 'Posh Boy's got balls.'

She slapped him on the back and he looked all chuffed as though he'd been elected captain of the football team. I glanced up at the windows of the houses around us. One of them had curtains with a teddy bear print.

'I don't think this is a good idea,' I said.

Jules was nodding, bottom lip stuck out.

'You're right, Molls,' she said. 'The coat hanger only works with old bangers. This car's too new. The alarm will sound as soon as you touch it.'

Luca nodded at Jules as if she was his newly appointed crime adviser. They walked off, hunting for an old banger. Boy trailed behind, her little stump waggling in anticipation. It took a while for Luca to notice that I wasn't following. When he did he gestured at me with his long, dangly arms. I squeezed my shoulders tight.

'*It's not right*,' I whispered.

Luca squinted, trying to decipher what I was saying. Jules heard just fine though, rolling her eyes and jutting her chin in the air.

'Here we go!' she cried.

Boy barked. The sound echoed around the street.

'Control your dog,' Luca told Jules.

'*She ain't my dog!*' Jules hissed.

She picked Boy up and fed her some Quavers from her pocket. Luca scurried over to me.

'It's not fair to just take their things,' I said. I made sure to keep my voice low so Jules wouldn't hear.

Luca shook his head as though I'd made a simple mistake.

'The people on this street own two cars minimum. They won't even notice it's gone.'

The rows of cars were all parked neatly beside the kerb. There were family cars, camper vans, two-seaters with soft tops, all shiny and buffed with little air fresheners shaped like fruit hanging from the mirrors. The snakes slithered.

'You don't know that,' I said. 'They might be really struggling. They might be elderly. They might have a disabled child and need the car to get them to hospital.'

I could hear Jules sighing. She wandered over to us, Boy still in her arms, but I didn't look at her, I looked at Luca. I could see he was thinking about what I was saying.

'Just because they live in a nice house doesn't mean they don't have problems,' I said.

Luca jerked back as though I'd slapped him. Jules didn't notice, nudging him gently in the ribs.

'She's got moral on us recently has Molls. Seen God or summat.'

I didn't like the way she said this, all dismissive. I felt the heat prickle up my neck, my shoulders draw in even closer. I looked at the can in her hand. I wanted to snatch it and empty the contents down the drain. She'd be fuming if I did that.

'I'm going back,' I said.

I turned around before Jules could see she'd got to me. If she saw that, she'd tell me I was too soft. Every time I disagree with her, she tells me I'm too soft. I don't mind it most of the time, but this wasn't about me; it was about the people who lived here.

I kept my head low, not knowing where I was going or whether Jules and Luca would follow. I saw a rat scurrying along the side of the pavement, its long pink tail flicking out behind it. I slowed down, thinking about the rat eyes from the night before. How they wouldn't stop staring, as if they were trying to tell me something. Then I remembered my dream.

When I looked up, there was a police car at the bottom of the road. It was so bright and luminous with its reflective yellow-and-blue checks that I didn't understand how I hadn't seen it earlier. It must have just arrived. I scanned the houses and saw a man in uniform at the door of a cottage. I almost turned to run back up the road but the policeman had spotted me. The sour taste in my mouth turned rotten. He looked away and I began to whistle.

Back when I was deep in the habit, me and Jules would go on the rob together. Rusby said no one ever suspected girls so it was best that way. Truth was he'd been caught so many times that he'd been banned from the city centre. In any case, me and Jules worked pretty well together. I'd be the lookout while Jules went and filled the pockets of her oversized camo jacket and cargo pants. When I saw a shop assistant looking suspicious or a security guard coming I'd do this whistle. It couldn't be an obvious whistle or people would look at me and we'd both be in for it so I did a quick 'Follow The Yellow Brick Road' melody. Then I'd leave and meet Jules at our safe spot for that part of the city. The front of the Town Hall, for example, or next to the Brian Clough statue.

We didn't have a safe spot in Bingham, but I whistled my tune loud and quick as I passed the policeman, then carried on whistling so it didn't sound suspicious. When I got to the square at the bottom of the street, I turned, hoping to see Jules and Luca behind, but they weren't there. I thought of going back to Manor Cottage or to the station.

Then I saw the Buttercross monument and decided I would sit underneath it, right in the middle, so that they wouldn't be able to miss me.

The slabs were cold and my hip was aching as I sat cross-legged. The seconds seemed to drag on for hours, and I thought about what Luca said about time being relative. The seconds plodded on. Tick. Tick.

I looked at the houses at the end of the street. They were big buildings, painted white with panelled glass windows. We had a nice house once. When I was little. No mansion, mind, but a nice semi in the suburbs. Beautiful lawn, a shiny car in the driveway. From the outside, everyone must have thought we had a great life, that we were the perfect family. But no one knows the inside of something unless they live in it. I pulled at the rubber bands on my wrist. I didn't want to be thinking about that but the policeman had brought it all back. I whistled again, hoping the sound would swallow the memories. But other memories took their place. The magistrates' court by the canal in Nottingham. Feeling giddy as I looked up at the tall glass entrance. How I'd sat in a denim jacket, a maxi dress and sandals because I had no other clothes to wear. I couldn't borrow anything because I was eight months pregnant and nothing fitted. I remember sitting in the reception, watching all the solicitors and barristers walk by in their pressed suits and shiny shoes. They glanced at me, but only for a second, as if I was something they'd seen out of the corner of their eye but realized was nothing important. I wanted to tell them that I had been going to be a solicitor myself. It's what had been planned for me. But what did it matter? What was planned wasn't what I was. And what was I? A homeless, pregnant thief sitting on a bench in a magistrates' court with a boyfriend who had a season ticket for the place but was nowhere to be seen.

I shivered. The memories were taking over. My parents. Rusby. Those dark, fragile days. I pulled a bunch of rubber bands from my wrist and began twisting and looping them together until I had legs and a body, two rubber-band plaits. I was so focused that I didn't hear the barking. Then I saw Boy running towards me across the square. A fuzzy ball getting bigger and bigger. I tucked the half-formed body into my jacket pocket.

'Good girl!' I said as she jumped into my lap.

I squeezed Boy tight, feeling her heart thudding in her tiny body like the beat in a stereo speaker. One by one the streetlamps switched off as the blue dawn turned to day. I saw the police car drive around the square before leaving. I couldn't tell if there was anyone in the back. Boy licked my chin. She carried on until two figures came marching down the street. Then she jumped out of my lap and ran straight to Jules, who was trying to get Luca to turn back. But Luca's expression was steel. When he saw me, he headed to the Buttercross and stuck his hand out. I clasped his palm, feeling the firmness of his grip as he pulled me up.

'We can still do it,' Jules was saying. 'He's gone now, ain't he?'

Luca shook his head.

'Not with what you just told me.'

Jules flapped her arms down hard to her sides.

'I already told you! He ain't gonna recognize me!' she said. 'I'm not in his jurisdiction.'

'She's broken her probation,' Luca said. 'Wasn't supposed to leave Nottingham. That's why we just spent the last ten minutes hiding behind a bin. Thanks for the whistling thing. You saved our necks.'

He was looking at me with that impressed look. I felt my cheeks tingle as I blushed.

'Yeah, ta,' Jules said, but in a begrudging way, as if she'd opened a birthday present to reveal something she didn't want.

She scrunched up her beer can and threw it on the ground. Then, seeing Boy for the first time, bent down and scooped her up.

'End of adventure, then,' she said.

Luca pulled the straps tight on his rucksack.

'No, not the end,' he said, starting to walk away. 'Just the start of Plan C.'

Jules looked at me, confused, and then followed Luca.

I picked up the can and threw it in the bin.

The Magic Art of the Psychotic

I saved a boy from drowning once.

He'd been squatting on the bank of the lake at the local park – hand stretched out to a toy boat floating on the ripples, body straining forward as his fingers wiggled towards the sails – and lost his balance, falling head first into the water. There wasn't a dramatic splash, just a dull plop, as though a heavy rock had been thrown in. No one seemed to notice he'd fallen, apart from me, or that he was flapping his arms and legs in a way that was moving him further and further from shore.

I dived straight in. I was eleven at the time; I'd started my rookie life-saving course at school so it seemed logical that, if I could rescue bricks from the bottom of a pool in my pyjamas, I could save this boy.

His hair was the colour of fire. I remember searching for it as I front-crawled through the murky water. The rotten stench of stagnating water was in my nose, the sludgy algae entering my mouth and making me gag, but I kept going, watching the fire of his hair get closer and closer until, finally, I grabbed him around the shoulders, flipped on to my back and began short firm kicks towards the shore. The boy clung tightly to my arm, his body relaxing into mine as he coughed and spluttered. This is it, I thought, I'm going to be a hero.

That's when I got stuck.

Something, a reed or an old rope, was wrapped around my ankle. I tried to kick it off but the harder I kicked the more we were dragged under the water. Our heads plunged down, then back up as we gasped for air. I began choking, my mouth filling up with the stagnant taste of lake water and death. The boy began wailing.

I don't remember how we got out of the lake, but when we did the boy was still crying. Even when his parents came rushing to his side he kept his eyes closed, chest heaving in and out with each sob. I knew how he felt; my chest was stinging, the foul taste of death still swimming across my tongue. I wanted to sob too.

The father ran over to me. He had the same fiery hair, freckles scattered across his pale face. I waited for him to hug me tight and thank me a thousand times over. Instead, he held me firm by the shoulders.

'Next time, call for help,' he said.

When my mother came, her face was thunder. She ignored everyone telling her to wait for the paramedics and took me to the car park. She pushed me on to the back seat of the car and climbed into the front. I looked at the back of her head, her hair in a perfect French twist, highlights running in horizontal lines. She glanced at me in the rear-view mirror, dark eyes buried beneath furrowed brows.

'Don't tell anyone about this,' she said. 'Especially your father.'

She switched on the ignition as I shivered. There was a blanket in the boot, but I didn't ask for it. That's the thing with my family: you never called for help, even if you were drowning.

The sun was lily white as we followed Luca through Bingham. It shone through the gaps between the shops and on to the cobbled pavement. Jules was telling us again about the man who looked like Flash Gordon and how he'd held his head, weeping.

'I mean, it's like the man never had his head nutted before,' she said. 'Bloody knobhead.'

She'd obviously forgotten the car debacle. As long as we were moving, she didn't care too much what we were doing. Even when her phone kept ringing she didn't slow down, just took it out of her pocket, glanced at the screen and declined the call.

For a long time, we were walking in loops. Jules didn't notice, she was too busy gabbing, but I recognized the same red telephone booths and veg stalls, the Chinese takeaway and dry cleaner's that looked like a solicitor's office. I didn't ask Luca where we were going; he seemed to have a plan and I didn't want to interfere.

'You've got to let the wind guide you when you're on the streets,' Robin Hood had told me. 'You're not a caged bird any more; you're wild.'

It was past midday when we turned on to a new path with grass verges and arching trees. A heritage-green sign said 'BYWAY'. Boy was following us, shoving her head in bushes and ditches. The sun was shimmering through the leaves, creating a dappled light across the path and on our faces. Robin Hood said they have a word for this in Japanese: *komorebi*. He had travelled a lot when he was a CEO. We used to have nice conversations about his travels and I kind of wished I could tell him about mine now. To be honest, I missed Robin Hood. And Big Tony and Yasmin from Glasgow. I even missed Private Pete and his skin infections.

We walked straight up the byway, Jules telling us how – after nutting him – she'd kicked the Flash Gordon man in the balls so he'd know what *real* pain was like. As she demonstrated the kick, fist tight round her bevvy, leg snapping out, Luca stopped walking. His feet stayed stuck to the path, but his body wobbled forwards and backwards as though there was a big magnet beneath him. We stopped too, watching Luca staring down at his feet. Then he turned around and headed back the way we'd come. We both began to follow but he paused again. Jules was being quite patient, holding her bevvy lax in her hand, strands of her hair still at crazy angles from the night before. She was looking at Luca with curiosity, like he was a rare animal. It was only when Luca turned, set off again, hesitated, and spun round for the third time that her neck blotched poppy red.

'What the **FUcK**, Posh Boy?'

Luca scratched his chin like he was solving a mathematical problem, lips pulled to the side, eyes darting round like steel balls in a pinball machine. Eventually he sighed and shook his head.

'I can't do it,' he said.

'What can't you do?' Jules said. 'Walk up a **FucKinG PaTh**?'

A cloud covered the sun, and the *komorebi* vanished.

'Shall we rest for a bit?' I said.

I tried to say it cheerily to break the tension, but the words only riled Jules further.

'Rest from what exactly?' she said. 'We've only been **WalKinG**.'

Luca didn't seem to hear Jules at all. He looked at me, nodding as we made our way to the grass verge and took off our rucksacks. The grass was damp so we both sat on Luca's trumpet case. I could feel the warmth of his body pressing into mine. Boy came and curled up in front of us as if we were a fire. I glanced up at Jules. The clouds were hovering like a dark canopy, heavy and foreboding.

'Only for a bit, Jules,' I said. 'You can have a fag.'

Her face was tight as she pulled out her rolling tobacco.

'I can have a **FaG** walking and all,' she muttered.

She didn't sit down with us but kept muttering to herself. Luca was clearly having another mathematical think because he was scratching his chin again. He pulled a bit of bread from his pocket and broke it up for the birds as he had in the graveyard. It seemed like a ritual he had to do before a big decision. Maybe Einstein did a similar thing.

Jules took a drag from her cigarette and then held it by her side. The darkness was hanging over us, birds gathering at our feet.

'Does a lot of **THinKinG**, this one,' she said, gesturing at Luca. 'Like you in that way, ain't he, **MoLLs**?'

She took another drag, puffing out smoke in big curls. Dog-walkers passed by, spying from the corner of their eyes. I knew what this would lead to; if we lurked too long they'd call the police, reporting us for committing the grand crime of looking suspicious. That's probably what happened this morning with the police car: *You must come, Officer, there are unknown people walking our quiet market town streets.*

It began spitting with rain. Tiny little drops hit Jules's face but she didn't wipe them away. She pointed her finger at Luca. It looked aggressive the way she did it: long digit wobbling, fingernail bitten down into a jagged blade. But I could see by the way she was holding her shoulders that this was her version of being calm and reasonable.

'I've told **MoLLs** and I'm telling you,' she said to Luca, '**ThINking** never helped no one.'

Luca's mathematical frown dropped. He pushed each of his fingers down, counting off examples.

'The theories of space and time; the invention of the steam engine, telephone and penicillin; the creation of art, literature and music . . .'

Jules flapped her hand at him, shaking her head like she was teaching a toddler to stack cubes.

'*Naaaah!*' she said. 'That's not what I'm talking about. Thinking doesn't help the likes of *us*.'

Luca stopped counting and looked at Jules.

'All it does is send you more mental than you already are,' she said.

It was a reflex comment, like the babble that comes after a big cry, no judgement or malice attached. Jules may think the world is full of psychotics but it's not some godawful thing that she believes needs to be purged from the face of the earth. It's not something that *scares* her like it might other people.

'Everybody has their dirty laundry,' she'd once explained to me. 'Some stains are harder to see than others. Especially the crazy ones.'

If Luca had known Jules's philosophy on the subject he might have reacted differently, but he didn't so he took the comment personally. He stood up tall; the birds hopped away.

'I am *not* mental,' he said.

He held himself tense, staring at Jules, hard and cold. I could see the dark canopy moving over his head. The rain was heavier now, big droplets splashing against the concrete path.

Jules laughed.

'Yeah, and I'm Kate Middleton.'

Luca took a deep breath as his lip curled into a sneer.

'I am not mental.'

I was hoping Jules would hear the kick in his voice but the two of them seemed immune to each other's moods. Jules searched the ground for Boy, then tucked her under her arm and waved her cigarette daintily in the air as she put on her posh Kate Middleton voice.

'I live in a big palace, don't you know? Me and my darling Wills walk the corgis every morning and pick up their royal shit with golden baggies.' She made kissing noises at Boy's face. *'Only the best for you, my sweet.'*

I got the giggles. I couldn't help it. Jules is hilarious when she does her Kate Middleton. It's nothing like the actual Kate Middleton but it's still dead funny. Jules began sniggering. Then she straightened out her face and gestured down to her camouflage outfit.

'Do you like it, darling? Vivienne Westwood just insisted I should have it.'

Jules spun around as if on a modelling shoot, looking over her shoulder at me with a pout. Boy didn't know where to look. I laughed so hard I rolled on to the grass. I was hoping Luca would see the funny side – she did the pose perfectly – but when he stepped towards Jules his body was shaking. He pointed at his chest.

'I am NOT mental!'

The dog-walkers looked at us as Luca's voice bounced off the grass verges and sent the last few birds flying. Boy jumped from Jules's hands. I pushed myself to a standing position, hoping I'd think of a way out of this but Jules was already snarling.

'WHo do you ThiNk you're taLKinG to, POSH BOY?'

She was clenching and unclenching her fists, making the knuckles flash pink and white. Luca backed off. His body, so tall and firm, suddenly shrank. It was like watching plastic shrivel in a fire.

Jules kept her eyes on Luca as she bounced up and down.

'WHO tHe FUcK dO you tHINk You ARE?'

Luca had never seen Jules on a berserker before. Considering the amount of time we'd spent together he'd had a good run. But now the veins were throbbing in her neck as rainwater rolled down her cheeks. Her eyes bulged from her face like a zombie ready to rip into his flesh.

Luca looked as though he was going to wet himself.

'Sorry,' he said quietly.

But it was too late for that; the volcano was erupting.

'You MEN aRe All THe FUCKinG SAMe!' Jules screamed. 'AcTING aLL NicE To StaRT wiTH tHEn—'

She smacked her hands together.

'—BOOM! You'rE yeLLing aT deFEnceLESs WoMEn, ThROwING YoUR FiSTs AbOUt. RAPING ANY FUCKER WHO GETS IN YOUR WAY!'

The dog-walkers were no longer walking but standing at the sides of the path with umbrellas over their heads. Luca's cheeks burnt red.

'Now, hang on a minute!' he said.

Jules was hopping about so quickly now it was like she was in a boxing ring ready to swing. *Ding! Ding!*

'No, YOU haNg on, MATE!' she cried.

She thrust her finger into Luca's chest as one of the dog-walkers lifted a mobile phone from his pocket. The rain lashed in slanted lines. I picked up Boy as she whimpered.

'YOU BLOODY HANG ON!'

I pushed the wet hair from my face, put my soothing voice on and imagined I was a masseuse in a luxury spa.

'It's OK, Jules,' I said. 'He meant no harm.'

Jules looked at me as though I'd just pissed on her leg. She took her shaking finger with the jagged nail and pointed it at me.

'DON't PReteND YOU'rE AnY BEtter! You'RE JuST LiKe thAT BitcH, DoNNa.'

I clamped my lips. You're as good as finished when Jules starts talking about Donna.

'FuCKed me RIghT Over, DiDn'T ShE? ThE LiVerPooL SLaG! AnD you'll dO THe SAmE, MoLLs. MARk mY woRDs, yOu'LL DO IT!'

I looked at Luca with wild desperation. Back in Nottingham, I could turn on my heels and leave the scene knowing that, after an hour or two, I'd come back to Jules having an intense discussion with some poor sod about her love of pygmy goats. Of course, I'd later hear how she'd kicked the shit out of a bin or punched a wall and fractured her hand but when I got back she'd be all tranquil, the venom bled clean from her veins. But there was no leaving Jules alone in this town; she'd rip the whole place to pieces.

Luca was scratching his chin again. I shook my head. Deep thoughts were not what we needed. He straightened his back, placing one hand behind him, elevating his already BBC-newsreader voice to new heights.

'*Now, Ms Middleton,*' he said. '*That is no way for a lady to talk.*'

Jules looked over at him as she hopped from side to side.

'WHAt the FuCk YoU TaLking aBouT?'

Luca held his butler pose.

'*I'm merely pointing out, milady, that these are your royal subjects.*'

He swept out his hand as if presenting the pedestrians to her. Jules looked at the spectators standing on the verges in their raincoats and wellingtons. Suddenly they moved on, looking at anything – the trees, the sky, the dog turds on the side of the path – as long as they weren't looking at us. Jules stopped hopping. She glanced at the pedestrians, then at Luca, then back at the pedestrians. Then she stared at me. Her gaze hovered over my face as her brows twitched.

Luca jabbed me in the side with his elbow. I put Boy down on the ground and stood up tall, pulling out the sides of an imaginary skirt before crossing my ankles as I curtseyed.

'*Your Highness*,' I said.

The whole of Jules's body flopped. She looked back at the pedestrians and released a devil-like grin. She stood up tall, holding her cigarette in the air.

'*Please forgive me, darlings*,' she said, all Kate Middleton again.

Nobody looked at her. It was like 'The Emperor's New Clothes' except, instead of people staring so as not to upset the King, they were looking away so as not to upset Jules. This only made her louder.

'*No need to stop, of course! I'm the people's princess, haren't I? Just like one of you.*'

She stood there, sucking at her cigarette and tossing her head around. The rain got lighter, until eventually it stopped. Me and Luca looked at each other and smiled. I felt a rush race up my body. It was like we'd climbed bloody Everest.

Luca picked up his rucksack and swung it on to his back. Then he picked up my camping rucksack as well as his trumpet case and even picked up Boy, which was the first time I'd seen him touch her. I think he was still in character because he did all of this with a masterfulness I don't think he'd have pulled off as himself. He turned to Jules, voice back to normal.

'Come on, Princess,' he said. 'We're nearly there.'

*

A charity worker once put barriers around Private Pete as he slept in the doorway of an unused office. It was a yellow, foldable barrier with warning triangles plastered across it and exclamation marks inside the middle of each shape. On the front, a sign was tacked on:

THIS MAN HAS REFUSED TO TAKE AN OFFER OF THREE NIGHTS IN A HOSTEL.

When Jules saw it she leant over the barrier and gave Pete a prod.

'What's this notice about?' she said.

Pete stuck his face up, hoodie draped over his head.

'I don't know, but that lady keeps going on about it,' he said.

That's when we saw the television crew coming towards us. There was a man with a camera, another one with a big mic, and a woman wearing ten layers of foundation. She seemed excited to see us, asking if we knew the 'gentleman' and if we wanted to make a comment about the barriers and sign. I shrank back, looking away from the lens. The last thing I needed was my face broadcast across the nation.

'Yes!' Jules said. 'Yes, I do bloody well want to make a comment!'

She pointed at Pete.

'Lord knows how this man hasn't had the shit kicked out of him. The general public love kicking the shit out of the homeless and that's without a bloody sign. And what's with the warning symbols? What you warning people *of*? "Smelly homeless bastard lives here"?'

The woman asked if Jules could say the comment again without swearing. Then again without the 'smelly, homeless' bit. Then again without the swearing. They kept on doing takes like this, trying to get a clean version. I sat down next to Pete.

He pulled himself up when he saw it was me, scratching the back of his neck where his psoriasis was; stress made the itching worse. He said it was true, he *had* refused a place at a hostel but the hostel was in Derby and he was on bail in Derby for begging so he couldn't go back there. Besides, he'd had hassle in the hostels there from young lads taking the piss out of him.

'You know, because of my scabies,' he said. 'They wouldn't touch me but threw things at me and called me names. It got too much in the end.'

He tried to tell the charity worker all of this real nice and polite, and she'd nodded as though she understood, so he curled up in his sleeping bag and went back to sleep. The next thing he knew there were barriers around him and a woman with a mic, shouting at him about a sign and did he think it was dehumanizing? He didn't really know what she meant by dehumanizing until she read the sign out to him and he figured it out.

'And it *was* dehumanizing, Molly,' he said. 'It made me feel like scum.'

The reporter got a call on her phone and told Jules she had to get to another story. Jules protested, saying she had a great headline for her report, but the crew packed up and left before she could tell them what it was.

We both shuffled up so Jules could sit down and roll a cigarette. She was still livid about the whole sign business.

'The bloody cheek of it,' she muttered. 'If only I'd caught her doing it, Pete, the mouthful I'd have given that lady! But they don't want to listen. No one wants to listen to the likes of us.'

When she said this, I thought about the reporter, how she'd asked Pete about the sign and had told him it was dehumanizing. I thought about how Pete would never have realized it was dehumanizing unless she'd said that and would have considered it as just another day on the streets. And I realized then that perhaps people did want to listen. Perhaps they wanted to know our stories. Perhaps they wanted to understand. Although this charity worker had been brutal, the majority of people were good sorts – even the God-botherers – and knew that they could easily be in our position. It was bad luck that we'd ended up where we were. Or a few bits of bad luck. Or bad luck after bad luck after bad luck, until you're spinning around with all the bad luck and don't know where to look. Some people say you make your own good luck in this life. Those people have never been homeless.

I looked over at Jules as she finished rolling her cigarette, little strings of tobacco scattered over her lap, and thought about all the trouble she'd been through.

'What was the headline?' I asked her. 'You know, for Pete's story.'

She took in a deep drag. Then she blew a fat cloud of smoke out before fanning her hand in the air as though the words were being spelt out in front of us.

'"Beggars CAN be choosers",' she said.

It was funny because it was the opposite of what I'd been thinking, but of course it was true. You can't choose your circumstances, but you can choose how you react to them. And right then, we reacted by bursting into laughter.

As we walked the streets of Bingham, Jules performed royal waves for everyone we passed. Every so often she'd stop, and I'd pull out my imaginary skirt and curtsey. The more she stopped, the lower the curtseys became until my knees were nearly scraping the pavement. This amused Jules no end. She kept making snorting noises and slapping Luca on the back with a newfound sense of camaraderie. You'd never have guessed that a few minutes ago she'd been screaming within an inch of his face. That's the thing with Jules: when she's done with her rage, she's done. She doesn't go on about it, dragging her ill feeling into every petty argument. My mother was the queen of that, and we didn't even have to be arguing for her to start banging on about my past mistakes.

'This is like the time you wet yourself in that brand-new satin dress,' she'd say. 'You can't help but ruin things.'

It didn't matter that I'd been three at the time or that I didn't even remember doing it.

There are people who've robbed Jules of all her money, kicked the shit out of her and reported her to the police for things she didn't do, and she's still on chatting terms with them.

Except for Donna. I don't think she'll ever be on chatting terms with Donna.

Our clothes were still damp from the rain, but I was too busy watching Luca to care. He walked ahead with his wiry limbs and trumpet case. You'd never have guessed he had it in him but the way he'd handled Jules was magic. His hair glowed in the morning light like a big curly crown and I imagined two giant grey wings sprouting from his shoulder blades, stretching out to reveal an array of iridescent feathers. He was King of the Byway. King of the Pigeons. King of the whole of Bingham.

The road was quiet with detached houses set back from the pavement. We were in proper countryside territory now: big old drives with four-by-fours, huge lime trees and privet hedges lining the fences. The houses were like manors, with dozens of windows gleaming like teeth and little plaques with names like 'Willow Cottage' by the main entrances. On one of the houses all the wood – the garage panels, the doors, the window sashes – had been painted a soft sage and twisting ivy was winding up to the roof. A big long conservatory ran the length of the house. It had oversized potted plants inside, leaves squashed up against the glass.

Luca stopped in front of the house. He put Boy down and then placed his hand on the latch of the gate. He clicked it open and walked up the path.

'What you doing?' I said.

He stopped to look at me.

'Plan C,' he said.

Me and Jules looked at each other. Sometimes we don't even need to say anything; we know we're thinking the same thing. This time we were both thinking: *He tries to steal one car and now he thinks he's a grand thief.*

'Are you coming?' Luca called.

He didn't turn around, just carried on walking as we hovered at the gate. You could hear the crunch of his trainers against the gravel; he wasn't even trying to be quiet. Boy followed him without glancing back. Her hind stump was wagging along with her tail.

Jules's brows were knitted into a frown. Her hair was still wet, her camo jacket damp and sagging on her small body. She watched Luca for a second and then shrugged, clicked the gate open and followed him up the path.

The slithering was happening in my gut again. I looked up and down the street, knowing if I stood there for too long it would look suspicious. So I followed them both, closing the gate behind me. I had to squeeze my arms around my stomach just to keep steady on the gravel.

Even the stones were classy: white and caramel pebbles, all neatly organized in a curving stream up to the door. There was a BMW in the drive but Luca didn't seem to care if the owners were in. The slithering turned to thrashing. I knew I wanted no part of whatever foolish plan he'd conjured up, but at the same time I couldn't make myself leave. When I got to the front door I saw a plaque beside it that read 'Cherry Blossom Lodge'. You couldn't rob a place called Cherry Blossom Lodge. It'd be like mugging a children's book character.

Luca raised his hand to the knocker. It was the shape of a lion's head, a brass hoop through its mouth. I saw its teeth flash as though it was going to bite Luca's hand off.

I picked up Boy from the path. She released a little yap. '*Luca*,' I said.

He must have heard the panic in my voice because he turned to me with a teacher-like reassurance.

'Don't worry, Molly,' he said. 'I know what I'm doing.'

He took hold of the knocker and banged three times. He was going to do it; he was going to knock on these people's door, push his way through and rob them of everything they owned. Probably elderly folk, I thought. Probably elderly folk with heart conditions. I knew I should be running, getting myself away from this dead-cert disaster, but my feet were fixed as if they were sunk in mud. I felt the frozen panic I'd get as a kid, knowing that something awful was about to happen but not knowing how to stop it.

The Guardians of the Gate

My grandma thought she could see ghosts. Whenever we visited she would tell us to be careful of Michael in the kitchen who'd been thrown off a horse and not to mind Mabel who lived in the attic and had been murdered by her husband fifty years ago. She said these things casually, as if giving us the history of an antique and not apparitions who were haunting her house. One time, when my mother was out of the room, Grandma leant in so close that I could smell the washing powder in her clothes.

'You see them too, don't you, sweetheart?'

She was looking at me with bright emerald eyes surrounded by peachy folds of skin. I nodded even though it wasn't true; I saw lots of things, but never ghosts. But I didn't want her to think she was the only one. I didn't want her to feel alone. So I nodded and, when I did, she clutched my arm.

When my mother came back in she saw how Grandma was holding on to me and told me we needed to go. When she got outside she waited until we were at the end of the road before turning to me. She was a tall woman, taller than other mothers, with hair so immaculately neat it looked like it belonged on a mannequin.

'Your grandmother's crazy, remember that,' she told me. 'She's been living in that ghost world all of my life, dragging me around to seances and spiritualist churches. Telling everyone I had the gift too.'

She glanced around the street as if checking for spies. I searched my mother's face intently, noting every flicker and flinch as she spoke. I'd seen the bitterness before but there was something new in her expression, a small tremble of vulnerability.

'She paid more attention to those stupid ghosts than to her whole family,' she continued. 'She didn't care how people talked about us, how people *looked* at us. My poor father, he never got over the embarrassment.'

It was the most I'd ever heard about her childhood and the most I'd ever hear.

'Still, you have to stick by your family,' she said, 'even if you can't stand them.'

I frowned.

'Why?' I asked.

She looked confused, as if she didn't know the answer. Then she patted the back of her hair.

'Because that's how things are done,' she said.

She turned away, walking towards the car. And I, not knowing any better, followed.

You could hear the cups tinkling on their saucers as we sat in the living room. They were pale blue with pretty roses in the middle. Every time I took a sip I had to be extra careful. Just squeezing the handle made me feel like the whole thing would shatter.

We sat quietly as Luca's mother mucked about with a giant clear teapot. She was doing some business with a tin full of dried tea leaves – inserting some into a special chamber at the top of the pot then squishing more in – and we were all watching as if she was performing heart surgery and any disturbance might make her snip the wrong tube.

Luca's dad, who Luca said was not his dad, had turned ashen when he'd seen us standing at his door. He ushered us in with a big strained grin that quickly fell off his face when the door slammed shut. He was a tall man, thin with a carefully cropped ginger beard that clashed with the toffee-brown hair on his head. He said his name was Stuart but we were to call him Stu.

It took a moment for him to notice Boy in my arms. When he did, he grimaced as though I'd brought in a dead creature.

'We don't have animals in the house,' he said.

'She's an assistance dog,' Jules said.

Stu frowned, staring at Jules as if she too was a dead creature. He kept his eyes on her as he called down the hallway.

'Joyce! We have visitors!'

It took a moment for Joyce to appear but, when she did, it was like a goddess had floated into the hallway. Trumpets, fanfares and a shaft of white light would have been fitting. She was a tall woman, broad enough to carry the world and its problems, though no one would ever imagine asking her. Her body was a series of rolling curves, as smooth and defined as piped icing on a cake. Her skin was as rich as dark melted chocolate poured into a pan and her short spiral hair, cut smoothly around her head, was distinct and neat, like coconut shavings sprinkled across her scalp. This woman was good enough to eat.

She didn't falter when she saw Luca, just scooped him into her arms as though she'd been expecting him all along and directed us into the living room, insisting we call her Joyce, before sliding off to the kitchen to fetch the tea.

As we watched Joyce filling up the cups I glanced around the living room. It was like one of those interior design magazines and we were sitting right on the cover, getting in the way of the decor. The walls were painted a milky duck-egg colour, the tables and bookcases made of matching dark wood with printed cushions spread across the sofas. On the walls were crazy paintings in traditional frames. Splashes of maroon with cubes of cream, wiggling lines and neat circles painted over and over each other until it made you dizzy looking at them. They were hung up neat like in a gallery, which made me think they were probably done by some famous people and not just something Luca had brought back from GCSE Art (which is what they looked like). I liked the sculptures though, standing on shelves and nailed high on the wall. African masks and carvings of animals. A gazelle on the mantelpiece, a giraffe by the window. On the table beside me was a hippo with its head tilted to the side and mouth open like it had just spotted me and was about to ask a question.

As soon as Joyce finished pouring, she balanced her cup and saucer on her palm and looked over at Luca.

'Well, it's *rarely* lovely to see you, darling,' she said.

Her voice was proper posh. Even posher than Luca's, saying '*rarely*' instead of 'really' like that. It made her sound like royalty but not Jules's Kate Middleton royalty, the real Kate Middleton royalty. She shuffled back into her chair, back straight, sipping at her tea with her pinkie pointing out. I imagined her sitting on a throne in Buckingham Palace, fur-trimmed cape on her shoulders, the crown jewels balanced on her head.

Boy was sniffing around the carpets and furniture. Stu, who sat with his legs stretched out, feet crossed at the ankles, watched her with beady eyes.

'We don't have animals in the house, do we, Joyce?' he said.

Joyce looked down at Boy as though it was the first time she'd noticed her, which was a good acting job because it was hard *not* to notice a Border terrier with a missing leg.

Joyce waved her hand at Stu.

'Not a problem,' she said.

Luca sat slumped in his seat. Joyce smiled widely, teeth all neat like a picket fence.

'You must tell us all about what you've been up to,' she said.

I could see the shape of Luca's eyes was the same as his mother's, but otherwise he was all Stu. The thin face, the tight lips.

'See how I'm already getting the Spanish Inquisition?' Luca said to me.

Stu stiffened in his armchair. 'I don't believe one question qualifies as the Inquisition, Luca,' he said.

Luca looked at me again and rolled his eyes. I felt myself blush, like I'd taken sides in a war I hadn't known existed. Luca took his shoes off and began doing his thing with the socks. Peeling them off layer by layer, arranging them on the floor in neat little rows. Joyce watched him carefully from the side of her eyes.

'You've got a beautiful house here, Mr and Mrs—' I began. As soon as I started I realized I didn't know Luca's surname.

'Bargate,' Joyce said.

I looked over at Jules. She shrugged as though this had been the most obvious thing, that Luca would steal a credit card from his parents.

'*Please* call us Joyce and Stu,' Joyce said. 'We feel so old when we're called Mr and Mrs.'

Luca looked up from his socks.

'That's because you are old.'

Jules snorted with laughter.

'*Luca*,' Stu said with a warning in his voice. It sounded well practised, like he'd used it many times before.

Joyce managed a nervous smile.

'It's all right, darling, it was just a joke.'

'I think you'll find it's an evidence-based fact,' Luca said.

He was putting his socks back on now. I didn't realize how barmy his whole sock business was until we were there in the living room with the shiny dark wood and the perfectly printed cushions. It was like watching a prince pissing in the palace fountain.

Jules was staring down at her cup.

'What's this tea, then?' she said. 'Not normal, is it?'

Joyce smiled. 'Earl Grey,' she said.

Stu placed his cup and saucer on the table beside him.

'Horrible stuff,' he said. 'But apparently that's what *everyone*'s drinking. You can't hold your head up in Bingham if you haven't got a cup of Earl Grey.'

Jules grinned.

'Well, in that case . . .'

She drained her cup and smacked it down on the coffee table.

'. . . pour us another.'

She smiled, all friendly, but Stu was straining at the jaw as he bent forward and filled her cup. We all watched as he poured, as though Stu was now doing the heart surgery.

It was then that I saw the girl standing in the doorway. She can't have been more than six; springy Afro hair tied in bunches that sat like clouds on either side of her face. Her skin was milky brown like Luca's, dark eyes scanning the room before settling on him. Luca must have felt the gaze because he turned to her, his eyes losing their narrowness.

'All right, Cora?' he said.

The girl blushed as everyone looked at her. I gave her one of my big smiles, the type that swallows up my whole face.

'Are you Luca's sister?' I said.

She glanced at me and then nodded, running over to Luca's side. Boy came straight over and sniffed her shoes. She seemed scared at first, but Luca bent over and gave Boy a rub on the head to show she was friendly, so Cora bent down and did the same. This got Boy excited, licking at Cora's face, which made her giggle.

'Be careful, Cora,' Stu said, which seemed like a stupid thing to say. Boy was as dangerous as a puddle of mud.

Joyce had put her cup of tea down and wrapped her hand around her knee. She was rocking gently back and forth, cheeks puffed out as though they were ready to burst with questions. Eventually she shrugged.

'Staying over?' she asked Luca.

Luca cricked his neck to the side. You could see he was trying to hold back the sarcasm.

'Just tonight,' he said. 'Got to keep moving.'

I thought he was going to tell her about the people following us but he just bit down on his lip.

'If that's all right?'

Joyce looked sort of pleased with herself when he said that. Then she sucked in a deep breath that made her huge breasts billow out.

'And your friends too?'

She didn't look up at us as she said it, just stared aimlessly at her knees. Luca rolled his eyes.

'*Obviously.*'

Luca's dad clenched the arms of his chair.

'Now look here, Luca—' he said.

Joyce laughed. It was such a sharp, shrill laugh that I almost dropped my cup.

'Stop being a grumpy old man,' she said. 'He's been in a bad mood ever since the cricket scores came up.'

She didn't seem to say this last part to anyone in particular but when she stood up she looked down at me and Jules and smiled her picket-fence smile.

'Of course, you're both welcome,' she said. 'We have plenty of space. Come on, girls, I'll show you to your room.'

Jules raised her brows. As we walked out, I glanced over at Luca. He was looking at me with eyes that said 'Sorry'. I didn't know what for.

After we first met, Jules became my bunk-buddy, sharing shop doorways with me and finding unused basements in warehouses. You had to be over eighteen to get a place in a hostel and I wasn't then. Although Jules could have got herself a place, she stuck with me. But the homeless life isn't an organized one. There'd be times we were supposed to meet in the evening and she wouldn't turn up, too absorbed in family dramas or out on an almighty bender. Then I'd set up my sleeping bag under the bridge near the Navigation pub. Something about being next to the canal appealed, even though it was a hazardous spot to sleep. Drunk people were the worst; pissing on your sleeping body or pouring kebab meat over your head for 'a laugh'.

I'd spend nights under that bridge with the pigeons cooing in the rafters above, wondering what it would be like to have a proper place to live. I'd imagine being in a living room with a smouldering fire, people curled up on armchairs, reading books, watching the television. It created this feeling inside me that I've never really felt. Not happiness or contentment. Something simpler. Something basic. It made me feel safe.

You can't feel safe sleeping rough though, not when you don't know who'll be walking past, not when you're so exposed. I couldn't relax under that bridge, even with the pigeons to keep me company.

But in Luca's house I felt something like safety, like a tiny bead of security was locked in my heart and just being in this house, being with Joyce, made it grow bigger. I didn't know if Luca felt the same way; he seemed to hate the house and Joyce along with it. But he had come back here. If your car is on fire you don't get back in the driving seat.

Except, perhaps, when you can't find another escape.

Joyce showed us to the spare room. Jules flung herself straight on the bed, bouncing up and down as Joyce found some extra bedding.

'Sorry it's only a single,' she said.

Jules shuffled up the bed, placing her hands behind her head as she spread out flat across the white linen. Joyce looked down at Jules's Doc Martens, mud caked into the treads. I sat on the end of the bed hoping that Jules would prop them up on my jeans but she just shuffled further back, putting marks across the sheet.

'It's all right. We'll just do sardines, won't we, Molls?' she said. 'Head to toe, like.'

I nodded and smiled as Joyce tied the gingham curtain back with a matching gingham strap. The whole room was doused in pale blue-and-white gingham: the curtains, the bedspread, even the vase on the windowsill had a che-quered stripe running around the base and lip.

Joyce looked distracted as she passed me a pillow and some towels.

'I would give you Luca's room, but I turned it into an art studio a few months back. I don't think he'll be happy when I tell him.'

I smiled up at her again.

'It's lovely in here. Thanks.'

I watched as she squeezed her shoulders to her ears.

'You both must be *star*ving,' she said. 'Get yourselves sorted and I'll order us a Thai curry from the local.'

Then she left the room. I could tell Luca had something against his mum but I've learnt it's best to make your own decisions about people. So far, Joyce had treated us real decent.

'Did you hear that?' Jules said, smacking me on the arm. '*Thai curry.*'

She closed her eyes as her head sank into the pillow.

'Now you're talking my language.'

I went to the bathroom to wash my face. Just being in the house made me realize how dirty I felt. My hair was greasy and there was black grime beneath my fingernails. Of course, my hair was always greasy, the black grime standard, but being in a clean environment made me feel even dirtier. I tried to scrub at the filth but my skin was getting red and raw so I decided to have another go in the morning. Light was flooding the landing as I made my way back to the bedroom. I looked through the large arched window at the top of the stairs and straight into the back garden. It looked like a park, it stretched so far. Pear trees and lavender bushes all neat along the borders; an elaborate birdbath beside big egg-shaped wicker chairs swinging from hooks. Right at the end of the garden I could see Luca sitting on a swing set with Cora as Boy dug up the flowerbeds. Cora looked really absorbed in what he was saying. Then the ground began to wobble, the trees and bushes trembling. Neither of them seemed to notice this, nor the tiny cracks emerging in the neat, grass lawn.

'In dreamland again?'

Jules was leaning on the doorframe of our room. She had a yo-yo in her hand, snapping it up and down, smooth and practised.

'Something's wrong,' I said.

She looked at me with a raised brow.

'You're right,' she said. 'He won't stop texting me.'

I didn't need to ask who.

'He doesn't know where we are, does he?' I asked.

Jules shoved the yo-yo into one of the pockets of her cargo pants.

'Rusby couldn't find his own arse if you paid him,' she said.

She turned and walked back into our room. Of course Jules didn't know about the knife. She didn't know about Rusby's network of lowlifes, of what they did to that boy. She barely saw me the whole time I was with Rusby, which was exactly how Rusby liked it. Rusby always got what he wanted in the end.

The snakes were slithering inside me again. I closed my eyes, trying to tuck all thoughts of Rusby away as Joyce called us down to the kitchen. He couldn't touch me here, not if I didn't let him.

The food smelt delicious, coconut and lemongrass filling the air. The kitchen was twice the size of the living room, with a huge cream Aga along the back wall and a marble-topped island surrounded by chrome stools. There was still room for an enormous oak table, big enough for a banquet. Stu was sitting down already with the *Financial Times* held so you could only see his neatly clipped fingernails. Joyce had arranged the takeaway food in a selection of hand-painted ceramic bowls and set out plates and cutlery with cloth napkins as though we were at a fancy restaurant.

'This is proper *lush*!' Jules said, pulling her silver knife and fork set from her jacket pocket. She sat down at the head of the table, tucking the napkin into the collar of her T-shirt.

Luca came in with a packet of jelly babies in his hand. Cora was carrying Boy, which was difficult because, even though she was a small dog, Cora was a small girl, so the ratios only just worked. Before Stu could say anything, Joyce smacked her hands together.

'Bon appétit!' she said.

Jules had already loaded her plate. She scooped a fork-ful of rice and green curry into her mouth and her eyes went dreamy. Cora had Boy on her lap as she sat at the table but Stu lowered his paper and Cora quickly placed Boy on the floor.

'There's last night's chicken in the bowl over there,' Joyce said to Boy as though she could understand English. Boy sniffed at Cora's feet.

'Oi! Food,' Jules said, clicking her fingers and pointing to the bowl by the double-doored fridge.

Boy trotted over to the chicken and gobbled it up.

Joyce unfolded her napkin, flapping it out with a quick firm shake and placing it across her knees. I tried to do the same.

Everything went quiet as we ate. Joyce sat all upright, using a knife and fork to cut her string beans into small pieces. Stu was putting food on Cora's plate, slopping sauce all over the table. Luca was finishing his jelly babies while Jules scrolled on her phone, shovelling curry into her mouth until her cheeks bulged.

'So, how did you all meet?' Joyce asked.

Jules glanced up from her phone, then began speaking through full cheeks. Bits of string bean and baby sweetcorn tumbled around her mouth like tea towels in a washing machine.

'Well, this is how it happened, see. Luca got chatting to my mate Robin Hood, who put him in touch with Suzie who volunteers down at the shelter. When he got down there, he began chatting with my mate Big Tony, who brought him to this party I was having on account of me being found not guilty in court.'

Stu put down his paper.

'Court?'

Jules pushed another forkful of rice into her mouth.

'Just a little misunderstanding regarding my probation. They reckon I breached it, which I kinda did, but they couldn't really prove it in court so they let me off. Good job as well because it was my last chance, if you know what I mean?'

Cora, who'd been watching the conversation like it was a tennis match, looked up at Joyce.

'What's *probation*?' she asked.

Jules opened her mouth to explain but Joyce dived forward with a bowl in her hands.

'Anyone for noodles?'

Jules stuck her hand up and we passed the bowl to her end of the table. This only stopped her temporarily. She was in one of her rambling moods and you can't stop Jules when she's on a ramble.

'It's all because of when I got jutted by Stacey Unwin,' she said, piling the noodles on to her plate, bamboo shoots and spring onion spiralling in thick, long strands. 'Never had a problem with her till this one day she jutted me in the back. Later she got jutted herself so the police, thick planks of wood they are, thought I was the one responsible. Doesn't matter that I hadn't realized I'd been jutted until an hour after and that I was in A&E when she got jutted herself.'

Stu was looking puzzled.

'What does *jutted* mean?' he asked.

Jules pulled her box of toothpicks from her inside jacket pocket and wiggled one inside her mouth.

'You know, *shanked*,' she said, putting the toothpick on the table and pushing another forkful of noodles in her mouth.

He still looked puzzled.

Jules stood up, clenched her fist and performed a stabbing motion. Stu's face turned ashen, the ginger in his beard accentuated by his pale skin. Jules sat back down.

'Did me right in the back when I wasn't looking, sneaky cow,' she said. 'Then there I was, walking around like I hadn't a care in the world, when Molly here says to me, *Jules, I think you've got something in your back.*'

They all looked at me. I smiled sort of weakly. Jules was breaking every etiquette rule imaginable. I wasn't as posh as the Bargates, but I came from the same background, with formal sit-down meals where people barely spoke let alone discussed stabbings. The streets had equalized me and Jules, but we weren't on the streets now and I hoped that, seeing the shock on everyone's faces, Jules would realize it.

Except, of course, Jules didn't realize it so instead stood up to recreate the moment she found the knife in her back. She looked over her shoulder and performed a series of expressions: shock, anger, the way she nearly fainted. Then she sat back down again and carried on eating.

Everyone was quiet. Jules pointed to her plate.

'Proper delicious, Mrs Bargate,' she said.

Joyce jumped slightly and then shook her head as if to say it was nothing. We all said how nice the food was, except for Luca, who wasn't eating.

There was quiet again. Jules was right; the food was delicious. We'd only had the croissants that morning and I had to stop myself from piling my plate up like she had; I could have eaten buckets of the stuff.

'*Psst!*'

I looked over at Jules, who was leaning towards me. She tried to act casual as she pushed her phone across the table top. I read the message on the screen. It was from Rusby.

Tell Molls I'm getting close.

My skin prickled as though the temperature had dropped. An image flashed through my mind: Rusby out there in Bingham, walking amongst the beige and grey people, his red baseball cap a siren on his head. I tried to shake the image away.

'So, come on, out with it, Luca,' said Stu, arms crossed on the table top. 'Tell us what you want.'

Joyce shot her husband a glare at precisely the same time Luca did, and Stu shot one back at each of them. Glares were zipping round like laser beams.

'Not now, Stuart,' Joyce said.

Stu shook his head. 'Come on, Joyce, we don't see him in months and then he turns up with—'

Jules suddenly stopped eating. Her broken eye bulged. 'With **whAT?**' she said.

You had to give him credit; Stu heard the edge in her voice straight away. He adopted a soft, mollifying tone.

'I haven't got a thing against you, girls, honestly. It's just your friend Luca here has put me and his mother through hell recently and the only time he ever seems to call is when he wants something.'

Luca was sitting with a fork in his hand. He'd piled some coconut rice on to his plate and was twisting his fork in it, this way and that.

'It's true, isn't it?' Stu said. 'What did you come for?'

He had that same intense look Luca had given me at the party.

Luca shrugged.

'Just saying hello,' he said.

Stu laughed, but not in a kind way.

Cora's bottom lip stuck out like rubber. She sat up tall in her seat.

'I think it's nice he's saying hello.'

She said it like a grown-up. Like the voice of adult reason.

Stu tossed his head back.

'You'd think it was nice if he blew up the Houses of Parliament.'

He looked back at Luca, pointing at Cora.

'She worships you, this girl. Lord knows why.'

Joyce stood up.

'Anyone for yellow cah-reh?' she asked.

I didn't realize she meant *curry* until she ladled it on to our plates. The liquid spread across the patterned ceramic like an oil spill.

'You're going to make him go away again,' Cora said. She'd whispered it but we all heard. It was heartbreaking the way she said it and even Stu knew to shut up. He picked up his newspaper and pulled it up in front of his face again.

'Not at the table, darling,' Joyce said.

Stu snapped his paper down, his cheeks flushed. I was expecting him to start bellowing but he just folded the newspaper in half, pulled his chair closer to the table and began eating.

We kept on like this for a good five minutes, nobody saying anything, the clinking of cutlery the only sound; it was just like the meals I had growing up. Then Luca dropped his fork.

'Why would I ask *you* for anything, *Stuart*?' he said, spitting the name as though it was dirt in his mouth. 'It's not like you're my *real* dad.'

We all looked at Stu, who was clenching his knife and fork with such force that they were shaking. He clanked them down on the table.

'For God's sake!' he said. 'This again?'

Joyce tried to mumble something reassuring but Stu was looking at Jules and me now.

'I *am* his real dad,' he said.

'And I'm a bloody Ferris wheel,' Luca said.

'Enough!' Joyce said. 'Please, Luca, just for one night.'

Cora's eyes were glazed with tears.

'Some have meat and cannot eat, some cannot eat that want it . . .' I said.

Everyone stopped and looked at me as though I'd gone mad.

'But we have meat and we can eat, so let the Lord be thankit.'

I smiled. They stared.

'I try and remember that every time I have a really nice meal,' I said.

Joyce blinked.

'Is it a quote?'

Jules was still staring at me.

'Yeah,' I said. 'But I can't remember who said it.'

I could remember; it was Robert Burns. My mother made us say it as a sort of prayer at dinner. Sometimes we sang it, if she was in a good mood.

Cora frowned.

'Some have sweets and cannot . . .' she began.

Joyce chuckled.

'Meat, darling. It was meat.' Then she looked over at me. 'Maybe you can teach it to us?'

And so that's what I did.

The Queen of the Wheat Field

That night, I dreamt that I was under the bridge by the Navigation pub and Luca was crouched in the rafters above, surrounded by an army of pigeons. His coat was made of slick grey feathers, long and shiny and puffed up around the shoulders, and his hair had been gelled down until it was almost flat. If it hadn't been for his square glasses, I wouldn't have recognized him.

In the dream, Luca was King of the Pigeons; the other pigeons held him in the highest esteem, pulling and preening his feathers, bringing him treasures from across the city, placing them at his large, clawed feet. He spoke to them in coos and warbles and they respected everything he said. I sat curled up, watching the whole routine as though it was a show.

When I saw the toads coming up the canal path I didn't think anything of it. They were only green specks at first, hopping in arcs, but when they got closer, I saw that they were the size of public bins. One of them locked eyes on a pigeon and, with a flick of its elastic tongue, swallowed it whole. The shape of the bird slid down its throat, pressing against its bottle-green skin. The other pigeons flapped away, but the toads just stretched their tongues out and caught each one until all you could see were pink fleshy tongues stretched out like bubblegum, grabbing pigeons from the sky.

Luca was still in the rafters of the bridge having his feathers preened. I stood up and shouted a warning but he couldn't understand my human language so ignored me.

When I looked back down the canal I saw that the leader of the toads, charging ahead of the others, was different from the rest. His teeth were yellow slabs and there was a red baseball cap perched on his head. When he saw me, he cocked his head to the side.

And that's when I ran.

I woke up with images of toads and feathers flashing before me. I looked for an anchor to the real world, then spotted the gingham curtains and remembered where I was.

The sun was shining through gaps in the curtains. As a kid, I'd lie in bed looking at the light streaming through, dust particles dancing, waiting for my alarm to ring. As soon as it did I'd get myself ready, race down the stairs and make sure he'd left for work. I'd know because his work shoes, all buffed and shined, wouldn't be on the rack any more. Then I'd go and pour a bowl of cereal and put bread in the toaster for Mother and stare at the clock in the kitchen, waiting to leave for school.

I was always waiting to leave.

I rolled over. Jules wasn't in the bed. It shouldn't have surprised me; she can never stay still for long.

On the landing, dresses were hanging across the banister as though drying, but they weren't damp. They had long flowing skirts and wild patterns in mad colours. I wondered if Joyce was trying to show me how nice her things were, though that didn't seem in her nature.

I took a shower, the hot water sprinkling from a shower-head so large it looked like a giant sunflower. The water fell like rain in shampoo commercials, where women stand in wheat fields with arms spread wide as they spin deliriously. I didn't think Joyce would mind me using her shower gel so I put a spot on my palm, trying not to waste any. It smelt of Apple Blossom and Bliss. I shaved my legs and armpits for the first time in ages, making sure to wash all the hairs from the razor afterwards. Then I walked out on to the landing, a towel wrapped around me, a newer, shinier Molly. I saw the dresses hanging and I picked up the plainest, a white cotton summer dress with flowers embroidered across the neckline and hem, and took it back to my room.

As I slipped the dress over my head I heard a buzzing coming from beneath the bedcovers. It was Jules's Nokia. For a second, I thought it was Rusby and I shuddered at the thought of his voice, but when I picked it up I saw 'MUM' written across the orange screen.

'Hello, Mrs Squires,' I answered. 'It's Molly.'

I heard a sigh.

'Oh, thank God! I was beginning to think something terrible had happened.'

I'd met Jules's mum a couple of times for Sunday roasts. People think the homeless have nothing to do with their families, but most keep some contact. Jules even stayed with her mum occasionally, but never for long.

She's a thin woman is Jules's mum, blonde perm too big on her tiny body, a crucifix always hung around her thin neck. Her mouth, circled in pink, waxy lipstick, never stopped moving, spouting off opinions about immigrants, drug addicts and gay people, bunching them all together as if they were the same. It was the opinions that always led to them falling out. Jules had too many of her own to listen to her mother's.

'I've been calling constantly,' Jules's mum carried on, 'and she's not been answering her phone. I keep telling her, "I don't care if you're not talking to me, Julia, you still need to pick up your phone" . . . You don't know where she is, do you, love?'

I didn't want to give too much away – the relationship between Jules and her mum was a delicate thing, not to be messed with – so I just said no.

'She's going to drive me crazy, that girl!' she said. 'You know she still hasn't been to the hospital? They say they can't tell me anything but they keep sending me the letters.'

I gripped the phone, hard. I must have missed something; Jules had never mentioned the hospital to me. Her mother sighed.

'You'll tell her to come home?' she said. 'I know we don't always get on but things have changed. I've been talking to my hairdresser; she's a lesbian, you know? I told Julia all about it.'

I told her I'd talk to Jules and she told me what a good girl I was. When I hung up I slipped the phone in the side pocket of my rucksack so I wouldn't forget it. I knew something was serious; Jules never kept secrets.

When I went down to the kitchen Stu was cooking something in a cast-iron pot on the stove. Boy was curled in a ball by the oven, staring up at Stu, who would occasionally glance over at her in annoyance. When he saw me, he nodded in a polite way and then got back to stirring. The rest of the family were in the conservatory, which was more like another wing of the house than a conservatory. There were shiny terracotta floor tiles, an array of mature cacti and large bi-fold doors left wide open. Everyone was sitting around a circular table with a huge potted palm tree towering behind them. It rose up to the roof and spread its fat leaves across the glass.

Joyce turned in her seat. She was wearing an orange headwrap with a spiralling knot tied expertly on the top and had large Hollywood sunglasses balanced on her nose.

'Morning, Molly, sweetheart!' she sang.

She looked me up and down. I felt my cheeks burn as I stood in the summer dress. She'd think I was a thief. Perhaps she'd punish me: feed me bread soaked in salt water, destroy my favourite things, put stones in my shoes in the morning and make me keep them there until I came home from school.

Joyce grinned.

'You found them!' she said. 'Luca was telling me you didn't have many clothes so I thought I'd leave out my old dresses. Don't you look *divine* in that?'

I smiled crookedly. It was hard for me to remember that not all mothers are the same.

Joyce turned her head to look at Luca and Cora. 'Doesn't she look *divine*?'

Cora was munching on a bowl of cornflakes. She was wearing purple jelly shoes with sparkly silver bits that caught the light as she swung her feet beneath the table. She looked up at me and grinned.

Luca was sitting on the other side of the table, a large mug with a painting of waddling baby ducks in his hands. His hair was kind of fluffy, like teddy fur out of a dryer; I guessed he'd had a wash too. He had a new T-shirt, sky blue with 'REASON' across it. His eyes darted from me to the ducks.

'You look nice,' he said. His cheeks flushed as he said it. Joyce grinned and then spotted my canvas shoes. They were scuffed on the toes, the laces tinged a dirty grey.

'Maybe we can do something about those too,' she said.

I sat down next to her.

165

'It's fine,' I said. 'I like them like this.'

She nodded slowly as she sipped her coffee. She was sitting perfectly upright, as though she was about to start a yoga sequence, so I sucked in my stomach and sat upright too.

'That's a pretty necklace,' Cora said, pointing at the key hanging around my neck.

Joyce lowered her sunglasses.

'Yes, lovely,' she said. 'Where did you get it from?'

I looked over at Luca whose eyes were a wide NO. I wrapped my fingers around the key.

'A friend gave it to me,' I said.

Luca smiled, pleased with himself. It was such a small word, 'friend', but it packed so much meaning. Just saying it made me feel like the hairline fractures running through our souls were being plastered together.

A loud bang came from the kitchen.

'It should be right in here. Why isn't the goddamn thing in here, Joyce?'

I hoped Jules hadn't 'borrowed' something expensive. She had rules when staying in people's houses: don't out-stay your welcome, dispose of your fag ends in a bin and borrow whatever you like.

Joyce wiped the corner of her mouth with her napkin even though she'd only been drinking coffee and hadn't eaten anything yet.

'If you would excuse me,' she said, pushing her chair back and slipping into the kitchen.

'*Hey.*'

I looked over at Luca, who was bent towards me.

'Yep?' I said.

He raised his finger to his lips even though I hadn't spoken loudly.

'I found the card,' he whispered, eyes darting to the kitchen.

I leant forward.

'The card?'

He rolled his eyes.

'The credit card,' he said. 'It fell down the back of my rucksack.'

I sighed; at least Jules hadn't borrowed that. Luca put his finger over his lips again.

'It means we can leave,' he said. His hands drummed on the table top. 'The sooner the better.'

'You're leaving?' said Cora. She looked at me accusingly, as though this was my idea.

I tried to keep my voice low.

'We don't need to rush off so quick, do we?' I said.

Luca opened his mouth but he was all agitated so just sat there puffing.

'I mean, shouldn't we wait for Jules?' I asked.

'Why would we wait for her?'

Stu came into the conservatory with the cast-iron pot, sweat dappled across his forehead. He hadn't heard Luca, but Joyce had; I could see it in her forced smile.

'Couldn't find the serving spoon,' she said, and then looked at me. 'I hope you like porridge.'

Stu dropped the pot in the middle of the table. Joyce rearranged it so it sat symmetrically on the heat mat. Steam was flowing out, the thick smell of oats floating out with it. I looked at Stu.

'I love porridge,' I said. 'It's one of my favourites.'

Luca looked at me sharply like I was a traitor, but I wasn't even lying. When I was little I went through a phase of eating porridge for breakfast and lunch. My mother thought it was a punishment but I'd have had it for dinner if she'd let me.

Stu sat down, rubbing his hands together. He didn't notice Boy jump on to one of the spare chairs.

'Best thing for keeping you regular,' he said.

Joyce rolled her eyes.

'Oh, *rarely*, Stu,' she said. 'Not at breakfast.'

She began spooning out the porridge. It was thick and gloopy. There were strawberries and raspberries heaped in bowls. They looked proper lush. I felt bad for Jules and then remembered she always found something to keep her going.

'Can dogs eat fruit?' Cora asked.

Boy had somehow managed to get her head in the bowl of strawberries.

'Oh, for goodness' sake!' Stu said. But he didn't stop her.

Joyce gave me her sun-goddess smile. It was all you could see; the rest of her face was covered by her big tinted lenses.

'So, Molly,' she said. 'Where's your friend Jules today?'

'She's popped out for a bit,' I said. 'She has friends in the area.'

Joyce frowned.

'In Bingham?'

Luca put his mug down.

'You're right, Mother, you can't possibly have friends in Bingham unless you have a four-by-four and live within a three-mile radius.'

Joyce raised an eyebrow.

'Where you got this sarcasm from, I don't know.'

I looked up at the conservatory ceiling. *Komorebi* was seeping through the palm leaves.

'What a lovely day,' I said.

Cora grinned at me, two teeth missing from the top row of her gums.

'I'm going on a bike ride,' she said.

I squeezed my shoulders up tight, stretching my eyes wide.

'Ah, that sounds brilliant,' I said.

Joyce tucked in the edges of her headdress.

'I like to sketch in the countryside. Luca's told you I'm an artist?'

Luca rolled his eyes. Stu was trying not to roll his.

'Of course,' I said.

She looked all pleased, as though I'd let out some secret. I'm a great liar if it's for the right reasons.

'Can Luca and Molly come with us?' Cora asked.

Joyce's smile faltered for a second and then eased back into a curve.

'Why not?' she said. 'I have a spare bike I never use. Luca, you could use your dad's fold-up.'

'I've no intention of going,' he said.

Joyce tensed. 'Molly?'

My mouth was filled with porridge. I tried not to look at Luca as I replied.

'Tha woo be lub-ley,' I said.

Everyone laughed but Luca.

After saving the fiery-haired boy from drowning, I wouldn't swim again. Every week my parents would take me to the swimming pool and I would stand at the edge, looking down at the water. Instead of blue and white tiles at the bottom I saw reeds and old ropes ready to entangle my legs.

My parents would stand behind me in full swimming gear, waiting for me to dive in.

'She won't do it,' Mother would say.

I heard him sigh.

'Give her a chance.'

'She's had lots of chances. All you ever do is give her chances.'

I looked to the other side of the water. On the bench, my swimming bag was wiggling.

'You give her too much attention,' my mother said.

'And you don't give her enough. Which is how we ended up here, isn't it?'

I watched as a hand pushed itself out of the swimming bag, followed by a head with plaits. Then another head, followed by another. A team of Rubberband Girls stood on the bench and raised their arms in a cheer.

'Let's go home,' Mother said.

I jumped in.

Joyce decided we should use the BMW. The inside of the car was cream with leather seats, an integrated satnav on the dashboard. It smelt of shoe polish and excess. Cora insisted I sit in the back with her and Boy so she could tell me about her school friends, what she wanted for her birthday and why she didn't like butterflies. She even sneaked one of her bracelets into my hand when Joyce wasn't looking. It had bright plastic beads, all different shapes and colours, with the word 'L-O-V-E' spelt out on four cubed beads. I pulled out the Rubberband Girl I'd started making under the Buttercross. I weaved more bands into its body to make arms. Cora watched me as though I was doing a magic trick. When I passed it to her, her eyes were round with excitement. She held it like treasure. We spent the rest of the journey grinning at each other.

Luca had stayed at the house to go through his things in the garage. He was cross that they'd been moved in the first place and also cross with me for agreeing to go with Joyce and Cora. He wouldn't look at me before we left.

Here's my rule: if someone doesn't tell you they've got a problem with you then you should act like they don't until (*a*) they get round to telling you, or (*b*) they get over it. You'd be surprised how many times the result is (*b*). Now, Jules *always* tells you if she's got a problem so you don't have to wait for either option. I like that about her because things get dealt with quickly. But I could tell Luca kept things buried deep down. The problem with people like that is they only get things out by exploding.

Joyce pulled up by a bunch of wheat fields with trees dotted like lampposts alongside the hedges. She took a while to decide where to set up her easel. Eventually she propped it on a mound by a big oak and sat down on a camping stool. Then she listed a set of rules for Cora and Cora kept nodding her head without listening, waiting for Joyce to finish so we could set off.

I put Boy in the basket on the front of Joyce's bike. I was worried she'd jump straight out but she put her front paws over the edge and looked ahead expectantly.

'How did she lose her leg?' Cora asked.

'I don't know,' I said. 'But she does fine without it.'

Cora nodded.

'It's our differences that make us interesting,' she said. 'Luca told me that.'

I smiled, trying to remember that for the next time he made a quip about Jules.

The bike was a bit stiff and Cora was way faster than me. But after a while we found a few dirt tracks and rode at the same pace. I hadn't ridden a bike since I'd left home (there was no point having one on the streets; they only got nicked). It was nice to be moving all smooth and effortless, the breeze in my hair, the wheat sheaves glowing in the sun like they were ablaze.

We had a couple of races. Boy's ears flapped back in the wind. Sunrays shone warm on our back as we sailed through the wheat, the wind blowing our clothes, plastic beads glinting on our wrists. It sort of felt like my own little girl was riding beside me, that if I closed my eyes and opened them she'd be right there, copper-red pigtails sailing behind her, nose covered in freckles.

Then I saw a figure.

He stood in the distance, a tall dark thing, hands shoved in his pockets. I hit the brakes.

'Who's that?' I said.

Cora stopped ahead of me. She looked across the landscape, caught sight of the tall thin man and shrugged. I tried to focus, to see how he was holding himself. The clothes on his body billowed in and out. It was Rusby.

'I'll go check,' Cora said.

I gripped the handlebars.

'No, Cora!'

But she'd already started. I began to pedal. He must have been following us all this time, waiting to get me alone.

Except I wasn't alone. I was with Cora.

Rusby's arm reached up as if waving. It looked like a friendly wave but nothing stayed friendly with Rusby for long. Above me the birds were gathering in a big black cluster. They created a whirlpool in the sky. Boy began barking.

'Wait!' I screamed.

I could hear Cora laughing as she pedalled ahead. She thought it was a game. The noise of the birds grew louder, as if they were warning her to stop. I squeezed the brakes, tipped the bike to its side and rested a foot on the ground. Boy leapt out, running straight after Cora. I leant forwards.

'CORA! *STOP!*'

Her back tyres spat out a cloud of dust. She put her feet on the ground and came to a halt. Boy ran straight past her, then circled back as I caught up. Cora's expression was wrinkled with confusion.

'It's all right, Molly,' she said. 'It's not real.'

I looked down the field. The fabric was still billowing in and out but I could see now that it was nailed to a pole. Above me the birds scattered.

It was just a scarecrow.

Molly Becomes King of the Beasts

I see the things no one else sees: fireworks exploding in a crowded living room, grey wings sprouting from the back of an ordinary man, scarecrows that look like an enemy. They're real to me, but not to others, so I try not to tell anyone about them. Except, of course, Rusby. I told him the first time I met him.

It was in the queue outside the old church building where we got free lunches. It was a popular place to go for a hot meal, a pudding and a friendly face. Usually Jules would be there, chatting away to whoever would listen, but she'd made amends with her mum and they were on a shopping trip. No matter how hard her mum tried, they always ended up at the army surplus store.

I'd been queuing for about five minutes when the man in front, dressed in a green raincoat and a pair of yellow wellingtons with faces drawn on the toes, began mumbling and laughing and wagging his finger up and down.

I didn't realize he was talking to me until he spun around and grabbed my shoulders with his thick fingers. He put his face close to mine and shouted like an evangelical preacher, *'You are the devil and you will not tempt me!'*

I can't remember much about his face other than his eyes, so wide you could see red veins weaving through the white. That's when Rusby stepped from the back of the line, taking the man by his arm, twisting it behind his back and shoving him against the wall. The man struggled at first, still spouting about temptation and the devil, but then two charity workers came out of the church, split them up and took the man to the side. Rusby stood by me, tall and broad, twice the man he'd be a few years later.

'You all right, sweetheart?' he said. Then, before I had a chance to reply, 'Don't mind if I nip in here, do you?'

He pointed to the space in front of me and slipped straight in. I looked back at the man as he brought a crucifix out of his pocket and started pointing it at the sky. Rusby rubbed his hands together and shook his head.

'Bloody nutter,' he said. 'Thinking you were the devil.'

I crossed my arms and shrugged.

'Everybody sees things, I guess.'

He froze, but then smiled, front tooth crooked in an otherwise perfect set.

'Oh really?' he said. 'What is it you see, darling?'

I shrugged, feeling my cheeks burn.

'All sorts.'

He nudged me on the arm.

'I bet you do.'

I didn't know what he meant. I don't think he did either. But the comment made us both laugh. As the doors opened he followed the queue as it shuffled forwards.

'This is the thing,' he said, looking over his shoulder at me. 'A man should never put his hands on a woman . . . Unless it's consensual, of course.'

My cheeks were burning again.

'But nah, seriously,' he said. 'I would never let a man disrespect a woman. Stick with me, sweetheart, and I'll make sure nobody touches a hair on your pretty little head.'

I was young. I believed him.

When we got back from the wheat field, Joyce made us all lunch. I sat on a chrome stool by the marble island in the kitchen, watching her toss olives and feta and salad leaves into a mixing bowl. She did it real elegant, splashing vinaigrette and sprinkling in bright peppers from jars as she went along. It was kind of relaxing watching her do it. I got to thinking that maybe I should tell Joyce about the whole Rusby situation, that maybe she could give me some sage advice. She seemed the type to give sage advice, like she knew about the world, not in the streetwise-survival way me and Jules did, but in the reads-thick-books-and-knows-stuff way. But, before I could say anything, she was washing her hands and calling for Luca.

I took the salad and went to the living room where Luca's dad was sitting with the *Financial Times* in front of his face again. I thought it best to leave him to it and sat down in the armchair opposite. Cora wasn't hungry and had gone upstairs to watch an episode of *Doctor Who* online, taking Boy with her. She hadn't told anyone about the scarecrow.

When Luca came into the living room he was covered in dust. Joyce strolled in with ceramic dishes full of bread rolls and began pouring us all a glass of red wine. People look down on the homeless for drinking during the day but it was OK there in the living room. Perhaps it's *where* you drink that matters. I thought I'd tell Jules that later.

Luca gave me a half-smile, which I was glad about because it meant he wasn't cross any more.

Joyce leant back in her chair, folding one leg beneath her bottom and holding her glass like a goblet. She started talking about a 'breakthrough' on her painting – something to do with contrast and lines. She talked non-stop and with such intensity it didn't matter if I concentrated or joined in.

'Enough about me,' she said eventually. 'Tell me more about you, Molly.'

I shrugged slowly.

'What do you want to know?' I said.

'Oh, the usual,' she said. 'Where you're from, what your parents do.'

She leant back as though waiting for a big long yarn. Luca stiffened in his seat but didn't say anything. I kind of wished he would because I hadn't talked about that stuff for a while. Nobody really asks about your family when you're on the streets. They know it's dodgy ground.

'I was born in Nottingham,' I said. 'My mother works in PR. My dad's a policeman.'

I don't know how I did it, telling the truth all smooth and easy when just saying the words felt like pins were being pushed into my windpipe.

'A *policeman*,' Joyce said, looking over at Stu with raised eyebrows.

As soon as she said that I knew I should have lied. This was the whole problem, people being impressed with job titles, people thinking it defined a person.

'And what type of work do you do?'

I wrapped my palms around the head of the wine glass. It was such a big glass that my fingers didn't even meet. I looked down at the burgundy pool.

'I'm not working at the minute,' I said.

I took a gulp of wine, hoping that'd be the end of it.

'Studying?' Joyce said.

Luca was poking his salad, pulling out the pieces of feta and pushing them into his cheek.

'Give it a break, Mother,' he said.

Joyce raised her eyebrows, ready to object, but when she looked at me she must have seen how awkward I was feeling. She lowered her glass.

'I'm sorry, Molly, I wasn't trying to be nosey.'

Luca stuffed another piece of feta into his mouth.

'Yes, you were.'

I held the glass tighter in my hand. I felt guilty being so cagey. Joyce had been so nice, giving me a bed, food, the dress, taking me to the wheat field, letting me borrow her bike. It seemed the least I could do was to tell her the truth.

'I used to work on the streets,' I said.

Her expression blossomed with hope.

'Performance?' she said.

I looked at Luca. I hadn't told him yet. I hadn't told him anything really. If he'd asked I would have. I really would have. I pulled the rubber bands on my wrist, feeling the sting as they smacked my skin.

'No,' I said. 'Sex work.'

Stu lowered his paper. He did it the way an actor might in a spy film, all slow, eyes peeking over the top. I looked down at my glass as the room went dark. People expect you to look a certain way when you're a sex worker. Six-inch heels, fishnet tights, rouged lips and mini-skirts: the ultimate fancy-dress prostitute. Some of the parlour girls dressed that way but when you work on the streets you just want to keep warm. Denim jeans, a thick coat and canvas shoes were my uniform. The men never seemed to mind.

I kept looking at the glass in my hands, red droplets sitting along the rim like blood. I didn't want to see the expressions on their faces.

I should have explained it better. How I'd never planned it. How when me and Rusby got together and into the habit it was the only way. Better that than him robbing and getting put in the nick again. At least this way he wouldn't be hurting anyone else. Just me, if things went wrong. I opened my mouth to explain but then I closed it again. It's not unique, my story. Plenty of girls did it, lads too, though I never saw much of them. Yasmin from Glasgow had worked in a massage parlour, which she said was better because you got protection, but they would never let someone like me in. The problem with parlour girls is they look down on the streetwalkers because they themselves have better working conditions and better pay. Of course, the high-end lasses look down on the parlour girls for the same reasons. Truth is, to most people we're the same no matter how much we get paid – a bunch of sluts, slags, hookers and whores.

Stu folded his paper.

'Well,' he said. 'It is the oldest profession in the book.'

Joyce's jaw tightened.

'Stu!'

He shrugged, eyes wide.

'It is!'

I wanted Jules with me. She'd have bulldozed over the conversation, talking about how she got her broken eye or what happened after she got jutted. The giraffe ornament was looking at me from the windowsill, the gazelle eyeing me from the mantelpiece. Hanging from the ceiling was a string of mahogany birds, cawing and laughing.

'I don't do it any more,' I said quickly.

I should have said that straight away. That, and how it was never something I enjoyed. Some girls do, but they don't tend to be the ones doing it in the back of someone's Ford Fiesta on an industrial estate, needing money for the next hit. Yasmin from Glasgow said it wasn't as bad as some jobs. That working in door-to-door sales for eight months had made her suicidal in a way that the parlour never had. Both were similar; you gave parts of your soul to your customers. You just gritted your teeth and grinned through it so you could pay the bills. But you can't really explain this stuff to people who've never been through it. They feel they have to share their point of view and I'm not really into debates, particularly ones where people only care about what they have to say.

'I'm trying to get on a better path now,' I said.

The Yellow Brick Road, I told myself. *The Yellow Brick Road*.

Joyce's expression was caught between revulsion and confusion. She couldn't really hide it, even though I could tell she was trying. No other profession can leave such a sour taste, not the way prostitution does. Except maybe traffic wardens. That's why I make sure to smile at them.

I couldn't look at Joyce any more and I couldn't look at Luca. I hoped he would be more understanding, that he'd know it was just a job I did once.

'What does your father think about this?' Joyce asked. Her voice was low and soft.

I looked her hard in the eyes.

'I couldn't give a shit,' I said.

Luca chuckled. He looked sort of proud.

Joyce coughed, leaning over for the bottle.

'Well, it's all very brave of you,' she said. 'More wine?'

She had her goddess smile back, neck straight and teeth gleaming. It was so well practised that it would have fooled a lot of people, but not me. It was the same smile my mother used for strangers.

I put down my glass and glanced over at Stu, who had his head cocked back, examining me like some foreign artefact.

'I think I'll sort my bag out,' I said.

I shot out of the living-room door, the tiled floor, the wooden stairs, the cream carpet on the landing all a blur as I rushed past. I could hear Joyce calling for me but I was too knotted up for any more. I ran into the bathroom and locked the door. I stood holding the edge of the sink, trying to remember how to breathe. It was hard to focus, my head fuzzy from the wine and filled with wooden animals and scarecrows. I saw Joyce sprinkling berries on to her porridge, her hand covered with fur. When I looked up she had a bear's face, mouth snarling.

I hit the side of my head. My imagination takes over the truth sometimes. Like the pride on Luca's face. That was just what I wanted to see.

My face looked back at me in the bathroom mirror. It was pale and drained, blue veins swelling beneath my eyes. It didn't matter how nice my hair was, or how pretty my dress was, or how long I'd been off the drugs and off the game and how hard I'd tried to be a good, honest person; people always saw the worst. A shadow formed behind me in the glass. It was taller than me, with a hand reaching out. I slapped my head again. Then again. A pain rippled down my neck and into my limbs.

This is how it feels when you need a hit: pain in your joints, cramp, sweat, nausea, anxiety and the deep-down need to make everything disappear. I searched the bathroom for something to make it stop. I checked the medication in the bathroom cabinet. I read the labels but they were mainly vitamins and blood-pressure tablets. Then I came across a cluster of dark little bottles with childproof caps on the top and long words that I couldn't pronounce. I was going to take a bunch of them, mix them up and hope for the best, but then I saw the same name printed along the bottom of each one.

'MR L. BARGATE'.

I closed the bathroom cabinet and leant my head against the mirror. The pain had eased but the images were still swirling. I knew what I had to do. I had to leave.

My grandmother saw ghosts, but she didn't like them. She told me they bothered her at the most inconvenient of times. But then, just before she died, she told me she was glad she could see them.

'I'm never alone,' she said.

train, or some other last-ditch attempt that would probably land us in hot water. Then I'd have to deal with Rusby.
He'd still be mad at me for the beer-soaking and he'd think
I owed him. I started to feel heavy at the thought of this
so lay down on the bed and pulled my knees to my chest.

They weren't always so bad, the punters. Some were
young lads who'd preferred a sure bet to a night on the
town full of rejection. Some were older men who didn't
want anything but a chat. I'm a good listener so I didn't
mind those. But sometimes, when I was standing on the
streets in the middle of the night, clinging on to my denim
jacket, bouncing up and down in my red canvas shoes to
keep warm, I'd see a car pull up beside me and know by
the way the man was sitting, the slump of his shoulders,
the leer in his eyes, that there would be trouble. By the
way he wouldn't speak as I leant down and asked how
he was doing, but would carry on leering like I was some
kind of insect he wanted to pull the legs off. I'd get that
slithering feeling in my gut, the cold wet crawling along
my spine, and know that I shouldn't get in the car, that
this man would do horrible, terrible things and I wouldn't
have any right to complain because I'd asked for it, hadn't
I? But when these men came, and I saw what they were,
I knew that Rusby would be around the corner watching. He'd get fisty if I turned away a client even though
I'd turned them away because I thought they'd get fisty
themselves. Rock and a hard place. That's where girls like
me always get stuck. So I went with these men, trying to

make chit-chat about the weather, acting cheery as they drove me down a real dark alley, and I knew Rusby, for all the use he was, was getting further and further behind. So I'd do what they said, take the insults and slaps and the fear, because that was my job. That was how I survived.

I only realized I was crying when Luca put his hand on my shoulder. He'd crept through the bedroom door. I wiped the wetness from my face but couldn't stop the sniffing, couldn't stop my body shaking, couldn't stop the snakes slithering.

Luca slipped on to the bed, curling his body around mine. He didn't say anything as he shuffled one of his arms under my neck, draping the other over the top of me. His body was warm. It felt like I was in a cocoon of Luca, all snug and protected. Then I felt his breath hot on my ear.

'It's OK, Molly,' he said. 'It's over now.'

The Cowardly Lions

It's hard to let go of the past.

Once, Private Pete got temporary accommodation in a bedsit and spent a week sleeping on the floor. The bed was too comfortable; it kept him awake. When Big Tony first came back from the army he said the worst thing was not being told what to do every minute of the day; the freedom drove him crazy. Yasmin from Glasgow said she couldn't ever have a loving relationship because all she'd seen was the worst side of men.

I'd been invisible for so long – the Stillness Lessons, disappearing down dark alleys and being a ghost on the streets – that it felt hard to be seen again. By Joyce and Stu; even by Luca. But when you stop being seen, you stop existing. And when you stop existing, that's when you give up.

I must have dozed for a few minutes because the next thing I knew Luca was gone. I went to the bathroom and washed my face with a gloopy gel. It was minty and made my skin raw and tingly, which was exactly how I felt inside.

I don't know why, but as I was scrubbing I got to thinking about Robin Hood outside the Tourist Information. I thought about how, when he was packing up one day, we started having a real nice conversation about corrupt politics and reclaiming power from 'the man' when, all of a sudden, he fixed me with pain-soaked eyes. I asked what was wrong and he told me it was his daughter Emily's birthday that day. It shocked me dead centre because I didn't think Robin Hood had kids; he always seemed the loner type. I asked how old she was and he said that she wasn't any age, not any more.

'She drowned on a sailing holiday ten years ago,' he said. 'She was twenty-two.'

I felt a sharp twist inside my chest. When you lose someone like that it leaves a hole inside you that you can never fill again. Nobody can see it but you're hollow for the rest of your life and even if you can make a shot of things and somehow feel happy again, that hole will always be there.

'You look a bit like her,' he told me. 'She had the same eyes as you.'

He smiled at me, grateful even though I hadn't done anything. After that I couldn't go back to the Tourist Information. I felt rotten about it, but I couldn't be someone's daughter again, not when it had gone so badly the first time. Besides, I knew Robin Hood wouldn't read too much into it. People move on quick on the streets.

I suppose I got to thinking about this in the bathroom because I still had the feeling I'd had with Robin: like I needed to run away. But then I thought about Luca and how he'd held me and I knew I couldn't do it to him. So I went back to the bedroom and put the key around my neck. I tucked it beneath my dress and it glowed amber like a candle.

When I went downstairs I couldn't find Luca or Cora but I could hear Joyce and Stu talking in the kitchen. The door was cracked open and I could see Stu pacing up and down with his hands shoved into his corduroy trousers. I was going to walk straight in, get the awkwardness out of the way, but then I heard him speaking and there was something in his tone that made me stop.

'He's still got that stupid trumpet case with him,' he said. 'And don't even get me *started* on that girl.'

'Stu, please keep your voice down.'

I stepped away from the door. Stu was still pacing.

'Bringing that three-legged beast in here.'

'It's just a dog.'

'And that *Jules* friend of hers.'

Joyce didn't say anything. The temperature dropped; I could feel the sudden chill in the air. I wrapped my arms around my body.

'The way she was talking about that . . . *stuff*,' Stu carried on. 'Over lunch, for God's sake.'

Perhaps telling them over breakfast would have made it better, or while they watched the news. I could have whispered it to them while they slept, or screamed it from the rooftop. But, in the end, it doesn't matter how you tell a person something, not when they don't want to hear it.

It was so cold now that tiny ice crystals were forming above my head. Joyce was chopping something with quick little movements. Her back was towards me as I watched her shoulders lift and drop, lift and drop.

'So she's lived a little.'

I smiled when she said that. It's funny how people can be different from what you think. I thought Stu seemed relaxed about the whole thing and Joyce was disgusted. But I forgot that sometimes people need time to think.

Stu was standing with his hands on his hips now. He looked like a statue of a Greek god.

'*Lived* a little?' he said.

Joyce stopped chopping and looked over at Stu.

'OK, so I was shocked too. But *rarely*, Stu, it isn't a big—'

Stu tossed his head back.

'Don't get all bohemian liberal with me, Joyce.'

She sighed in that weary sort of way parents do with children. I liked Stu, I really did, but I could see how he'd grate after a while. He poured himself a large glass of red wine. He swirled the ruby liquid around the glass.

'You're overreacting, Stu,' Joyce said. 'She's a perfectly nice girl.'

, Stu moved out of my vision. I put my eye to a crack in the door. He was leaning against the kitchen worktop, stuffing green beans into his mouth.

'Yes, she's very *nice*,' he said, rolling his eyes.

Even though I knew I was about to hear something I shouldn't, that I ought to cover my ears and run away, I was frozen, ice crystals blooming in the air. I kept my body huddled by the crack of the kitchen door, muscles sucked in tight. The key to being invisible is to be in-offensive, small, harmless. People don't pay attention to you when they think you're not a threat.

Stu was still stuffing green beans into his mouth.

'And I'm cancelling my credit card,' he said. 'You can't stop me now.'

'But we need to keep track of him,' Joyce said.

'He's here now. How much closer can we track him?'

The ice crystals were beautiful, spreading out in frac-tal patterns. I looked up at them, then back through the crack as Stu tried to lower his voice but to little effect.

'Did you *see* her arms?' he said.

I could feel the ice crackles on my lashes as I blinked.

'Little scars all over them,' he said. 'She's a drug addict, I'm telling you. Heroin or poppy. Whatever they call it nowadays.'

Joyce crossed the kitchen.

'Just because she's a *sex worker* does not mean—'

Stu's voice boomed loud again.

'Pull the other one, Joyce! You can act all Mother Earth about the whoring but you know what drug addicts are like. Besides, I saw you put all your jewellery away last night.'

Joyce was pushing a tray into the oven. I had to strain to hear her over the clanking.

'Just because I'm sympathetic doesn't mean I'm an idiot,' she said.

Stu pointed at her.

'I knew it!'

The ice encased me. *Sympathetic*. I used to think that was a good word but Jules said it was an insult. Empathy meant someone felt what you felt, was trying to walk in your shoes. Sympathy meant they were looking down at you from way up high.

Of course that was what Joyce was doing. She didn't want to imagine what it would be like to live in my shoes. Nobody wanted to imagine that.

'Yes, yes, and I'm sure there's a terrible story behind it,' Stu said. 'But she's not our problem, Joyce.'

He held his hand up before she could interrupt.

'*Luca's* our problem. Is she really the type of person he needs right now?'

Joyce stopped real still this time. I couldn't see her face but I could tell by the silence that she agreed with him. When she spoke again her voice was faltering.

'I don't know what to do,' she said.

Her shoulders hiccuped but she hardly made a sound. Even when she cried she was graceful.

'He used to be full of potential,' she said, a wobble in her voice. 'Now he's walking the streets with smackheads . . . I shouldn't have said that.'

I guess it shouldn't have surprised me. This is how people think: *Once a smackhead, always a smackhead.* It's the same for criminals. Big Tony, for example; convicted of grievous bodily harm at least four times in his youth, but he learnt his lesson on the last conviction, nearly killed a man only to realize it wasn't the man he'd been looking for. He was a pacifist now, but that didn't mean anything when it came to finding a job. Once a violent nutter, always a violent nutter, and if there are thirty people going for the same minimum-wage job, why choose the convicted one?

Stu was getting excited now, hopping about on the spot. He knew he was on to a winner.

'Yes, you should bloody well say it, Joyce!' he said. 'It's not right. He's not right. Doing that thing with his socks, carrying that tatty trumpet case around.'

'That was Dad's trumpet case,' Joyce said.

Stu laughed.

'Yes, the man who told everyone Louis Armstrong was his personal mentor,' he cried. 'Living in a fantasy world. I wonder where Luca gets it from.'

'Now there's no need for that.'

'Yes, I know. Still.'

Stu took a gulp of wine. It was all quiet for a bit and Stu was kind of fidgety. He gestured outside.

'Did you *see* what he's done in the garage?' he said. 'Taking all his stuff out and categorizing it by themes for no goddamn reason. Have you seen the labels he's put on the boxes? He's worse than he was before.'

Joyce shook her head, firm and defiant.

'No, Stu. He's not that bad.'

Stu was still now, holding his glass tight to his chest.

'You said that last time, Joyce, and look what happened.'

There was a pause. The ice was packed so heavily around me I couldn't move.

'We have to get him sectioned, Joyce,' said Stu.

There was a pause. I could hear the tapping of Joyce's fingers against the worktop, the buzzing of the fridge, the throbbing of my heart in my chest.

'Maybe you're right,' she said.

The ice shattered, crashing down on the tiled floor. I backed away from the door. Then I ran.

Escape from the Guardians

Jules was sectioned when she was fifteen years old. One night, when we were sitting in the entrance of a betting shop, she told me all about it. It was the first time we slept rough together and a lady in a smart suit offered to buy us dinner from the local fried-chicken shop, no strings attached. She was a real nice lady, chatting to us in the queue about how her bastard of a husband had just left her and she felt like celebrating. After she'd gone Jules said that the husband leaving wasn't the real reason she'd stopped, that it was because of my big eyes, all innocent and vulnerable.

'Now my eyes are *crazy* eyes,' she said, stabbing her chicken with a plastic fork. 'Look at this one.'

She leant in close to me, pulling down the bottom lid of her broken eye. I could see it pointing in the wrong direction, red lines running through the white, pupil dilated wide so there was barely any iris.

'Now look at this one,' she said.

She pulled down the bottom lid of the other. It was green with ripples of hazel running through it.

'You'd think it'd be my dodgy eye that gives me grief but you'd be wrong,' she said. She jabbed just below her good eye. 'This is the one that hallucinates.'

She continued eating, chopping up the chicken with her fork.

Later, as we lay down on our boxes, pulling our sleeping bags up to our chins, she told me how it all began.

'It was a Saturday night, I remember because the Lotto was on and my family were mad into the Lotto. We made all these plans, how we'd buy a mansion and breed thoroughbred greyhounds if we won. Anyway, we were just sitting there, waiting for the Lotto results at the end of the news. The newsreader bloke was staring right down the camera at us, talking about a missile attack in Lordknows-where when, all of a sudden, he looks at me. "This is a message for Julia Squires," he says. I looked round the room to check if anyone else had heard. They were just staring at the screen. When I looked back, the newsreader's eyes were all wide and freaky. "Yes, that's you, Jules," he says. Frit me half to death! But then the Lotto numbers came on and I kind of forgot about it. A week later, there's a different newsreader and this time she's dancing and singing show tunes at me with a feather boa round her neck. Proper belting it out. Frickin' *hilarious* it was, Molls. You would have loved it. It was only when my good eye filled with tears from all the laughter that I realized I couldn't see her dancing with my dodgy eye. She was just sitting normal and looking all serious. And when I couldn't see her with my good eye I couldn't really hear her either. It was dead weird.'

I lay there listening to Jules, who couldn't really see my face because of how our bodies were angled away from each other. I think she was sort of relaxed there in the doorway, full belly, nobody to distract her, and so she just kept talking. I was feeling sleepy but I stretched my eyes wide. I needed to hear the ending. For the next few nights she told me pieces of her life this way. I could have written her biography by the end of it, I knew so much.

Thing is, people think psychotics are violent people. But the messages Jules got from the newsreader never told her to go and hurt anyone, they just told her to do daft things. Put all her mum's magazines in the washing machine, chop spy holes into the curtains. It was around about this time that she got into buying camo gear and survival equipment. When she locked herself in her room with a bunch of kitchen knives, screaming that the zombie apocalypse was about to begin, her parents called the police.

'The problem with being sectioned is all the other mentals that's sectioned along with you,' she said. 'They say prison makes you a better criminal. Well, mental health wards make you a better nutter.'

It was in the hospital that Jules met Donna. Love at first sight, she said. They'd stuck together until Jules was discharged. When Donna came out they became a proper loved-up couple. Which is when it all went wrong.

'If I was screwed up before Donna I was *demolished* after her,' Jules said.

It was the first and only time I heard Jules talk about Donna without an edge in her voice.

I found Luca in the garage with Cora and Boy. They were sorting through boxes labelled with capitalized words: 'GRAVITY', 'JAZZ', 'JOY'.

Boy was chewing on a deflated rugby ball and Cora was sorting through a bunch of empty Tupperware from a box that said 'TIME'.

'Ah, the perfect person!' Luca said. 'Can you explain to Cora why time is just a construct? You're better at explaining than me.'

I didn't say anything, just stood there with Jules's rucksack on my back and all our other baggage held in my hands. Luca stood up.

'What's wrong?' he said.

The bags were getting heavy. I dropped them on the floor.

'We've got to go, Luca.'

Cora looked up at me with her empty box of 'TIME'. I smiled at her to say it was OK, but kids are quicker than adults at knowing when someone's bluffing. Luca rolled his eyes.

'What have they done now?' he said.

I looked around the garage, deciding how to say it. It was a big place, bigger than some people's flats. There were boxes of acrylic paints, funny-shaped vases, classy-looking Christmas decorations made of ceramic, and then all of Luca's things stuffed into storage boxes in the corner. They were shoved on top of each other, with big white labels that read 'LUCA'.

Cora stood up.

'Can I come?' she asked.

'No, you bloody well can't,' said Luca. 'You remember what happened last time.'

She crossed her arms and stuck out her bottom lip. I could feel time weighing down on us, heavy as bricks. I had to say it. There was no way I could convince them both if I didn't say it.

I looked Luca hard in the eyes.

'They want to get you sectioned.'

The air froze again but quicker than before. Luca and Cora were covered in frost, bodies chilled in cubes of 'TIME'. The thing is, for me time isn't just a construct. It's a physical thing: heavy, cold, tight and thin as candyfloss, depending on the occasion. But I couldn't explain it to them then because I didn't have the words.

Luca pulled out a snow globe from a box marked 'ILLUSIONS' and threw it on the floor. A piece of plastic chipped off the bottom but it didn't smash. His whole face collapsed in on itself.

'I knew I shouldn't have come here,' he said.

Cora shook her head.

'They won't do it,' she said. 'They promised they wouldn't do it again.'

I looked down at the snow globe, glitter spinning so fast that you couldn't see the landscape inside. When I looked back Luca was on one knee in front of Cora.

'I've got to go,' he said.

She shook her head, pigtails flapping back and forth.

'No, no, no!'

He pushed her hair back.

'This isn't your fault,' he said. 'I know you'll think it is, but it isn't.'

She searched Luca's face for signs of deceit. Then she threw her arms around his neck.

'No, no, n—'

She sank her head into his shoulder so you couldn't hear the noes any more. It made me feel dented inside to see her that way. Somewhere in her future, sitting in her back garden or at the peak of Mount Fuji or in the doorway of a betting shop, she'd remember this moment and realize how it changed her for the rest of her life. I just hoped it would change her for the better.

'I hate them,' she said.

Luca wiped away her tears.

'It's not their fault either. Not really.'

'But you said—'

Luca put his hands in the air.

'You can't trust me. I'm mental.'

They were both quiet for a bit then began chuckling in the way that Jules and me do when we've got the giggles.

They rested their foreheads together. Then Luca's eyes sparked up.

'Do you know where Dad's car keys are?'

Cora's nose crinkled; then she nodded and ran into the house.

Luca stood up, shifting about on his feet as he tried not to look at me.

'It's not really stealing . . .' he said. 'I mean, they're my parents, for God's sake.'

I shrugged.

'It doesn't matter.'

His brows rose then fell again. He looked at the rucksacks at my feet.

'What about Jules?'

I smiled. You could tell he was reluctant to ask because it showed he cared.

'Don't worry,' I said. 'She'll find us.'

I thought about Stu, how he said I wasn't the right person for Luca. Then I thought about the medicine cabinet, full of pill bottles. I saw the trumpet case on the floor.

'So, your granddad and Louis Armstrong . . .?'

Luca's eyes lit up.

'He taught him the trumpet,' he said. 'That is, Armstrong taught my granddad. He used to tell me all these stories. The places they went to and the people they played with. Wait a minute.'

He rummaged through his boxes until he found 'JOY'. He pulled out a CD and waved it at me. Cora came hobbling back with Boy in her arms and a set of car keys hanging from her mouth. Luca took the keys as she passed Boy over to me.

'I'll distract them,' she said.

She was gone before we could say anything. I looked at Luca.

'Master criminal in the making,' he said. 'Let's go.'

The BMW was still on the drive. It made a quick beep as Luca unlocked it, but when I reached the boot it was already cracked open. I didn't mention this to Luca as I opened it wide for him to throw the bags in, yet it was still puzzling me as we slipped into the front seats. Then Boy began licking my face and I soon forgot about it.

I looked up at the big house: the sage-green sashes, the matching door. I don't think Joyce meant to pull me in the way she had. She was no Wicked Witch, no Queen of Narnia tempting me with Turkish delight. But I'd been pulled in just the same. I thought her life was something special, something I could grab a piece of for myself. But it was just a hall of mirrors. I could never be one of them, and Luca couldn't either, which was exactly the problem. He was like the palm tree in their conservatory, leaves pressed against the glass. He could grow in that climate sure enough but sooner or later his head was going to be pushed up against the roof, his shoulders forced out of joint because he just couldn't fit in. He needed an open roof; he needed to breathe.

Luca put Louis Armstrong in the CD player. 'What A Wonderful World' flowed from the speakers.

'Dad *loves* this car,' he said, grinning. 'He's going to kill me.'

As Luca turned the key in the ignition I heard a growling coming from the back seat. We both turned to look.

'For **FuCK's** sake!' yelled Jules, emerging from under a blanket. Her eyes were half open, a line of drool across her cheek. 'What's a girl gotta do to get some **kiP**?'

Boy began barking. Luca put his foot on the accelerator.

The Wonderful Town of Skegness

I wanted to go cold turkey from the heroin when I found out I was pregnant, but the midwife shook her head. She said it would 'risk the development of the foetus and cause it to suffer withdrawal symptoms'. It felt like she'd slapped me when she said that. The bundle of cells inside me was already hooked on the hard stuff and it was no one's fault but mine.

Rusby told me I could have an abortion. The bigger I got, the more he talked about it until I thought he'd force me down the clinic himself. But then he got caught burgling an old people's home with an offensive weapon and was put in prison again.

I thought the methadone maintenance programme would be a short-term fix before I got completely clean. Then they took Izzy away, Rusby dumped me for that Slovakian girl and Jules went on a bender somewhere near Yorkshire. It wasn't a good time to get off the methadone;

life was too unstable. But then one day I saw Robin Hood and realized things had to change.

I'd been avoiding him since he'd told me about his daughter but that day I needed company. I must have been looking particularly rough because, when I got to the front of the sandwich queue, he took me to one side, placed two Caesar wraps in my palms and then rested his hand on my shoulder and squeezed.

'Take care of yourself, Molly,' he said.

His grey eyes were kind and warm.

'What for?' I said.

I meant it. I didn't know why I should take care of myself. Izzy had given me purpose; I hadn't had any before her.

Robin Hood's eyes turned steely. He squeezed tighter, so hard it made me grimace.

'Because you'll never do any good in the world with your head in the gutter.'

I could tell he was sorry as soon as he'd said it, but I turned and left before he could apologize.

I went to the hospital chapel that night. It's warm and peaceful, open twenty-four hours though hardly anyone visits. Those few people who do are friendly; they nod and smile like you're one of them. I never have the heart to tell them I'm not.

When I got to the chapel I walked past the main section to the Islamic prayer hall. It was past all the prayer times so the hall was empty. I covered my head with a woollen scarf, took my shoes off and walked along the back, looking down at the specially made carpet, little oblongs with fancy designs all pointing east. Then I knelt down on one of the designs and clasped my hands together.

Sometimes you need silence to gain clarity and, kneeling on the prayer mat, I realized that Robin Hood was right to be angry with me. I was wasting my life, failing to live up to my potential, failing to do the things his daughter could no longer do. I was letting him down.

And then I thought of my own daughter, that little purple bundle placed in my arms, eyes squeezed shut, mouth stretching wide as she cried and cried and cried. If I ever wanted to see her again, as flimsy as that possibility was, I needed to be clean. I needed to be straight. I needed to be worthy.

Jules said I'd become moral because I'd seen God. But it wasn't God I saw in that prayer hall.

It was hope.

The signs were all pointing to Skegness. It would have been simple – roads long and straight, stretching through blankets of flat, grassy countryside – if it hadn't been for Luca's shoddy driving. Whenever we got stuck behind a lorry, he'd get rigid and panicky. Jules kept goading him to overtake, even when there was oncoming traffic, as Boy slept through it all on the back seat. Despite the power of the BMW Luca couldn't find the balls to fully commit so we'd pull in and out of the lanes like a yo-yo, horns blasting and other drivers giving us the finger.

Luca took it well, laughing off each near-head-on collision and pretending to wipe the sweat from his brow. Since we'd left Bingham, the darkness had lifted, replaced by rays of sunshine so bright that near-death couldn't weaken them.

We eventually passed a sign saying 'WELCOME TO SKEGNESS' with a picture of a fat fisherman, pipe in his mouth, mulberry-red scarf whipping behind him as he skipped along a sandy beach with a wide grin on his face. I sat with my hands wedged between my thighs, filled with the kind of optimism that gushes up from the very base of your spine and bursts across your face. I clutched the pillbox containing Izzy's hair between my legs. The metal was cold in my hands but I could feel it getting hotter, as if the hair inside was on fire.

Jules held a blanket to her chin as she sat slumped in the back seat. She'd guzzled rough whisky the night before and every time Luca swerved or bumped a kerb she'd clutch her stomach and yell out some obscenity. Even with the yelling it felt good having the team back together. It felt like we were back on track, that nothing could stop us now.

'Nearly there!' Luca announced.

The car swerved to the side as he bounced in his seat.

'Calm down, Posh Boy,' Jules said. Her hand was hanging out the window, a fag between her fingers. 'You're going to drive us into a ditch if you ain't fucking careful.'

Luca looked over at me.

'*Nearly* . . .' he whispered.

I leant over to him.

'. . . *there!*' I whispered back.

Jules rolled her eyes in the rear-view mirror.

'You're both bonkers,' she said.

I watched Jules stroking Boy's head in the mirror. The dog's eyes fluttered with each rub.

'Your mum called, by the way,' I said, light and breezy.

Jules jolted.

'What did she have to say?'

'Just wanted to know you were . . . *well.*'

'Bloody hell!' she said, scowling. 'She gets a new hairdresser and she thinks she's seen the light.'

Luca frowned and turned. The car swerved to the side.

'Keep your eyes on the road, Posh Boy!'

I looked back at Jules, mouthing, *Are you OK?*

She gave a nod, before mouthing back, *Thanks, doll*. Then she gave me a wink.

Luca told us his plan for Skegness. We'd find a nice B&B and book in straight away to make sure we didn't end up in some scummy dive. Then we'd do some of the tourist things, try to blend in a bit. When it all quietened down we'd start the search. Jules didn't ask what we were searching for. I don't think she was listening.

I could tell we were close when I saw the line of turquoise across the horizon. It was sparkling like the gems across the rim of a bracelet. It made me bubble inside just looking at it. You don't have sea in Nottingham, just concrete, canal and the odd patch of grass. You forget how blue the water looks, the shape of the waves. Canal water is black and green, narrow and bodiless, while the sea is *alive*: pulling you into its motion.

We circled the streets as Luca looked for a parking spot. The tourist shops were full of buckets and spades, comedy hats and spinning windmills made of brightly coloured foil. They rattled and glinted in the wind like milk-bottle caps in a magpie's nest. Jules pointed her finger out of the window as we passed a discount store.

'I am getting that hat,' she said.

When we parked she was out of the car, heading straight for the stalls. Luca looked at me, distressed: we were going off plan.

'All part of the adventure,' I said.

Luca went to get his trumpet case out of the boot, me still clinging to the pillbox in my hand. He added a strap and wore it across his body.

'Shouldn't you leave that here?' I said. 'You know, keep it safe.'

Luca shook his head. He leant in and whispered, 'We need it for the mission.'

I nodded as though I knew exactly what he meant but to be honest I'd kind of forgotten about the mission. I knew it was important to Luca but just being in Skegness was enough for me. Breathing in the salty air, seeing the turquoise horizon, knowing what this place meant.

I wasn't supposed to know where they had sent Izzy but the social worker had left the adoption file open in our last meeting. By the time she saw my eyes scanning the sheets it was too late. I remember how she carried on talking as though nothing had happened, shuffling forward on her seat before carefully folding the file shut.

I slid the pillbox into the front pocket of my jacket, picked up Boy from the back seat of the car and followed Luca down the street. We found Jules outside a gift shop by a hat stand, a baseball cap with panda eyes and ears rammed on her head. I don't know how she made it look so good, standing there puffing away on her fag, but somehow it worked. She nudged me in the ribs.

'Now, distract the shopkeeper so I can do a runner,' she said.

When I looked over at the counter Luca was handing a credit card to the man behind the till.

'Get yourself one too, Molly,' he called.

I got a purple hippo cap with two white teeth hanging down from the visor. I think it was meant for children but it fit my head just fine.

Jules wasn't too impressed with Luca when he got back. You could tell she'd been all geared up for the run.

'Dipping into the bank of Mum and Dad again?' she said, straightening out the ears on her panda hat.

Luca looked down the street as though Jules hadn't said a word. There were amusement arcades lining the road, big spangled signs over the doors, machines flashing and blinking with lights. There were ice cream and dough-nut stalls, and about twenty different fish and chip shops. Luca held his face to the sun for a second. He must have forgotten his plan and the B&B because suddenly he was turning away from the town and facing the sea.

'Beach,' he said.

The only time I ever saw Donna was when I accompanied Jules to meet her in the Company Inn, a Wetherspoon's in the red-brick British Waterways building by the canal. Jules wanted me there for moral support so I sat on one of the high stools near the bar as she perched on the edge of a leather sofa, bobbing her shoulders up and down and then flexing her head from side to side. She'd brushed her hair out that morning and had even gone to the perfume counter in Boots. I thought that she was going to be on her best behaviour, but when Donna finally came and sat down next to her I was still petrified.

I'd been expecting a larger-than-life character: dyed pink hair, tattoos, body-piercings, the works. Instead, this woman was tall and pear-shaped, long blonde hair match-ing her flowing dress. She wore large amber beads that shone against her skin. I'd never had piano lessons but, I thought, if there was a picture of a piano teacher in the dictionary it would probably look something like her.

The tension dropped from Jules's body as Donna leant forward and hugged her. When she was released, Jules sank sideways into the squashy sofa. I could hear Donna's

voice rolling and dipping in a soft, Liverpool accent, hyp-
notizing Jules like a snake charmer's music hypnotizes a
cobra. Soon I got distracted by the food coming out for the
lunch crowd – steaks and lasagne, chicken wings and battered cod. I imagined sinking my teeth into a burger, feeling the juices spill into my mouth, when suddenly Jules
bolted upright from the sofa. Her face was poppy red.

'WEll YoU caN FUck riGhT oFF!' she bellowed.

She'd stormed off out of the pub as I scrabbled around
on the floor for my rucksack. By the time I'd caught up
she was halfway down the canal, ranting at pigeons and
cyclists about how love was a pile of horseshit and you
could stick it where the sun don't shine. And marriage?
That was the biggest pile of horseshit and you wouldn't
see her committing to it, not in a million years.

Then she stopped and had a think.

'Except to myself,' she said. 'I'd marry me-bleeding-self
if I could. That would show her, LiVerPooL SLaG!'

We walked so far down the canal that we left the city.
There were only trees lining the paths, and the odd dis-
used factory and canal boat. I knew one of the factories
well: the broken panelled windows, weeds wrapping
themselves over the frames. I'd bunked there when I was
getting clean off the methadone. I spent a whole week
hiding out with nothing but a meagre stock of food, water,
vodka and painkillers to keep me company. They say the
only substance that can kill you if you go cold turkey
is alcohol. I tried to remember that as I lay in the foetal

position, sweating, shaking and sobbing through the agony: the pains in my body, the pains in my head. Whenever I wanted to give up, to ring someone for a hit, I'd think of Robin Hood. About taking my head out of the gutter and doing some good in the world.

The birds were singing, the smell of manure was in the air, and although it was cold the sun was bright, shining down on us as Jules stubbed out her fourth roll-up on the top of a bin. We sat down on a metal bench by a big willow tree and I asked her what had happened.

She was reluctant at first, but she couldn't keep it in.

'Only asked me to go to her bloody *wedding*, didn't she? Cheeky sod. I thought she wanted to . . . Well, it doesn't matter what I thought.'

She didn't look at me, just finished rolling her fifth cigarette and lit up. She blew a funnel of smoke up into the tree.

'Why does everyone else get a happy ending, Molly?' she asked.

I looked out across the canal; the sun was setting, turning the water burnt orange. The thing about endings is there aren't really any, except the last one. But I wasn't going to say that to Jules, not in the mood she was in. So I thought of something else.

'If you write your own story, you can always have a happy ending,' I said.

Jules bit her bottom lip, chewing away at it as she deliberated my words. When I looked into her broken eye I saw the universe wasn't spinning, it was sitting there calmly in the middle of her pupil. She nodded, then stood up and held her arm out at a jaunty angle.

'Let's go write ourselves a story, doll,' she said.

I smiled, taking her arm.

The beach was full: old-age pensioners shuffling around in twos, families with their little kids, flying kites and riding the donkeys. My mother had a picture of me sitting on a white donkey. I don't remember the day it was taken but I remember the picture because it sat on the mantelpiece above the fire. I remember how I didn't like looking at that picture because he was in it, hovering in the background, ice-cream cone in his hand. You couldn't even see his face properly but it ruined everything.

Boy ran off and played with the kids running up and down the beach. There was a large group of children with four Asian women wearing bright saris with cardigans. They sat on deckchairs, hems fluttering in the breeze as the children dug holes in the sand. There was a toddler waddling around in a nappy, trying to dig like the other children and nearly falling into their holes. She was the most gorgeous thing: big chocolate eyes, chubby cheeks and a protruding belly that stuck out round and proud. I could have eaten her up.

I breathed in the smell of the seawater. It must be great to bring up kids here. I wanted to say this to Jules but I knew she'd look at me all disapproving and tell me not to get sentimental.

We sat down and took off our shoes and socks. This took Luca a while because of all the layers. He stuck his legs out straight and placed each sock across his jeans so as not to get sand on them, until his jeans were covered in patches of sock. Jules was watching him eagle-eyed until eventually his pale toes emerged.

'What's with the socks, Posh Boy?' she asked.

'I keep them on rotation,' he said, making a little circular movement with his finger. 'It's the only way I can make sure they don't stink. I can't stand smelly socks.'

Jules sat up straight and nodded.

'No excuse not to be neat,' she said.

Seeing as we were getting on so well I suggested we go for a dip in the water.

'I don't like the sea,' Luca said.

Jules looked at him as though he'd said he didn't like breathing.

'What you talking about?'

He gestured out ahead.

'Look at it.'

We looked out at the water. The gentle lapping of the waves, the sparkling ripples, the slow turn of wind turbines along the horizon. Luca shuddered.

'It's so big and wide and *endless*. Just going on and on and on. I can't deal with it.'

He shook his head then looked at us.

'You two go though. I'm fine here.'

So me and Jules paddled in the water wearing our animal baseball caps. The water was icy and tickled our feet, then our ankles, then our calves. The wind was brushing against our faces, the smell of sea salt so strong you could taste it.

'So, what did the hospital find?' I said, keeping my voice casual as I ran my fingers through the water.

Jules sighed.

'It's just a lump.' She patted the side of her left breast. 'Probably just a cyst or something.'

The water pushed me back and forth.

'My aunt had cancer,' Jules said. 'You know, the fruit-loop one.'

Her panda ears flapped in the wind.

'So you came here to talk to her?' I said.

Jules kicked the water and shrugged.

'Nah,' she said. 'It wasn't that.'

She looked down, trying to hide her expression, and then I knew why Jules had hijacked the mission. Not because she wanted to speak to her auntie or escape her mum, not even to check I was OK – she knew I'd be fine. It was because she didn't want to be alone.

'You won't tell Posh Boy, will you?' she said.

I pulled my finger across my mouth like a zip.

She went back to kicking the water. I looked out at the open sea. I could see what Luca meant; it stretched on endlessly. It was like one of those ladies' saris, covered in sequins, unwound and rolling into eternity. But I liked being there, a small dot on a big sheet of blue. We were all just dots really, if you looked from high enough. Just one part of the pattern, one sequin in the fabric.

I must have been staring for a while because next thing I knew, Jules was sitting back with Luca on the beach. They seemed to be having an intense conversation that mainly involved her talking and him listening. He'd put his socks back on and had his map in his hand, turning it away from Jules as she spoke even though she didn't seem the slightest bit interested in it. I stood in the water for a bit longer then waded back to join them. The sand was gritty between my toes.

Luca shielded his eyes from the sun.

'You look like a mermaid,' he said.

My cheeks flushed. Jules looked all sharp.

'Have you been listening *to a word I've said*?'

I sat down beside them and Luca pulled his trumpet case on to his lap. He clicked the lid open to create a tiny crack and slid the map back inside.

'There's no point searching now,' he said. 'It's too busy. We'll have to come back at night.'

I looked at Jules's scrunched-up face. She glanced at his trumpet case.

'I need a bevvy,' she said.

We got a pack of strong cider from the town centre and strolled up to the Pleasure Beach. There was a huge Ferris wheel and carousels, comedy sunglasses and pink candy-floss hanging from stalls. The techno music was pumping and Jules was all set for a party but we couldn't start drinking because of all the kids so we got a packet of hot doughnuts instead. Luca bought a long tube shaped like a sword that was filled with jellied sweets. We found a nice bench just by the main gates where you could still hear the music.

Me and Jules ate the doughnuts and played the game where you let the sugar build up on your lips, waiting to see who licks first. Jules was chattering away, sugar showering her camo jacket. She told us the story of how she'd been attacked by a herd of cows the day before ('Cows are the most stupid animals of all. Stupider than dolphins!'). She was about to tell us how she'd ended up in the back of the BMW when she got sidetracked, reminiscing about her time as a car mechanic. I knew this was one of her false memories. Jules did a free taster course at the college once but that was it.

'Let's go,' Luca said.

He was looking up at the rollercoaster. It stretched so high I had to drop my head back to see the top. The tracks were shaped into crazy loops and zigzags.

'Yeah. Right,' I said, licking the sugar off my lips. He'd been scared by the sea, for crying out loud.

'No, really,' he said. 'It's stupid being here and not going on a ride.'

He looked over at Jules.

'Are you in?'

She shook her head, sugar powdered across her lips.

'No way, Posh Boy,' she said. 'Them things make me heave. Not a pretty sight for anyone, believe me. I'll stay down here with Boy and take care of the bevvies.'

She patted the four-pack as though it was her new bessie mate.

Me and Luca stood in the queue for the rollercoaster behind a group of lads in tracksuits and baseball caps. One of them looked at me suspiciously. He was older than the others and kind of familiar. Or maybe he just looked like every dodgy man in a tracksuit that I'd ever met.

He turned to Luca.

'Are you an Arab?' he said.

Luca glanced at the man and then up and down the queue before realizing the man was talking to him.

'Are you a salami?' he said.

The man's face knotted into a scowl.

'What?' he said.

'I'm as much an Arab as you are a salami.' Luca pointed at his hair. 'The Afro is a bit of a giveaway.'

The man looked at Luca's hair.

'Ah, good. Don't mind blacks,' he said. 'Just Arabs and Muslims. Can't stand Muslims.'

Luca raised his brows.

'That's a shame,' he said. 'I hear they're big fans of you.'

I snorted and the man looked at me, squinting as though trying to place me. But then it was his turn and his friends were telling him to hurry up. We managed to get a seat at the front as he went to the back. As soon as the safety bar came down Luca became twitchy.

'Have you been on one of these before?' he asked.

'Of course,' I said.

Then I realized he'd asked because he hadn't. It was funny really because there he was, privileged type brought up in a posh house with all that art on the walls and pony lessons and music lessons no doubt, and yet his parents had never taken him on a rollercoaster.

'You'll be fine!' I said.

The train jolted forward and Luca yelped as though he'd been bitten on the arse. The noise of the carriage creaking up the tracks didn't help matters. Our seats dropped back as we made the climb. You could see the whole of the beach, people scurrying along like miniature figures. The sea stretched out for miles in that rolled-out-sari way. Luca's eyes were fixed on it. I put my hand out.

'Hold on!' I shouted over the noise.

Luca grabbed it just before we plunged. Everyone was screaming, the wheels clattering against the tracks as we hurtled down. I clung on tight as the air blasted my hair back, making my mouth flap, my stomach rising up in my body as if ready to pop out. It wasn't until we began to loop that I heard Luca. He was screaming like he was being attacked by bees, gasping and shrieking, gasping and shrieking. Our hands kept banging against the safety bar but he wouldn't let go and then I was shrieking too.

The train slowed but I knew we weren't at the end because I could see the drop of the track below us. Luca loosened his grip.

'Thank God for—'

'Eeeiiii!'

I squealed so loud that Luca nearly crushed the bones in my hand. I looked over at him laughing hysterically and he looked back, whites circling his pupils, before laughing through the screams. We carried on doing this – laughing-screaming, laughing-screaming – right until the ride stopped.

When we got off Luca could barely walk straight. He was hiccuping with giggles and when he stumbled into me I wrapped my arm around him and giggled too until we looked like a pair of drunks stumbling out of a nightclub.

The lad from the queue walked past.

'I lied!' Luca screamed. 'I'm an Arab! And a Muslim! I'm an Arab bloody Muslim!'

The man glanced back at us then carried on walking.

'And I'm a salami!' I cried after him. 'An Arab, Muslim salami!'

'*Halal* salami!' Luca corrected.

'Yes, a *halal salami*!'

We both creased over, crying with laughter as we stumbled towards Jules. As the tears cleared I saw she was sitting next to someone. For a second, I thought it was Rusby but the belly was too round, shoulders too slumped. There were rips in the stranger's clothes, a muddy tinge to his leathery skin, wild hair stuffed beneath a black beanie. We homeless let off chemical trails; we follow each other like ants.

'*Heeeey!*' the man said as soon as he saw us.

He stood up, spreading his arms as though ready to give us a welcome-home hug. Luca slipped his hand into his pocket. I hoped it wasn't the knife he was clenching on to, but at the same time I knew that's exactly what it was.

'Hey *heeey!*' the man said, his face pulled wide like a squashed pumpkin.

Jules was chuckling as she sat with a bevvy and Boy on her lap. The man spoke in what sounded like Polish. The words rhythmic and beautiful. He was obviously drunk because, even in a different language, I could hear slurring. We sat down on the bench.

'He's been going on like this for the last five minutes,' Jules said. 'It's freakin' hilarious.'

The man was gesturing at Luca.

'My *phrrend,*' he said.

'You know this fella, Luca?' Jules asked.

Luca kept his hand in his pocket. The man came and squeezed his body between Luca and me.

'Yars, yars!' the man said. 'My phrrend *Looca!*'

He began jabbering again, all fast and emotional, slapping Luca on the back. He pointed at my hat and gave me a thumbs up.

'Very good!' he said. '*Superb* hats!'

He chuckled. Jules smiled.

'Cheers,' she said, raising her can.

The man lifted his hand and Jules, seeing it was empty, passed him a cider. Then she gave me and Luca one too.

'Igor,' said the man, pointing at his chest. '*Eeee-gor.*'

It was like a game of charades, trying to understand Igor, his body all gestures and mimes, the occasional recognizable word. I gradually figured out that he'd been roughing it in Lincoln before coming to the coast. He'd been trying to find work but a 'scumbag landlord' took all his money.

'I live in Skegness now; always chips to eat in Skegness!'

After he told us this, he seemed to remember something. He stood up and began grinding his hips.

'I know best place to party,' he said. 'You must all come!'

Luca frowned.

'*Now?*' he said.

Igor nodded enthusiastically.

'It happens all of the day,' he said and slapped Luca on the back as though he'd won the Lotto.

Luca shook his head.

'We have other business here,' he said.

Igor didn't understand. Luca shook his head again.

'*No. Come. Party,*' he said.

Igor's eyes welled up like he was about to cry.

'No party?' he said. 'My phrrend?'

'Come on, Posh Boy,' Jules said. 'One night on the town ain't gonna kill us. Besides, we've got time to waste, ain't we? You said so yourself.'

Luca thought about this for a second. Then he looked over at me.

What I really wanted to do was go on my own mission, but I knew this wasn't the time for it. I shrugged.

'Maybe just for a bit?' I said.

Luca clicked his tongue and stood up.

'For goodness' sake,' he muttered.

Me and Jules smiled, knowing that meant *yes*.

The Rescue

Rusby used to take me to the vintage shop by Nottingham station. It's a big old store with four levels filled with fur coats and crazy patterned dresses, board games and dainty crockery. Sometimes he'd let me buy something – a little brooch, a pair of velvet gloves or an ornament for the squat. He wouldn't come in himself. He liked everything new and modern.

'Second-hand is old tat,' he'd tell me. 'Vintage is old, fancy tat. Antique is dead people's old, fancy tat. No matter how you look at it, it's all tat.'

But he still gave me the money for the trinkets. He could have made me nick them but he liked to create the illusion that he was taking care of his princess. I fell for it; I thought the trinkets meant he cared. It was only after he left me that I realized the money he used was the money I'd earned and the value of the items was never more than a fiver.

One time I was looking through some bric-a-brac at the back of the shop and came across a metal pillbox covered in flowers. It was a tiny, beautiful thing, hand-painted with a small metal catch. I went to pay at the till but there was a ruckus by the entrance. The busker was shouting at one of the shop assistants. He was wilder than usual, his flat cap rammed low on his head, his beard a big shaggy mess.

'I told you, I don't care how much you give me for it, I just want to get rid!'

He was holding out his guitar to the shop assistant, a skinny pale man wearing a *Star Wars* shirt. It was the first time I'd heard the busker speak; he had an Irish accent with a musical tone that made his words sound soft, even as he shouted.

The sales assistant was shaking his head, telling the busker he wasn't in charge of buying. But the busker wasn't listening, just saying the same thing over and over again as he shoved the guitar at the poor bloke. I paid for the pillbox and put it in the front pocket of my denim jacket. Rusby was outside, smoking a cigarette.

I turned to the busker.

'Please don't sell it,' I said.

When he realized I was talking to him he scowled, a deep crease in his ruddy face. But then he must have recognized me because his expression weakened. I suppose it's hard to forget the girl who cries in front of you every time you play.

'Don't get involved, lady,' he said.

He looked back at the shop assistant but didn't speak, waiting for me to leave the shop.

When I got outside Rusby was making a deal on his phone. He spent most of his time on the phone talking to people I didn't know. He gave me a nod and put his hand out for the change. He didn't even care what I'd bought.

'Because if he doesn't get it to me,' he said down the phone, 'then I'll make sure everybody knows about it.'

I stood patiently, waiting for him to finish. Then, behind me, I heard the tinkle of the shop door. When I turned around I saw the busker coming out, eyes low, his guitar clutched firmly in his hands.

Igor's party was in the underground basement of an old bar. You could smell the damp as you walked in; the concrete floor was black and sticky, strobe lighting shooting neon beams through artificial smoke. The place was filled with sweaty bodies, music pumping DnB from large stereo speakers, and everyone moving wild and jerky, arms flailing, legs skipping up and down.

We'd tied Boy to a lamppost by the beach. I wasn't happy leaving her there, ears pricked up and whining as we walked away.

'She'll be fine,' Jules said. 'You don't get by with three legs unless you're a fighter. Tough as old boots, that one.'

I looked back at Boy, big eyes staring.

'Tough as new boots,' Luca said.

'*Old* boots,' Jules corrected.

'Surely new boots are tougher than old ones,' said Luca.

They carried on arguing about the toughness of boots until we arrived. The bouncers were huge ex-army types like Big Tony, bald heads and dressed in tight black shirts. Jules wedged her hat down further; I took mine off and stuffed it into my pocket.

'I'm the Panda tonight,' she said, pointing to her flappy ears.

The bouncers looked confused but let us in.

Luca paid for our entry fee but Igor took the lead, escorting us through the basement as though we were the members of a rock group and he was our manager. Luca wore his trumpet case diagonally across his back as though he had the world's smallest guitar, Jules strutting behind me with her panda hat as though she was the backing dancer and me at the front like I was the lead singer.

'*Cześć!*' Igor said, raising his hands to people he'd obviously never met before. Some of them glanced over with mild irritation, some with pure elation. Jules pushed past me, linking her arm through Igor's and doing her royal wave to the crowd.

'*How do you do?*' she said in her Kate Middleton voice.

This was lost on Igor.

When we got to the bar at the back of the room Igor lifted his hand, pretending to drink from a bottle.

'We get?' he said.

He looked at Luca expectantly. Luca sighed and ordered us vodka mixers in plastic bottles. They were aquamarine and glowed in our hands. Igor took a swig.

'Terrible vodka,' he said, a grin plastered across his face.

This made us laugh, even Luca, who pulled a plastic bag from his pocket.

'I bought these at the shop earlier,' he said. He passed a bunch of paper glasses around, giving Igor the pair he'd obviously bought for himself which I thought was pretty generous. The glasses had love hearts all over the frames and thick dark plastic for lenses. We all put them on and suddenly the world was alive with love hearts. Every time the strobe lights hit them the hearts would ripple in glittering reds, blues and greens. It was like watching a firework display of love.

Jules took hers off straight away and handed them back to Luca.

'Ta but no ta, mate,' she said. 'I see enough funny stuff without needing *props*.'

Luca smiled; it was the first time Jules had called him *mate* instead of *Posh Boy*. Igor spun around, trying to catch the light. I moved my glasses up so they were propped on my head like an Alice band.

'Ta, Luca,' I said. 'They're perfect.'

Jules rolled her eyes.

'Right!' she said, grabbing Igor's hand. 'We're going for a dance.'

She poked Luca in the chest, spilling blue liquid on his REASON T-shirt.

'You remember what I said,' she said, targeting him with her broken eye.

She held his gaze for a few seconds and then dragged Igor off to the dance floor. They bounced up and down like they had springs in their shoes.

'What was that about?' I asked.

Luca scrunched his face up as though he'd tasted something rotten. He leant in close. I could feel his breath against my neck. It felt as warm as a hug.

'I've been *warned*,' he said.

He made round scared eyes at me.

'About what?'

'You,' he said.

My expression dropped. He must have thought I hadn't heard right because he leant in even closer and began shouting loud.

'She said I have to be *careful* with you,' he said. 'Apparently you're deli-*buff*.'

A throbbing beat swallowed his words.

'What?' I said.

'Deli-*BUFF*.'

'*What?*'

He took a deep breath.

'DELICATE!'

He screamed the word just as the track finished. The dancers looked our way and then he had round scared

231

eyes for real. I snorted with laughter. The music started up again and a big stupid grin spread across Luca's face. He guided me to the corner of the room and we stood in an arched cubbyhole, leaning up against the cold brick wall.

'Apparently,' he said, 'if I do anything to hurt you, Jules is going to knee me so hard in the bollocks not only will I not be able to have children but my children won't be able to have children.'

I raised my eyebrows.

'Wow. That's pretty serious.'

'Pretty *impossible*, you mean.'

'Still, you'd better be careful.'

He shook his head.

'Tell me about it.'

He downed his drink.

'Want another?'

I hadn't finished mine but Luca went straight back to the bar. I knew we were getting merry on his dad's credit but I tried not to let it bother me. I remembered the paintings in their living room; one of those was probably worth all the money I'd ever had. They probably wouldn't even notice what Luca was taking. But when he squeezed his way back through the crowd Luca didn't have any drinks.

'It's been declined,' he said, lights flashing cyan and magenta across his face. 'That bastard stopped the card.'

This wasn't much of a surprise to me but I tried not to let it show. I shrugged.

'Not to worry,' I said.

'Not to worry?' Luca repeated. 'How are we going to pay for anything?'

I tried to shout over the music.

'We don't need it!'

He shook his head, sucking in breaths as if trying to find the words to argue.

'We're homeless, Luca!' I cried. 'If there's one thing we can do it's get by without money!'

He stared down at me, as still as a mannequin. His button eyes were looking right into mine in that way he did, as if he could really see me.

'Besides, we're here now and we're gonna find our fortune!' I cried. 'We don't need anything else!'

'Yeah,' he said, slowly nodding. 'You're right! We don't need anything. We're here. *We're bloody here!*'

I smiled. It was the first time he'd really listened to me.

'Let's dance!' I said.

We moved to the middle of the floor, dancing like the night we first met, guided by the rhythm, not caring about what other people thought. Luca's arms were batting up and down, legs akimbo, nearly knocking into everyone around him with his trumpet case. I swung my head and hips side to side, getting so hot and sweaty I had to take my jacket off, tying it around my waist before flinging my arms up and spinning around. My white skirt bloomed out like a tutu.

Luca's forehead was dripping with sweat.

'You all right, Luca?' I said.

He nodded in an exaggerated sort of way. I was about to suggest he take his trench coat off but he spoke before I could say anything.

'I'm tripping my tits off,' he said.

He shoved his hand in his pocket and then pulled it out. There was a little white pill on his palm.

'Igor gave them to me. Do you want one?'

I looked down at the white disc. You have to be careful with pills. If you're not with the right people and not in the right mood they can set you in a downward spiral. That and you don't know what rubbish is in them any more. Pure MDMA = OK. Rat poison and chemical bleach = not so OK. I took the pill and swallowed it dry.

The DJ played some banger tunes with beautiful vocals gliding over the racing beats. Luca went wild with it, grinning crazy as he swung around.

'You're the Little Mermaid!' he screamed.

I tried to think of a quick reply.

'You're the Wizard of Oz!'

He seemed to like that because all of a sudden he grabbed me round the waist.

'You're beautiful, Molly!' he shouted in my ear.

I scoffed as he pulled me in tighter.

'Don't be daft!' I shouted back.

He looked deep into my eyes. Synth music filled the room. The beams were flashing in fast pulses that could set off seizures. I liked the way he was holding me.

As though he was protecting me from something even though he couldn't really protect himself.

Then he leant in and kissed me.

I wasn't expecting it but as soon as it happened I felt we should have done it before. It didn't even matter that his lips were all stiff as if he didn't know what he was doing. Our mouths pushed into each other, my hand sinking into his hair as his hands clung to my waist. The curls were soft and bouncy, like pushing your fingers through foam in a bubble bath. I knew the pill had started to work already because I could feel that tingly feeling as if I was made of nothing but candyfloss. We became light as air, our feet lifting off the ground as we sailed high above the rest of the crowd, strobes of light illuminating our floating bodies. Below us everyone carried on dancing but we were flying high.

When Luca pulled away we were back on the ground. We looked at each other for a few seconds, panting as we tried to catch our breath. The music was getting faster and faster. I pulled my glasses over my eyes, dropped my head back and shouted up to the ceiling. '*Wahoooooooooo!*'

Luca picked me up and swung me around so that the room was spinning with love hearts. Sweating bodies were pushing and shoving against us and nobody cared. I felt like everyone else. Not a ghost, not an invisible nobody on the street, just another person in the crowd, like I was normal.

*

At home, in my room, fifteen years old, I'd looked up all the ways I could end my life: overdoses, nooses, slit wrists, carbon monoxide. Drowning.

The drowning appealed most because it felt familiar. Sinking into water – down, down, down – and never coming back up. So when my parents were at a party I tried to drown myself in the bath. I plunged my head deep, trying not to hold my breath, wanting the water to fill my lungs. Closing my eyes. Waiting to disappear.

But I always came back up, spluttering, kicking and gasping for air. The small body of water was no match for the fight inside me, the instinct to breathe. After several attempts, I lay wheezing in that bath, completely in shock.

I wanted to live.

Two panda ears bounced beside me.

'This is *brilliant!*' Jules cried.

'I know . . .!' I said. 'Where's Igor?'

Jules shrugged. I scanned the crowd and saw him leaning against a wall, his body bent over. He looked in a bad way, head lolling from side to side, fingers clawing at his forehead.

'What's wrong with him?' I said.

Jules shrugged again.

'Having a wobbly,' she said.

I pushed my way through the crowd until I could hear him babbling. He was speaking broken Polish and English and repeating the number forty-four.

'I bad man,' he kept saying. 'I bad, bad man.'

Jules was behind me. She took a swig from her bottle. I looked at her expectantly. She sighed.

'Apparently he was in the KGB or summat,' she said. 'He's been a miserable sod since he started talking about it.'

'The KGB?' I said.

Igor's eyes were red-raw around the edges, his lips trembling.

'Forty-four,' he said. 'Forty-four.'

He said it as though the number gave him excruciating pain.

'What's forty-four?' I asked.

'The number of men he's killed,' Jules said.

Igor nodded.

'I kill them,' he said. 'I kill them all.'

Big round tears fell down his cheeks, creating white streaks of clean skin against the layers of dirt. I put my hands on his shoulders, remembering what Luca had said to me.

'It's all right, Igor,' I said. 'It's over now.'

All of a sudden someone yanked my shoulder back. It was a firm, hard yank that stung down to the bone. Luca was next to me, glasses off, but he wasn't looking at me, he was looking at Igor.

He pointed his finger at Igor's face.

'I knew it!' he said. 'I knew I couldn't trust you.'

Igor panicked. He looked at me, tears rolling, eyes blinking.

237

'Why's he looking at you?' Luca said.

My shoulder was smarting. I rubbed it gently.

'I was just checking he was all right,' I said.

The lights shone in neon beams above Luca's head. He laughed.

'I *bet* you were!' he said.

Jules rolled her head side to side, stretching her neck muscles. 'Calm down, Posh Boy,' she said.

Luca grabbed Igor by the jacket and lifted him up against the wall.

'It's you, isn't it?' he said. 'You're the one who's been following me!'

'Forty-four,' Igor wailed. 'I kill forty-four!'

'*And I'm forty-five, am I?*' Luca cried.

Igor shook his head.

'My phrrend,' he said. '*Loo*-ca.'

Luca pulled Igor towards him, then smacked his body against the wall. Igor winced as his head hit the brick-work. I pulled at Luca's shoulders.

'You're hurting him!' I cried.

'*You want me?*' Luca shouted. '*You followed me and now you're here for me?*'

He thumped Igor's head against the wall again. A patch of crimson splattered against the brick.

'Get off, you little shit!' cried Jules.

She was pulling at Luca but he wouldn't budge.

'Stop it!' I cried, thumping him on the back. 'STOP IT, LUCA!'

He let go. Igor fell, shaking his head as he tried to focus. Luca stepped back and put his hand in his pocket.

'No!' I cried.

I saw a flash of metal and then Luca's legs were in the air. I could see the balloons on his socks as a large, thick man in black lifted him away. There were hands on me, dragging me through the crowd. Another bouncer was carrying Jules.

'Wait!' I cried. 'I've dropped my jacket!'

He pretended not to hear me, pushing me towards the exit. He was tall with arms like boulders. I scanned the floor for my jacket but all I could see were feet. I thought of the pillbox stuffed in the front pocket, imagining it being crushed under someone's thick trainers. As the metal caved in so did my heart, denting and then breaking in two.

The Discovery of Luca the Terrible

The night after I'd tried to drown myself in the bath my mother found me crying in my room. She'd returned from another party so smelt of Merlot and cigarettes. I remember her stroking my hair clumsily, pulling it by accident and slurring as she spoke.

'You could be happy, Molly,' she said. 'You've just got to choose it.'

She'd said it before, when I'd scraped my knee or had fallen out with a friend. She made it sound simple, like choosing a drink in a bar. *Just a bag of roasted peanuts and a pint of happiness, please.* I tried to believe it. Whenever I felt down I'd think: *You're not making the right choice here, Lara. You're not choosing happiness.*

But sometimes it's dead hard to choose it. Sometimes you can't lift your hand to get the barman's attention, let alone order the pint. At those times, you can choose happiness as much as you can choose being caught up in a big cyclone and whisked away to a fantasy land.

The thing was, he hadn't done it for ages and had been real good to me. So when the Social came to visit a few days before and began asking questions, like if I was happy at home and was there anything I wanted to tell them, I said that I was really great. And of course they looked at our house, with shelves full of books and polished ornaments, and they looked at my mum who was a PR agent and my dad who was a policeman, and they decided that whoever had phoned up about me was just trying to cause trouble for a hard-working, wholesome family. 'Probably jealous,' I heard one of them say to my mother. I remember her face straining so hard to stay neutral yet twitching at the mouth. The social workers didn't see it though, just packed up their things and left. That's when I realized that the world is blind; we don't see things as they are but how they make sense to us.

If I'd known what he was going to do to me later I might have told the Social about the cold salted bread, stones in my shoes, the Stillness Lessons from Mother. I might have told them about what he'd done to me before even though I was trying my best to forget. But then maybe they still would have done nothing. Both he and my mother were untouchable and I knew I couldn't wait for anyone to help any more. I wasn't a princess locked in a tower. No knight would come on a galloping horse to rescue me.

I was the Rubberband Girl, strong and stretchy, with the power to bounce somewhere new.

So that's what I did. I cut my hair, changed my name, packed a rucksack full of clothes and rubber bands, and threw all their photos of me in the fire.

The spell was broken. I didn't belong to them any more. Lara, the girl they'd brought up, was theirs, but Molly, the girl I became, she was mine.

Luca was digging in the sand.

He'd found a bucket and spade next to a sandcastle and was making holes along the beach. It was a child's spade, so he was on his knees, digging in the ground with short sharp thrusts, showers of sand flying over his shoulder.

It was night, the streetlamps our only light. Me and Jules sat in a bus shelter overlooking the beach. Except Jules wasn't really sitting. She was pacing up and down the pavement, then perching on the bench, before jumping up and pacing again. A trail of smoke followed behind her as she puffed on a cigarette.

The wind was blowing hard against my bare arms. My hair kept blowing in front of my face and hitting my cheeks. After a while I stopped pushing it back and let it blow. I was trying to keep my body still, the way I'd been taught, trying to quieten my mind and forget what had happened. But I could still see it. The force of the knocks. The clash of skull against brick. The splatter of blood.

We last saw Igor on a trolley being taken into the back of an ambulance. His head was bandaged up, tears leaking from his bloated eyes.

'I kill forty-four!' he was crying. 'I kill forty-four!'

Jules was ready to jump in the ambulance with him but then we realized Boy was missing. All that was left around the lamppost was the old rope, still knotted but with no dog. It was hard to tell if she'd wiggled free or if someone had taken her.

We marched up and down the street, shouting 'BOY!' into the darkness. We gave up after an hour and followed Luca towards the beach.

Jules was perched on the bench again.

'Let's get out of here, Molls,' she said.

She walked away. It was as if, because she'd made up her mind, I had too.

'Where are you going?' I called after her.

She stopped and turned around. She looked at me as though I was simple.

'Home,' she said. 'Back to the squat.'

She rolled her eyes, getting all mardy.

'But how? All our stuff's in the car.'

Jules waved her hand as though this was nothing.

'Aunt Janice.'

I frowned. Jules rolled her eyes again.

'The fruit loop with the figurines. She'll help us. Now let's get *moving*.'

Luca had stopped digging and was talking loudly to himself, rocking back and forth, studying the map clutched in his hands.

'I bet she's petrified, poor little sod,' Jules said, looking out at the streets. 'I don't know why I care, she ain't even my dog!' She turned and glared at me. 'Are you coming or what?'

The waves were getting louder as they crashed against the shore. I didn't move.

'Look,' Jules said. 'I wasn't gonna say anything, Molls, but you need to know.'

Her face was kind of pale under the glow of the street-lamp. She had that solemn expression people have when they're about to tell someone a relative's died. She angled her body away from the beach, leant in close.

'That map he's got,' she said. 'It's a sham.'

I must have looked confused because she began huffing and puffing again as if I was really putting her out by making her explain it all.

'When we were on the beach earlier, I saw it in his hands. It's not even a fucking map! Just a load of squiggles and dots.'

I reached up for the key hanging from my neck. Jules put her hands on my shoulders and squeezed hard as she looked at me with her broken eye.

'You can't trust him, Molls,' she said. 'He's a liar.'

Jules thought being a liar was far worse than being psychotic. She didn't know that I'd lied to her the moment I told her my name was Molly.

I looked down at the rubber bands around my wrist. Snapping the bands was a trick that diverted the pain in my head to pain in my wrist. I used it when I felt like I was drowning on dry land, snapping it when my mother said I loved ruining things, when someone told me I was lucky to have a policeman as my dad. I realized that this was the exact sort of moment when I'd usually pull it back, take the hit, feel that short rush of adrenaline. But I didn't feel like snapping it. There was no point hurting myself any more.

Luca was still rocking back and forth on the sand with the piece of paper in his hands. His trumpet case was strapped to his back, digging into the ground as he rocked. It was like a part of him had broken down, like he'd carry on rocking until he wound down and rusted.

Jules was waiting for me to move.

'Luca!' I called.

He didn't look my way but got up, moved, dropped to his knees and began to dig again.

'For Lord's sake!' Jules said. 'Have you been listening or what?'

I got up and walked down the beach.

'*Luca!*' I cried.

I could feel the sand trickling in through the holes in my canvas shoes, cold and damp.

'Daft cow!' Jules cried as she ran after me.

The closer I got, the louder his voice became.

'It's here,' he was saying. 'Somewhere here.'

The wind was whipping up the sand, creating mini-cyclones and spraying it against my skin as I approached. I reached out my hand, touching Luca gently on the shoulder. He pulled back so hard he toppled to the ground.

'Get your hands off me!'

His eyes were wild, filled with hatred. He hadn't looked at me like that before. It was the same way punters looked after the act, as if I'd made them do something animal and debased.

Jules came up behind me, gasping and out of breath. She tugged at my sleeve.

'He's past help, Molls,' she said. 'You saw what he did to Igor.'

I kept still. Jules kept on tugging.

'I told you once, Molls, and I'm telling you again, he's a fucking psycho.'

Luca stood and pointed at Jules's face.

'Stop calling me that!' he said.

It was dark on the beach but I knew Jules's eyes were round and veiny. The shadow of her body rose on its tiptoes.

'**PoINt THAt FiNGeR aT ME aGaiN aNd I'LL BiTe ThE FuCKer OfF!**'

Luca stood there for a second. He lowered his hand and stepped back into the light of the streetlamps, deflated.

'You know what makes us human?' he said. His eyes kept darting between us, stringing out the tension. Then he raised his fingers to his temple. 'Mental pain. Not caused by physical threat or hunger but by *other people*. Animals, now, they only care about survival. Us? We care about *feelings*. If someone likes the clothes we wear, the car we drive, the stupid words we use. We let other people control us even when they're *fickle, selfish, careless bastards*!'

He flung his spade down. It wedged deep into the sand. I wondered if he was talking about me. It stung me dead centre when I realized he was.

'Don't care about anyone,' he said quietly. 'You'll be a lot better off.'

He flopped down on the sand, hugging his knees to his chest with his head low as if bracing himself for a collision.

Jules was bubbling beside me.

'Igor would be a lot better off if you'd cared a little more about **HiM**,' she said. **'He wouldn't be lying in CASuALTY RigHT NOW fOR a StARt!'**

It was a good point but Luca wasn't in the mood for good points. He clenched his fists. The pill had worn off but there was still a fierce buzzing in my veins and I knew Jules and Luca were feeling it too. They weren't a good mix right then; they were too volatile.

'It's all right, Jules,' I said. 'Go back in the shelter and I'll take care of Luca.'

The lamplight hit and I could see her brow knotting fiercely.

'What are you, HiS MOTHeR?'

I didn't reply. I could see her rolling her shoulders back.

'I want to go HOME!'

She stamped the ground as she said it.

I looked at her sharply, feeling my throat tense.

'We haven't got a home!'

I hadn't meant to say it all loud and passionate but that's how it came out. The words stayed in the air like stars in the sky. But they didn't sparkle, they blazed.

Jules threw her head back.

'Oh, here we GO!'

The pressure was getting to me. The universe wasn't in Jules's pupil any more but swirling beneath my skin, ready to explode.

'That's the point, isn't it?' I said. 'We're not *house*less, we're *home*less. We don't belong anywhere.'

Jules lowered her chin.

'I belong in my SQuAt with a nice beVVy and the telly on high volUME!'

I looked down; I was swaying from one foot to the other, creating a fortress of sand around my feet. I hugged my body. It felt so heavy, the weight of the universe, but I wanted to keep it there inside me because then at least it would be safe. I heard Jules clear her throat.

'Are you coMing or NOT, MoLLs?'

When I looked up Jules was right in front of me, squaring her shoulders, leaning her face into mine. I wiped the tears from my eyes. She always said I was too soft.

'No, Jules,' I said. 'I'm not.'

She was so riled up I thought she was going to wallop me, but instead, she took a step back.

'You'll regret this, Molls,' she said calmly, as though she was the most reasonable person in the world. 'Mark my words, you will regret this.'

Jules turned and marched through the sand, her camo jacket getting smaller and smaller until it was just a green smudge on the horizon. I knew she'd be bitter, taking it all personal. She'd say I'd betrayed her. That I was no better than Donna. I loved Jules to pieces but you've got to make your own decisions in life. Otherwise there's no point having one.

I dropped down on my knees beside Luca. He had the map in his hand, running his fingers across the page. The lamps cast enough light for me to see that Jules was right; it wasn't a map at all, it was sheet music. Musical notes wobbled up and down the page, spelling out a tune I couldn't read. Luca paused and then, as though he knew what I'd seen, folded up the paper and stuffed it into his pocket.

'It's near here,' he said. 'I know it is.'

The wind blew hard across the beach, the waves crashing loud and fierce as I tried to remember what it felt like when he'd kissed me on the dance floor. The tingling feeling, the whole room full of love hearts and how we'd floated up in the air. But when I looked around I didn't see love hearts, just darkness.

'Shall we find somewhere to sleep?' I said.

His shoulders were covered in feathers, slick and black, with two giant wings sprouting from his back. He was King of the Pigeons. But then I blinked and the feathers were gone, his wings grey and spindly, one broken right down the middle. I looked above his head, searching for the crown I'd seen when we were on the byway. But all I could see was hair.

'Did you fuck him?' Luca said.

It took a moment for me to reply.

'Who?'

He rolled his eyes like I was playing a silly game.

'*Igor.*'

I tried to laugh in a light-hearted way.

'Don't be daft.'

He narrowed his eyes, looking at me with a blistering force. I could still feel the pulse of the universe riding through my veins.

'I'm not being *daft*,' he said. 'I saw you touching him.'

My smile dropped. I shook my head.

'I haven't left your side since we met him.'

He laughed but in that unkind way. It was exactly like Stu, cold and mocking.

'Yeah, right,' he said. 'You just met him this afternoon.'

I tried to think of a way to explain it all logically to him so that he'd snap out of this mood. If I got the words out in a neat, clever way it would make everything better. But I've never been good with words. Not when I've needed them.

'They took Boy,' Luca said.

There was no point saying anything.

'They're all following me,' he carried on. 'Waiting for their chance. They sent Igor. They took Boy. And you, you've been in on it all along.'

He examined my expression as though trying to catch me out.

'I know what you are.'

He shuffled on to his knees, pushing his face close to mine. On his breath, I could smell the sweetness of vodka mixers.

'I know what you've *done*.'

I leant back, my body shivering. My arms were pale and goose-pimpled. The wind blew my hair across my face and I let it stay there, a veil in front of my eyes. Not because I didn't want Luca to see me but because I didn't want to see this version of him.

'I haven't done anything wrong,' I said.

I said it as though I was saying it to my mother. I said it as though I was saying it to my father. I felt strong saying it. I felt right saying it.

But Luca just laughed. I pushed the hair from my face. The wind was so hard it was stinging my cheeks. His expression was dead, voice low and gravelly.

'You're nothing but a crackhead whore.'

I didn't take my eyes off him. There was so much disgust in his face it made me feel nauseous, yet I didn't want to be the first to look away. But then, after a while, I couldn't take it any more and looked down at the sand. When I looked back up Luca was on his feet, back towards me, wings tucked away, walking off into the distance.

My body buckled to the side. The universe burst out of me, leaking into the night.

Attacked by the Wicked Wolves

Once there was a young girl who went with her friends to find a Wizard. He was the only one who could help them with their problems. After many misfortunes and adventures, the young girl and her friends reached the Emerald City where the Wizard ruled. At the gates they were told to wear green-tinted glasses to shield them from the brightness and glory that lay ahead. Later they found out that the city was not really made of emeralds at all, that the glasses created an illusion. They were one of the Wizard's many deceptions in his make-believe utopia. The truth was that the Wizard was a trickster, his whole life in the land a lie.

He could help the girl and her friends no more than he could help himself.

As I walked along the beach I saw the lights of Skegness Pier on the horizon. The round orbs glowed like fireflies caught in a web. I walked back on to the street and into the arcade, wearing my paper glasses to protect myself from the harshness of the lights.

Luca's part in my adventure was clear. He wasn't the Scarecrow with no brains. If anything he had too much going on in his brain, the way he overthought everything. He wasn't the Tin Man rusted up with no heart. His heart was big; I'd seen that in how he treated Cora. He wasn't even the Cowardly Lion. It took courage for him to leave his parents' house, to take his dad's car and reject everything that was expected of him. I'd been right when I said it in the bar; he was the Wizard of Oz. Caught up in his own lies, unable to help himself, let alone anyone else.

And now I had to find my own way home. Except there was no home, no Kansas, no Aunt Em. Just a lonely pier on the east coast of England.

I heard the high trills of the fruit machines and the clinking of coins in the penny pushers. Children ran past me, screaming with laughter, animal masks tipped back on their heads. I couldn't laugh with them; I couldn't even smile. I had a new feeling. Like I was nothing but a hollowed-out husk. Barely a real person at all.

I made my way out of the arcade and on to the pier, walking until all I could see were the fuzzy globes of intermittent lamps ahead. It was windy and bitter cold without my jacket, but I didn't care. Physical pain is only temporary; Mother taught me that.

I leant against the rail, took the glasses off and dropped them into the water. I watched them fall as waves crashed back and forth against the pier. It got me thinking that life was like those waves. Crashing back and forth, wearing you down to smaller and smaller grains until you aren't even a rock any more but just a piece of sand.

The first time he came into my room I was twelve. Mother was on a business trip in Aberdeen and was due back the following day. At first, he stroked my hair. I remember thinking how comforting it was, the way it is when dads do things like that. He was the only one who was ever kind to me. I suppose that made it a double betrayal.

He told me afterwards that it always hurt the first time. That after a while I'd like it. I'd liked the stroking so I thought maybe he was right. If anything, it got worse. Just seeing his shadow creeping into my room, stretching tall against the wall with a hand reaching out to touch me, made my limbs stiffen. I was frozen with panic, knowing something awful was about to happen but not knowing how to stop it. My lungs stopped working but the instinct to breathe always won, the same way he did. Which was why I tried to fight it in the bath. I wanted control: of my body and what happened to it; of my life and where it would go.

'You just want attention,' Mother said. Which is why she'd never let me go to the doctor. Even with the cuts, even with the bleeding down there when it was too early for me to bleed anywhere.

It's easy to let these things drown you, which is where imagination comes in. Whenever I saw his shadow in my room, I'd imagine I was stuck out in Kansas like Dorothy and that, at any minute, a cyclone would come and whisk me away. I would look up at the ceiling and imagine it swirling, swirling, swirling. This was the scary part of the story but it would be OK because soon the house would crash and he would be far away. I would be in a new land of Technicolor and singing Munchkins. Of course, my story would be a little different. I wouldn't try to go home. I'd stay in Oz for ever.

None of this is an excuse. Everyone has their sad stories and they don't always end up on the streets doing the things I've done. I've made my choices, some good, some bad.

The good: running away from my parents. The bad: Rusby, the drugs, the men in cars, getting pregnant when I couldn't even take care of myself. I guess most of my choices have been bad, even the one with Luca which felt so good to begin with.

I walked back up the pier and heard laughter. There was a group of lads in tracksuits sitting on benches. They weren't on the bit you were supposed to sit on but perched on the backrest, feet on the seat as they smoked. One was the man from the rollercoaster queue. I ducked my head, hoping he hadn't seen me, and walked over to the Hook-a-Duck hut. The yellow plastic bodies were bobbing around in a circle, with large painted eyes that looked surprised. I tried to think of a happy memory. If I could just find one happy thing I would at least feel better. But I couldn't find anything. Happiness wasn't a choice for me, no matter what my mother said.

'Want a go, luv?' said the lady in the Hook-a-Duck hut.

She looked at me all hopeful as she blew warm air into her hands. I shook my head and walked back to the side of the pier, bending my body over the rail and looking down at the water. It would be nice to drop right in and get smashed into pieces, all this suffering washed away in the tide. It wouldn't take much: a quick shuffle up on the railings, a deep plunge. Then I would be gone and nothing else would matter.

'She's over there.'

Suddenly I was full again, my organs all back in place and pumping hard because he was back, he was sorry. But when I looked around there was no Luca. There was Rusby.

He was standing in front of the man from the roller-coaster queue, looking at me with hooded, wolf eyes. He had his baseball cap low, drooling at the fangs as he swaggered towards me. I wanted to run, but my limbs were frozen, just like when I was a child. I knew something awful was about to happen.

'Told you I'd find you, didn't I, darling?'

I lowered my head and tried to walk towards the arcade. Rusby grabbed my wrist and tugged me back.

'Ah, ah, ah,' he said. 'You ain't getting away from me this time.'

His gang lined up in front of me. I recognized some of them from the time Rusby's knife was stolen.

'I've got friends waiting for me,' I said loudly.

One of the lads lifted his chin.

'Hear you've got a lot of *friends*. Right, Rusby?'

They chuckled. Or maybe they growled. Their amber eyes gleamed, teeth snarling as they swayed from foot to foot. They were the wolves and I was their meat.

'Give us a minute, won't you, lads,' said Rusby.

They backed away as he held on to my wrist. When I looked at Rusby's face, all my fear drained away. I'd thought this was the worst thing that could happen, Rusby finding me, but having him there smiling his broken-slab smile made me realize what a small, tiny nothing he was.

The boards of the pier began to tremble.

'The lads have got a nice place for us in town,' Rusby said. 'Just come with us and everything will be all right.'

The men prowled ahead. Rusby was a man of promises. Promises that he'd treat you better. Promises that everything would be all right. But, most of all, promises to other people.

I looked down at the boards. The gaps between them were widening, with little rubber-band hands poking up through the slits. I rolled my shoulders back.

'Fire!' I screamed. '*Fire!*'

Everyone inside the arcade looked our way. Jules told me there's no use shouting 'Help!' or 'Rape!' No one wants to get involved. But fire? Everyone wants to see fire.

Rusby tightened his grip.

'Are you crazy?' he said.

The Rubberband Army were climbing the rails and leaping to the surface of the pier. Hundreds of them, all different colours and sizes, arms raised up in battle.

'Yaaah!' they cried in unison.

I pulled my leg back and kneed Rusby hard in the balls. He crumpled like a puppet with its strings cut. The army's cries turned into cheers. I knew I should run but their cheering spurred me on. I kicked him harder and harder. I kicked him in his stomach and head. I kicked him until the blood was pouring.

'You! Are! Nothing!' I cried.

I kicked harder with each word. I looked up at the wolves, but they were all stepping back with fear in their eyes. I carried on kicking.

'You! Are! NOTHING!'

When I stopped, Rusby lay curled up in a ball, groaning and rolling on the boards. He glanced up at me, but only for a second, too scared even to look me in the eye. I stood panting as the Rubberband Army formed around my feet.

'I'm sorry,' Rusby was saying. 'Please, Molly, please.'

That was when the security guards came.

The Rubberband Girls began to run. I bent down and pulled off Rusby's jacket before dashing down the pier after them. I saw them running down a flight of metal stairs leading down to the beach. I shot down behind them and, as soon as my feet hit the sand, began to sprint.

The tide had come in and my shoes splashed straight through the water. There were Rubberband Girls running, jumping and somersaulting through the air by my feet, whooping and cheering. I could hear the commotion on the pier above but I couldn't tell if anyone was following so I ran all the way down past the rollercoaster, past the Ferris wheel spinning round and round. I imagined the wolves chasing me – paws pounding the ground, teeth gnashing – and tried to sprint faster. It was so dark that I could barely see anything so I closed my eyes, remembering how I'd sailed along on that bicycle in the wheat field. How I'd felt like I could go on for ever. I imagined the sun shining down on me, I imagined my little girl by my side until eventually I realized that there was no more cheering. I looked behind me but the beach was empty. I was alone. I was free.

It was only when I stopped running that I realized my legs were aching, my chest stinging like a thousand bees had daggered me. I dropped down at the top of a grassy sand dune, the jacket still clutched in my hand. I searched Rusby's pockets: a packet of cigarettes, a lighter, a couple of tenners, and then I felt something cold and metal. I thought it might be the pillbox, hair the colour of autumn inside, but then pulled out a switchblade knife. Funny how I tricked myself, believing that something smashed on a dance floor would be in Rusby's pocket. As if he cared about Izzy, as if he cared about us. I buried the knife deep in the sand, then swung the jacket on.

I'd never hurt someone like that before. I didn't know if I should feel guilty; he'd done the same to me and worse. I thought of his face as he fell. The wolves when they realized that the mouse they'd trapped was really a lion.

I laughed. A loud whole-body laugh that rattled out like a warning alarm.

I am the Rubberband Girl! Watch me twist and bounce out of danger!

I carried on laughing until I couldn't breathe any more, my body slumped to the side, chest wheezing as it tried to catch up with itself. I coughed out the last blasts until there was none left in me.

Even a Rubberband Girl can snap.

As I lay there on the cold sand, I tried to think of Izzy. I tried to picture exactly what her face would look like: the ginger hair, the freckles across the nose. But no matter how hard I tried, all I could think about was the day they took her away. The way she'd been so warm in my arms and how cold it felt when she was gone. She's the only thing I've ever loved without hesitation. An undiluted, pure love. I hoped she was happy. More than hoped. It made my heart burst, thinking she could be happy.

I curled up, tucking my knees deep into my chest. I closed my eyes and tried my best to disappear.

Away to the Sea

It was the noise that woke me. A gentle chorus of warbling voices. When I opened my eyes there was a blur of turquoise and purple, the curved pattern of feathers. My vision cleared and I saw them: a flock of pigeons strutting around me. I sank my head deeper into the sand but the birds only cooed louder, flapping their wings at me, pulling at the skirt of my dress with their beaks until eventually I gave in and sat up.

'*Come, come,*' they said, rising up and then landing a few steps ahead.

Or maybe they said *coo coo*.

I followed the birds as they walked in a line, stumbling down the sand dune, into an empty car park, wandering up the streets as I brushed the sand out of my hair and off Rusby's jacket. I walked past arcades and cafés with the shutters down until eventually I was on residential roads. The pigeons had flown to the skies now and when I looked up their bodies were forming the shape of an arrow. I followed and found others were following too. Women with pushchairs, a few men with book bags in their hands. They were all talking about the new term starting. Today was the first day.

It was only when I got to the school gates that I realized what the pigeons had wanted me to see. In the playground, dressed in bottle-green jumpers, grey shorts and pleated skirts were the children of Skegness. They were running and shouting, swinging on railings and whizzing around on scooters. I watched the parents walking through the gates with their children and wondered if one of them would guess who I was. If they had seen a photograph of me or would know from the way I stood there alone. I looked at all the girls, searching for flame-red hair, but there were too many. Any one of them could have been my Izzy.

Except she wasn't my Izzy. Not any more. I gave up all rights to call her mine the minute I let them take her from my arms. She probably had a new name; they could have called her whatever they liked because they were her parents, people with good steady lives, enough to make them good parents, at least on paper. But then my parents were good on paper too. That's why, when I was filling in the adoption papers, I'd made sure to say, *Choose someone who'll love and take care of her. I don't care about anything else.* They'd looked at me with this patronizing smile as though of course that was what they'd do. But I knew from all the stories I'd heard on the streets that foster care and adoption isn't as clear-cut as that. The agencies make mistakes the same way the Social had when they'd come to see me. Nobody was perfect.

Then I saw her.

A girl with a white polo-neck shirt, grey skirt and socks that went up to her knees. She was skipping in the centre of a yellow circle painted on the playground, pigtails bouncing up and down with each jump. It was her; I knew it was, not because of the ginger hair or the freckles like Rusby's but because of the eyes. Big and innocent, just like mine.

'Izzy,' I said quietly to myself. I wanted to run and scoop her in my arms, to cling on to her and for her to cling back. But of course I couldn't do that. I wasn't a mother to her. I was a stranger.

I wiped a tear from my eye as I caught sight of two women chatting near Izzy. One was tall and gangly, wearing a long tie-dye skirt; the other was older with jeans, arms crossed firmly under her bosom. Tie-dye looked like she'd feed her child with special beans from the Peruvian mountains. Jeans looked like she'd feed her child a full English every morning. It didn't matter either way; both were better than me.

The whistle blew. Izzy wrapped the rope around her hand and ran up to an old woman on a bench. The woman's hair was pure white and rolled into tight curls; a walking cane rested beside her. Izzy pecked the woman on the cheek three times and then ran into the line, chatting rapidly to the girl in front of her. I could see Rusby in the way she was talking so fast. The old Rusby, before he became so harsh.

I sniffed back my tears and then looked to the skies. The pigeons were gone, leaving thin wisps of cloud in their wake. I hugged my middle, trying to squeeze out the hollow feeling inside, then felt something sharp digging into my wrist. When I looked down I saw it was the jagged beads of the bracelet Cora had given me. They were all different shapes and colours with four cubed beads in the middle. On these cubes, spelt out in capital letters, was the word 'L-O-V-E'.

I walked back to the beach, following the signs with the happy fisherman, then sat on the bench in the bus shelter. I looked out to the sea. The tide had washed away Luca's holes so it looked like nothing had happened. The water was grey today, as though someone had dropped a storm cloud right in the middle of it. But it looked calm too. Settled. It seemed more beautiful somehow.

It was only when I heard the panting that I realized Luca was sitting beside me. He had his trumpet case by his feet and Boy in his hands. She went berserk when she saw me, yapping and trying to scramble out of Luca's arms so she could lick my face. I looked at Luca. His eyes were soft, the hatred drained.

'I found her by the car,' he said. 'Jules was right. You can't get rid of her.'

She was still scrambling, back stump wagging, so I went ahead and took her from Luca's arms.

'Don't be mad at me, Molly,' he said.

I walked away. All I could think about was Igor's head smacked against the brick, Luca shouting at me and being left out with the wolves. It was my own fault really; I should never have trusted him. I should never trust anyone.

I could hear him getting to his feet; then I felt his hand on my shoulder. I knocked it off. When I looked back at him my jaw was clenched. No one was ever going to touch me again. I carried on walking.

'*I'm a psycho!*' he cried.

I looked back. His chest was heaving in and out like he'd been running for miles. I stood sideways, not sure which way to go. He walked up to me and placed his trumpet case on the ground before kneeling down and unbuckling the lock. He opened the case out flat, not even trying to hide what was inside.

I knelt too, putting Boy down beside me. The case was full of pieces of paper, and bottles and boxes of what looked like medication. There were neatly printed labels that read 'MR L. BARGATE', like the ones in his parents' bathroom. The bottles were filled with brightly coloured pills. The paper was covered with handwriting and shredded along the edges. I went to pick out a piece. Luca was prickly about it, but nodded. The first one said *Do not pay heed to people with green eyes*. The next one: *Daisies*.

Sunflowers. Daisies. Blood. I picked up one more, pulling it out by the corners: *The thing that makes us human is SHAME.*

Luca kept his head low. He patted the heap.

'They're my thoughts,' he said. 'Or at least some of them.'

The sun glinted off the lenses of his glasses. It looked like he had no eyes, like he was an eyeless, soulless man.

'Before I met you . . .' he began, but he was too tense to finish.

He dropped his shoulders and tried again.

'Before I met you I was in a mental health ward,' he said. 'I'm not very well, Molly.'

I put the pieces of paper back in the case.

'I know,' I said.

He frowned.

'How do you know?'

I shook my head.

'I told you before,' I said. 'I don't care.'

He thought about this a second.

'I guess you've figured out there isn't any fortune either?'

He looked kind of hopeful, as though he wanted me to still believe it. It was only then – as he looked at me full of anticipation – that I realized I'd never believed it. The hope drained out of his face.

'I thought it was real,' he said. 'My granddad used to always leave me little codes everywhere so when he left me this case, with the key and the map—'

'Sheet music,' I corrected.

His eyes widened.

'I thought it was a map,' he said. 'I thought there was a code in the notes. I thought it was leading me here. Then, on the train, I thought I saw someone following us. Then I thought it was Igor. It seemed to make sense. It seemed real. That's the scariest part, when it seems so real.'

He sighed heavily.

'Why did you come?' he asked. 'If you knew there wasn't any fortune, why did you stay with me all this time?'

I could feel the tightness in my throat. I stood up, about to walk away again, but the sun passed behind a cloud and I could see through his lenses to his wet, pigeon eyes. I couldn't do it. I couldn't stay mad with him.

'I liked you,' I said.

Luca sniffed.

'I've really messed up, haven't I?'

I wanted to tell him that he hadn't, that everything was OK, but it wouldn't be true. I've been making excuses for the rest of the world for too long.

'I've got to go, Luca,' I said.

'Wait.'

He pushed his fingers beneath his glasses and rubbed at his eyes before fiddling through his pockets. When he got up he handed me three twenty-pound notes.

'I took it out before the card was cancelled,' he said. 'Like an emergency reserve.'

I shook my head.

'I can't take it.'

'Yes, you bloody can. Besides, I've got the car. I'll take it home, say sorry. Then Mummy and Daddy can take care of me just like they've always wanted. Sorted.'

He smiled and looked down at the money. I had enough to get back to Nottingham but I liked letting Luca think he'd helped me. The same way that he was trying to pretend he'd go home even though I knew he wasn't ever going back there. I curled my fingers around the notes.

'Sorted,' I said.

He didn't let go and we both stood there holding the money as though we were holding on to each other.

'It's been great, Molly,' he said. 'Really something.'

He let go and bent down to close his trumpet case. Except he couldn't really close it because Boy was sniffing inside it.

'Wait,' I said.

I dropped on to my knees. Boy had her paw on something, a small compartment built into the lid, covered in the same crushed velvet as the lining.

'What's that?' I said.

Boy took her paw off. Luca stared at the box and then stuck out his bottom lip and shrugged. I pulled the chain from around my neck, and pushed the key gently into the hole on top. It slipped right in.

'You're *kidding* me!' Luca said.

I left the key sitting in the lock and sat back on my heels. I've always seen the things no one else can. I took a deep breath and nodded at Luca. He nodded back; then he turned the key and lifted the lid.

Inside was a clear plastic bag. It had been folded so you couldn't see the contents. Luca pulled it out of the box and unfolded it. The bag spread out like a piece of wrapping paper, bigger and bigger until you could see a lump of metal and the bright shape of something fabric with patterns across it, and a black and white card. Luca held it close to his glasses.

'It's a mouthpiece and a bow tie,' he said. 'Granddad never wore bow ties.'

'What's on the card?' I asked.

Luca pushed his hand into the bag. He pulled out the objects one by one. He'd been right: there was the mouthpiece to a trumpet, brassy and smooth, and an undone bow tie with paisley patterns all across it. The card had a picture of Louis Armstrong on it; in the corner was his autograph and a short message written in pen: 'To a great student and friend.'

Buildings lifted from their foundations, the sea spinning around us in a blur of wild colours as we knelt, frozen on the beach.

'I knew it!' Luca said, nearly throwing the objects into the air.

I laughed.

'Be careful!' I said. 'They must be valuable.'

Luca's expression became serious.

270

'Stu always made out Granddad was crazy. But it was true. This is proof that it was true.'

He collected the pieces and clung on to them real tight.

'I know, Luca, but be careful.'

He looked down at his hands before pushing the card, mouthpiece and bow tie back into the centre of the bag, trying to fold the plastic in the same way as he'd found it. He placed the bundle into the secret compartment, clicking the lid shut and hanging the key around his neck. We both knelt there, staring down at the box. Then Luca looked up at me.

'What should we do now?' he said.

It was the first time he'd asked my opinion.

'Let's go for a walk,' I said.

Luca was bouncing as we made our way down the beach. His trumpet case was strapped over his shoulder, covering the 'EAS' on his REASON T-shirt. I knew he was getting the wrong idea. Now that we'd found the fortune, he thought it was all fixed. But nothing was fixed because the two of us were still broken. The hairline fractures weren't hairlines at all; they were fault lines running down the landscapes of our souls.

I walked right up to the water and, even though I knew he was scared of that big rolling sea, Luca followed. I didn't say anything, just felt the wind knock against my body and listened to the sound of the water lapping the coast. I bent down, untying the laces on my red canvas shoes.

'Look, Molly,' Luca said. 'I'm going to go back on the medication. I was stupid to come off it anyway. I'll get myself straight and then . . . Maybe then we can . . .'

I took off my shoes and socks and stepped over the bundle of them as they lay on the sand. The water tickled my toes, cold and foamy.

'Then we can . . .?' I said.

Luca smiled as though it was obvious.

'Be together,' he said.

I smiled back.

'I'm no good for you, Luca,' I said.

He shook his head with a sudden panic.

'That's not true!' he said. 'I've never been as well as when I'm with you. You don't want to *know* what I'm usually like.'

The smell of candyfloss floated in the wind as the funfair came alive. I could see the clunking of the Ferris wheel as it turned on the horizon.

'Besides, I wouldn't have found those things without you,' he said. 'I was right in choosing you. I was right in trusting you.'

I looked back out at the sea. The wind tossed my hair back and forth.

'I'm sorry about last night,' he said. 'About Igor. About what I said. You're better than that. You're so good, Molly. I've never met anyone with so much *goodness* in them.'

I've never had someone say those things. Not Rusby, not Jules, not my mother or father. When no one sees your goodness you start forgetting it's there.

'I'm not special, Luca,' I said. 'I'm just another homeless girl.'

He laughed. Then he sighed.

'You're extraordinary,' he said.

My cheeks were hot and stinging. I wiped the tears from them. Then I felt his hand roll over my shoulder and squeeze.

'I love you, Molly,' he said.

He didn't mean it. Of course he thought he did, but it wasn't love Luca felt, it was infatuation. It wouldn't last. Like Rusby when he told me he loved me. Like my dad when he stroked my hair. That wasn't love, no matter how many times he told me it was. Even Izzy, who I thought would be my one guarantee, could never love me because she would never know me. I turned to Luca with tears in my eyes. He stepped closer.

'Please say I can make this better.'

I looked behind him at the empty beach. It was like we were standing in a bubble, two figures cocooned in a snow globe of 'TIME'.

'I've got an answer,' I said. 'About what makes us human.'

Luca was quiet.

'OK,' he said.

'Imagination.'

He was quiet again.

'Because', I said, 'without it you'd never be able to imagine what it was like to be someone else. And you wouldn't care so much, would you? You wouldn't want to help them.'

The tide was getting closer, almost touching our feet.

'Is that the right answer?' I asked.

Luca smiled; then he shrugged.

'Better than any I've come up with.'

I tried to smile too but I couldn't because of what was behind me. A shadow, stretching tall, reaching out to touch me. I didn't have to look to see it. It was always there. You can try and let go of the past, but it won't let go of you.

I pulled the L-O-V-E bracelet from my wrist and pushed it into Luca's palm.

'Goodbye, Luca.'

I turned, walking into the sea.

Luca's voice was faint when he called out to me.

'What are you doing?'

The water soaked the hem of my dress as I waded up to my knees. I knew he'd be too scared to come after me.

'Molly,' he said louder. 'Seriously, what are you *doing*?'

The water was up to my thighs now. The waves pushing me as if they couldn't decide which way to take me, as if they couldn't decide where I belonged. Pebbles loosened beneath my feet as the water reached my hips, my waist, my chest, until my toes were hovering over the seabed. It wasn't like the water in the bath; it was stronger. My body wouldn't be able to fight it. Not this time.

My legs gave way, body sinking into the water.

'Molly, get out of there!'

I could hear Boy barking but I didn't look back. There's no use looking back. Instead I swam ahead, watching the waves coming towards me. I wanted to be sucked in, swallowed up by the big greyness of the sea. I was a rock being washed back and forth, back and forth. Soon, there'd be nothing left of me but sand.

That's what I wanted. To be nothing but sand.

'Molly!'

I plunged my head beneath the surface. Bubbles zoomed across my vision and sounds became gulps: distorted, muffled. In one blinding flash I saw all the colours of the world. I saw the stars, the galaxies. I saw seaweed and feathers. I saw all meaning and then I saw that it was all meaningless. Pieces of paper from Luca's trumpet case floated by my face.

They watch you.

Frangipani socks.

HELP!

The ink was spilling out of the paper, swirling into the ripples. A drop of ink can turn a puddle black, but in the sea it just spreads out and becomes more sea.

The ink was spiralling towards me. I watched as it reached out, touching my fingers.

Then everything disappeared.

Molly's Wish

This is a happy story. This is an adventure.

The light was shining. Beautiful and golden. Circles of colour then copper red blooming behind my closed lids. Stars twinkled; fireworks exploded. It was day and night and the end of everything. I could feel a dozen hands grabbing at me. Tiny rubber-band fingers tugging at my body.

I didn't want to open my eyes. I didn't want to see what death looked like. I shook my head. Then the pain kicked in.

I heard voices and beeping machines. My head was heavy and I couldn't move my limbs. I blinked until my eyes focused, seeing the daisy print of the curtain, the white squares of ceiling tiles. Then, when I turned my head, I saw Luca reading a magazine out loud to himself. Except of course it wasn't to himself, it was to me.

"'The growth of the Himalaya and Tibetan Plateau is thought to have had a major effect on global weather patterns and climate change . . .'"

He was reading from a scientific journal. Lord knows where he'd found it. He was actually very good, speaking like he was giving a lecture at a big old university. I listened to him for a bit longer; then I cleared my throat. It was so weak that he didn't even hear me.

'Luca,' I said.

When he looked at me it was like an afterthought. His back stiffened.

'I'll call a nurse,' he said, springing to his feet.

'No,' I said, pulling myself up against the pillows. 'I'm OK.'

He looked at me, unsure, then eased back in his chair. We were in the corner of a ward by a window with a mesh cage. There were other beds with patients and visitors by their sides. It was noisy, the smell of disinfectant in the air, and all I wanted to do was sleep. Luca gave my hand a gentle squeeze. Then, as quick as lightning, his face turned to thunder.

'What the *hell* were you doing, Molly?'

I thought of the water swallowing me up, the sight of his words floating past. I thought of the wolves chasing me down the beach, the way he used to cough when he came into my room.

I shrugged.

'It doesn't matter,' I said.

Luca's brow knitted.

'Yes, it bloody matters.'

I looked at the machines beside me, the tubes in my arms. The last time I was in a hospital I had been giving birth to Izzy.

'I jumped in after you,' Luca said. 'I lost my notes.'

I looked at the floor but I couldn't see Luca's trumpet case. He followed my gaze.

'It got lost in the sea,' he said.

I imagined all the bottles and pieces of paper bobbing along the water. Then I remembered the plastic bag. I tried to sit up.

'What about the things?' I asked.

He sighed and put his hand in his pocket, throwing the plastic bag on to the bed. You could still see the colour of the bow tie. Luca remained irritated.

'Sorry,' I said. 'I thought you'd be too scared.'

'So did I. But there I was . . . *doing it.*'

He slumped back, part proud, part traumatized.

'Thanks,' I said.

There was a pause; all you could hear was the pumping of machines. I looked around Luca's feet.

'Where's Boy?' I asked.

Luca didn't respond and, for a moment, I thought he'd gone and lost her again. Then he leant down to his leather bag and lifted the flap. Boy was curled up in a ball, fast asleep.

'Jules was right,' Luca said. 'She's as tough as new boots.'

'Old boots,' I said.

He paused; then he looked stern again.

'You're the last person who should be trying to kill themselves,' he said. 'I mean *rarely*, Molly.'

The 'rarely' made me grin; he'd said it just like his mum. Then I frowned. I didn't know what he meant. I had a million reasons to want to die. But I liked that he couldn't see them.

'I have a daughter,' I said.

I hadn't planned on telling him. But planning was never something I was good at. I hadn't planned on drowning either. It just seemed like the best thing to do at the time. Luca rose from his seat.

'I'm going to call the nurse.'

'She's called Isabelle. Izzy for short. At least she was before they took her. She'd be five now.'

I don't know if it's because I was telling him or because I was thinking about the hospital and them taking her away, but I started crying. The tears came out in big fat droplets that blurred my vision. I thought about seeing Izzy in the playground and I wondered if I'd really seen her or if I'd just really *wanted* to see her. I saw so many things that I couldn't even tell any more.

'Do you think she's happy, Luca?' I said.

He looked at me, bemused. I sniffed loudly.

'I'd give anything for her to be happy.'

I could hear the rev of engines outside, the tweeting of birds, the tinkle of an ice-cream van. Luca smiled with the same softness he used for Cora.

'Of course she's happy,' he said.

It was exactly the right answer.

I knew he was a good one. We were the same, me and him, even though we seemed so different. Like jigsaw pieces. If jigsaw pieces were all identical then they'd never fit together. That was us, two jigsaw pieces that made no sense on their own but slotted together to make a finished picture.

Luca took my hand again and we sat there quiet for a bit.

'I'm going to make sure this never happens again,' he said. 'I don't care about myself any more. That was my problem, you see? I've never cared about anyone but myself. Except now. Because I care about you.' He squeezed my hand tight. 'I'm going to help you, Molly.'

It was such a sweet thing to say, even though I didn't believe it. People think they can help you but they let you down. They don't mean to, but they do. That's fine. All you've got to remember is not to believe them.

'Thank you, Luca. You can call the nurse now.'

He gave my hand a little shake as though we'd done a deal; then he got up. When the nurse came she pulled the curtain around my bed and asked Luca to wait outside. He looked reluctant but I told him it was OK. Before he left he picked up the plastic package then kissed my hand like he was a gentleman and I was a lady.

'I'll wait for you, Molly,' he said. 'Always.'

After he'd gone the nurse looked at me as though I was the luckiest girl on earth. It made me wonder if I'd been wrong, if perhaps he'd meant it when he told me he loved me. Then she prodded and poked me, saying I was good for not fussing. I think I was too tired to fuss.

'We have someone to see you,' she said.

I thought maybe it was Jules come to berserk at me. Then I thought it was Mother and him. For a moment I thought it might even be Izzy. Instead a tall black man came into the room with a bunch of papers. He was kind of round and soft-looking, like a big teddy bear.

'Hello, Molly,' he said in this real deep voice, smooth like honey. 'My name's Darren and I'm from the Social Services. If you don't mind I've got a few questions.'

I looked down at the rucksack Luca had left. I could hear Boy breathing.

'Am I in trouble?' I asked.

The man smiled but in a kind way; his whole face lit up.

'No, darling. I'm here to help you.'

Home Again

If you sit by Nottingham Castle where the tourists stand with maps and baseball caps and eyes that look without seeing, you'll hear a busker who, when he sings, bleeds his soul. Except you don't see him any more. I go back there and hope to hear that earthquake voice but the cobbles are always empty, people rushing by, not seeing anything but the narrowness of their own lives.

I texted Jules to see if she'd heard anything.

Probs glassing some fucker in the face :-) Jx

Jules doesn't live in the squat any more. She moved in to a flat near her mum in Bestwood so she could be close to the hospital. Her mammogram found that the lump was benign but they want to keep monitoring her. She says the breast cancer support has been amazing, far better than the mental health care, which seems to get less and less funding every year.

'Sickness is sickness as far as I'm concerned, Molls,' she told me. 'People forget the mind is part of the body too; it's all connected.'

She calls me every so often to give me these words of wisdom as well as the latest gossip: how Big Tony got a job in a gaming shop and has been made assistant manager, how Private Pete has gone a month without contracting any diseases (because she lets him shower in her flat once a week), how Rusby got his Slovakian bird pregnant and is bunked up with her somewhere near York. Sometimes when she's speaking, I hear Polish in the background.

Everything changed for me the day I woke up in hospital. After the social worker left I kept thinking about all the help. So much of it. The doctors and nurses, the social worker and Luca. I'd never had so much help. I didn't know what to do with it.

I'd planned to tell the social worker I was fine, to make up some lie about how nearly drowning was an accident and that I had a place to live and I didn't need anything. But the words didn't come out. He kept talking to me in his honey-glow voice about programmes available and how I didn't have to do anything alone if I didn't want to, and the lies crumbled in my mind.

Fuck it, I thought. What's the point of humanity if no one helps anyone? What's the point of humanity if no one's brave enough to take the help? You can say what you want about people, but we all have this thing inside us. We care about others, whether we want to or not.

So I took the help. Both Luca's and his. And now I'm in shared housing, which is good some days, bad others, depending on who you're sharing with. I'm getting qualifications in basic English and Maths, which means I can then get one in Social Care. My supporting officer thinks I'd be really good in a care role, if people are willing to look past my shoplifting record. Which, it turns out, some people are. I'm even on some meds to help with all the things I see. I wasn't sure about them at first – seeing things had helped me through some tough times – but it turns out I had something better than the hallucinations. *Imagination.* No meds can take that away from me. It's what makes me human.

It's still hard, of course, what with all the government cuts. You can see the stress wrinkles of the people who work in the housing associations and homeless shelters. They barely have enough to live on themselves let alone help me, but it makes me all the more grateful when they do.

Luca comes to see me at the shelter sometimes and we go on walks together, sitting in parks and cafés. He's been busy himself, of course. The day after I nearly drowned he was all over the news.

MAN ALMOST LOSES ARMSTRONG FORTUNE WHEN SWEPT OUT TO SEA

Someone who worked on the pier had filmed the whole thing and, before you knew it, Luca was an internet sensation. A news crew came to interview him as he held up the Louis Armstrong memorabilia. He hardly said a word, eyes darting about as the reporter stuck a microphone under his chin.

He hasn't decided what to do with the Armstrong items. Jules said he was bonkers for not putting them on eBay straight away; the bidding would have gone mental. But it was never about the money, not for Luca.

Besides, he's doing well without all of that. He's been taking his medication and he has his own studio flat where he lives with Boy. It's been good for him, taking care of another being, even when that being only needs food, water and a couple of walks a day (which, for Luca, is probably the maximum he could cope with). He's been studying part-time on a computer science programme and working part-time on an IT helpdesk. Turns out Luca's quite good with computers. They make logical sense, he tells me, unlike people.

'That's a good thing though,' I said. 'Life would be boring if everything was logical.'

He looked at me, shaking his head.

'You're always thinking from another angle, Molly,' he said with a grin. 'That's why you're on my team.'

We talk a lot, me and Luca. About the future, but also about the past. It's good to let someone know about the things that have happened, even if they can't be changed. It's the secrets that gnaw away at you.

The first day I got back to Nottingham I went to see Robin Hood at the sandwich giveaway. He was in the middle of bollocking some poor sod for throwing his carton by the side of the bin but he stopped when he saw me, big grin across his face. He was all questions: where I'd been, how I was. He said I looked well, but I could tell he knew I'd been through something deep and troubling. He placed his hand on my arm.

'It's good to have you home,' he said.

I welled up. All this time I'd thought home was something beyond me, kept far away in a room with sofas and fireplaces. But home wasn't a semi-detached house in the suburbs. It wasn't a nook under a bridge, or an abandoned community centre or a derelict Manor Cottage.

Home was the place you felt safe. Home was the place you were respected. Home was the place you were loved. And right then, home was outside the Tourist Information with Robin Hood.

They've become great mates, Robin Hood and Luca. They have long discussions about economics and whether the human race is doomed. Sometimes, when we're chatting, Martin looks at me all wistful and I know he's thinking of his girl. I know he's thinking of how much I look like her and how, in a funny way, I'm carrying on the life she never had. I don't mind being a second daughter to him any more. Anyone would be real lucky to have a dad like Robin Hood.

I was one year clear of drugs the other day. I didn't want to make a fuss about it but I thought I'd celebrate by going to the castle. I'm a proper Nottingham resident with a Citycard now so I can get in for free. What I like to do best is walk the castle grounds. It's not actually a castle any more, that part was demolished hundreds of years ago, but inside there are still some of the tapestries, potteries and paintings. It used to make my blood bubble, knowing someone had lived in such luxury as the poor rotted in the dungeons below and their families starved in the nearby slums. But then I read an information board about how a mansion was on the castle mound and how that mansion was burnt down by rioters when the residing duke opposed the Representation of the People Act. It made me feel there was some justice in the world when I read that.

If I was a duke, I would dress like the peasants and open all my rooms for them to live in. I'd smash all the fine china and pull down the chandeliers, handing out pieces of crystal to the cleaners and cooks before declaring Nottingham an independent state. There would be no rich or poor, only an exchange of goods and skills. No one would starve and everyone would have a home.

I carried on walking, imagining my rebel paradise, until I reached a huge oak, branches spanning over me like temple arches. Then I heard a voice singing over the wall. I froze, then ran to look over the edge. I could see the back of the Robin Hood statue, arrow pulled back ready to shoot, but I couldn't get a good enough angle to see beyond so I ran right down to the gates and out on to the streets. That's when I saw him in the same old spot, guitar strapped around his body, bleeding his soul all over the cobbles. I was so happy to see the busker that I nearly stumbled to the ground. He looked different somehow, with a new flat cap and neatly trimmed beard. Instead of the old parka he had a thick tweed jacket, and, when I looked at his face, I saw the fierceness that usually creased his features had softened. But the song was still electric, bolting through my nerves, striking me dead centre. Everyone was walking straight by like he was another invisible nobody on the streets. They were more interested in ghosts, kings and queens in castles than a person made of flesh and blood.

I went and stood right in front of the busker. If you do this, sometimes it forms a crowd, and I felt that today the busker deserved a crowd. But I guess the people were still not ready to see him – the pain of him, the anger as he pounded away at the guitar – because no one joined me. He had his eyes closed and was so deep in the song he was singing that, when he opened them again, he looked shocked to see me. Maybe no one had stopped and listened to him for a while. Maybe he recognized me from all those other times I'd sat on the bench as he played. Or maybe it was because I was crying. I couldn't help it; his singing always got me that way.

He looked embarrassed and fiddled with his strings. I opened my mouth to tell him to carry on. But then he began playing again and, when he played, it was a different type of music altogether. It was springy, light and made my muscles relax like foam into water. And when he sang it was with a gentle, smooth voice you'd have never believed could have come out of him.

It was like he was singing just for me, about the past and how he couldn't run from it, and the darkness and how it drowned him. Then the beat got quicker and he was telling me how he came home after a long time and how the sun was shining, his heart racing because at last he was happy.

He'd read my life and was singing it back to me. It made me shine from the inside out. When he got to the chorus he was bouncing his foot, telling me to keep my head up, to keep my heart strong. People stood next to me. They could see him now. They weren't scared any more. It must have been a popular song because some of them were singing to the chorus. Then they began throwing coins into his guitar case; that's how unafraid they were.

I was so happy. I don't know if it was because the busker was being seen and heard for the first time, or because life was finally going somewhere for me, or because of the beauty of the song itself, but I felt a pure, golden joy. I bounced up and down to the music and the people bounced along with me, though maybe not quite as high. There was a big crowd now and I was in the middle of it, dancing and swaying, jumping and pirouetting as the busker sang and played. It was like we were in the middle of a carnival right there at the front of Nottingham Castle.

I only realized he'd finished when the crowd applauded. The noise of a thousand pigeons beating their wings thundered down the street, feathers showering us like confetti. I didn't see it; I felt it. Then when I stood still – heart pounding, face grinning so wide it hurt – I saw the busker shoving his guitar into his case and closing it as people tried to put money in. When someone asked if he needed help, he snarled.

The crowd spread out like beads rolling across a slippery floor. I thought I should go too but then the busker looked at me.

He nodded.

I nodded back.

We saw each other, flesh and blood, and in that there was something beautiful.

Acknowledgements

A book like this couldn't be written without a lot of research and the help of many organizations. I'd like to thank Pedestrian and Writing East Midlands for giving me the opportunity to work as a writer-in-residence in Kennedy House Homeless Hostel and, in particular, Ellene, who showed up every week and was so generous in telling me her story. I'd also like to thank New Futures Leicester, a great organization that works with women and men engaged in sex work, with little funding and a lot of love, and also The Bridge, who provide free food for the homeless and allowed me to volunteer for them. Also, I'd like to thank the people I spoke to who have been or are currently homeless: your insights were fundamental in the writing of this novel.

There were some great programmes and books that helped me, in a compassionate and informative way, to understand the whole topic of homelessness and sex work, namely *Stuart: A Life Backwards* by Alexander Masters, *The Sex Myth: Why Everything We're Told is Wrong* by Dr Brooke Magnanti, *Love for Sale with Rupert Everett* (Channel 4) and *On the Streets* (BBC Four). My biggest thanks have to go to the miniseries *Five Daughters* (BBC One), which opened my eyes to the lives of the homeless and of sex workers in such a powerful, beautiful way that it inspired me to write this novel. Art really can change people's lives.

Also, big thanks to my agent, James Wills, and editor, Lizzy Goudsmit, who have backed this idea since I first put it forward and helped me shape it into something wonderful. Your support, sage advice and quick reading have been invaluable. And to Tom Hill, who I think is the most organized publicist ever made.

And also, as always, big thanks to my loving friends and family; particularly Laura Aston, Katie Snaith, Farhana Shaikh, Judith, Ian and Iqra.

Oh, and of course John, who is still awesome.

Mahsuda Snaith is the winner of the SI Leeds Literary Prize 2014, Bristol Short Story Prize 2014 and was an *Observer* New Face of Fiction in 2017. She lives in Leicester, where she teaches creative writing and tries to find the time to read.

For more information on Mahsuda Snaith and her books, see her website at www.mahsudasnaith.com

Also by Mahsuda Snaith

THE THINGS WE THOUGHT WE KNEW

THE THINGS WE THOUGHT WE KNEW
Mahsuda Snaith

Ten years ago, two girls' lives changed forever. Now one of them is ready to tell their story.

The first memory I have of you is all knickers and legs. You had flipped yourself into a handstand and couldn't get back down. We became best friends, racing slugs, pretending to be spies – all the things that children do.

Ten years later, eighteen-year-old Ravine Roy spends every day in her room. Completing crosswords and scribbling in her journal, she keeps the outside world exactly where she wants it; outside.

But as the real world begins to invade her carefully controlled space, she is forced to finally confront the questions she's been avoiding. Who is her mother meeting in secret? Who has moved in next door?

And why, all those years ago, when two girls pulled on their raincoats and wellies and headed out into the woods did only one of them return?

'A breakout book from an incredibly talented debut writer. Read, weep and laugh' *Stylist*

'A delightfully fresh voice' *Daily Mail*

'An original coming of age novel' *Observer*